SPIRIT BLESSED
CHRONICLES

A New Legacy

AK WARNOCK
Illustrator: BREANN CRUZ

This is a work of fiction. Names, characters, places, and incidents are either the product of the author's imagination or used fictitiously. Any resemblance to actual events, locales, or persons, living or dead, is purely coincidental.

ISBN-13: 979-8-218-60476-9

Publisher: AK Writes

Cover design and artwork by: Breann Cruz

Printed in the United States of America

DEDICATION

This book is in loving memory of our first child,

our beloved furbaby, **Rikimaru Wiki Warnock**.

We will forever miss you and hold you in our

hearts.

Table of Contents

ACKNOWLEDGMENTS

This book is the result of not just our imaginations, but the incredible support, encouragement, and inspiration we've received along the way.

To our four amazing kids: Rhesa, Reilyn, Raiden, and Ragnar—you are our greatest joy and constant motivation. Thank you for your not-so-endless patience as we poured our hearts into this project. Your love and energy make everything we do worthwhile.

To our family and friends who cheered us on from the beginning, your encouragement gave us the courage to take this leap. Whether it was a kind word, a shared laugh, or a moment of understanding, each gesture reminded us why this journey was worth it.

A special thank you to our Mom (Rhesa Sharp Warnock), Granny (Sharen Kemmerer), Breann Cruz, Melissa Henson, Hannah Stuart, Amber Hoffman, Katherine Dunaway, Carol Henson—your belief in our vision and honest feedback helped shape this book into what it is today.

To our readers, thank you for stepping into the world we've created. We are so grateful you've chosen to spend your time with our story. It's your curiosity and imagination that bring our words to life.

Finally, to each other—as partners in life and now as coauthors. Writing this book together has been a true adventure, and we wouldn't want to share it with anyone else.

With deepest gratitude,

AK Warnock

Chapter 1

The sun began its ascent over the lush, wooded landscape of Ashenfall, casting gentle rays of golden light into the town. In a cozy house on Cypress Lane, the morning tranquility was interrupted by the sound of an alarm clock buzzing persistently.

In a small bedroom decorated with posters of knights and dragons, Winslow "Wiki" Isaac Kinney slowly emerged from his dreams, his consciousness still lingering in the realms of fantasy. He was an 11-year-old, who possessed an undeniable spark of intrigue and imagination. As he rubbed the sleep from his eyes, he swung his legs over the side of the bed, planting his feet on the soft shaggy carpet. His short, neatly trimmed hair framed a face adorned with a pair of sleek glasses, accentuating his sharp, inquisitive gaze. His slender frame held an air of quiet strength. With a yawn and a stretch, he greeted the new day with a mix of excitement and drowsiness.

The room reflected Wiki's spirit, a treasure trove of imagination and wonder. Shelves overflowed with books, each filled with tales of mythical creatures and heroic quests. A wooden sword leaned against the wall, a constant reminder of the adventures he had envisioned with his father who went missing years ago.

As Wiki made his way downstairs, the scent of pancakes and syrup wafted through the air, inviting him into the heart of the home. His mom makes the best pancakes, they are so delicious you could eat them without syrup.

The kitchen was a warm and inviting space, delicately decorated with family photos and a chalkboard displaying his little sister's soccer schedule.

"Good morning, my sleepy adventurer," Mrs. Kinney said, her hair in curlers, pouring a cup of orange juice and placing it on the table. "I know it's not easy waking up for school, but a good breakfast will give you the vigor you need."

Wiki grumbled an unintelligible response, his mind still clouded with remnants of dreams and a longing for the comfort of his bed. He took a seat at the kitchen table, his gaze fixed on the untouched plate before him.

The moment was interrupted by the energetic entrance of Wiki's younger sister, Willow. Her tangled curly hair bouncing, her pajamas speckled with colorful flowers, she radiated a youthful exuberance that seemed to defy the early hour.

"Morning!" Willow chirped, plopping herself onto a chair beside Wiki. "Ready to face another exciting day of learning?" she asked.

Wiki rolled his eyes playfully, stating, "Oh, you mean another thrilling day of math equations and history lectures. How can I contain my excitement?"

Willow giggled, her eyes gleaming mischievously, "Come on, Wiki! You know it's all about having the right attitude. Besides, maybe today will be the day you finally solve the mystery of why your socks always disappear in the laundry!"

Wiki scoffed, "As if solving the great sock mystery will be the highlight of my day. I've got bigger things on my mind, like... like saving the seas from an evil pirate crew!" Their playful jabs and teasing punctuated the sleepy atmosphere of the kitchen.

Mrs. Kinney smiled, a mixture of amusement and exasperation evident on her face. "Alright, you two," she interjected, trying to maintain a sense of order. "Let's save the epic battles for after school. Can we please have just one morning where you get along? It's not too much to ask, is it?"

Wiki and Willow exchanged a brief glance, amusement dancing in their eyes. Despite their differences, they understood their mother's plea and nodded in reluctant agreement. With a sigh, Wiki picked up his fork and began to mechanically eat his breakfast, his thoughts drifting to the adventures that awaited him beyond the school walls.

Chapter 2

In a quaint house on Oak Road, one street over from Cypress Lane, the sun's gentle rays filtered through the curtains, casting a warm glow in Harper "Hap" Elizabeth Jones' bedroom.

Surrounding her was a vibrant blend of passions taking form. The walls were covered with an eclectic mix of sports posters, showcasing her favorite athletes in moments of triumph and tenacity. Intermingled with these displays of athletic prowess were colorful drawings and posters featuring fantastical creatures: dragons soaring through stormy skies and fairies dancing amidst lush meadows. Harper's room served as a testament to her dual nature, where the world of sports and the realm of imagination coexisted harmoniously.

Harper, with messy hair and a mischievous twinkle in her eyes, greeted the morning with contagious energy. She possessed an infectious smile that could brighten even the gloomiest of days, radiating warmth and excitement to all who crossed her path.

She leapt out of bed, her feet hitting the hard wooden floor with a deep thud, sending a reverberating sound throughout the room. With a burst of enthusiasm, Harper pulled open her closet doors, revealing a collection of sports jerseys and athletic gear neatly arranged on hangers. She grabbed her favorite soccer jersey, a vibrant green with her lucky number 7, and quickly slipped it on with her worn-out baseball cap.

Downstairs in the kitchen, the aroma of freshly brewed coffee mingled with the scent of sizzling bacon and eggs. Harper's father, the operator of the stove and creator of good smells, bellowed, "Morning my little champion!" as he stood tending to breakfast. He was a short and stubby man filled with ambition and dreams who instilled in Hap a sense of optimism and adventure.

Hap responded with a yawn, "Good morning, dad!"

"Ready to dominate the day?" Mr. Jones asked, his voice brimming with gusto.

Harper grinned, her face illuminated by the excitement radiating from her father. She walked into the kitchen, eagerly anticipating the delicious breakfast spread before her.

She playfully bumped her father's shoulder, "You know it, Dad! I'm all about embracing the thrill of every moment. Why are you so excited today?" She laughed while grabbing some of the crispy bacon and putting it on her plate.

"I have a feeling that today is going to be a special day. A day that will change everything for our family," Mr. Jones answered as he buttered some toast.

Harper's eyes widened with nosiness as she grabbed a spoonful of fluffy scrambled eggs, "Really, Dad? What's happening?"

Mr. Jones leaned forward, a playful glint in his eyes, "I might just be getting a big promotion at work! The boss hinted at it yesterday, and I have a good feeling about it."

Harper's face lit up with delight, "That's amazing, Dad! Finally, the title of Senior Land Surveyor. You deserve it!"

Mr. Jones chuckled warmly, "Thanks Champ. Now, grab a seat, and let's eat BACON!"

As they finished their breakfast, a familiar voice floated through the front door. "Good morning, everyone! Mind if I join you?" called out Wiki as he stepped inside, his glasses perched on the bridge of his nose.

Harper's face lit up with joy at the sight of her best friend. "Wiki! Perfect timing. I was just about to head out to meet you." Harper stood up and grabbed her school bag.

With their backpacks slung over their shoulders, Harper and Wiki bid farewell to Mr. Jones.

"See ya later, Dad! I love you!" Hap yelled to her father as the friends started the journey to school.

Chapter 3

As Wiki and Hap embarked on their journey to school, the crisp morning air enveloped them, carrying the scent of blooming flowers and the whispers of rustling leaves. The sun's rays peeked through the branches, casting a dappled pattern on the winding path that led them through the wooded outskirts of Ashenfall.

Wiki adjusted his glasses, his inquisitive eyes scanning their surroundings with a sense of childlike wonder and inspiration before he said, "You know, Harper, sometimes I feel like there's more to this world than meets the eye. Don't you ever get that feeling?"

Harper's eyes sparkled with excitement, her strides matching Wiki's with an easy rhythm as she said, "Oh, definitely! I mean, just look at these woods. They're teeming with secrets, I'm sure of it. Who knows what mystical creatures or hidden treasures are lurking just beyond our sight?"

Wiki nodded, a smile tugging at the corners of his lips, stating, "Exactly! It's like there's a whole universe waiting to be discovered, right here in our small town."

They laughed and then walked in comfortable silence for a moment, the distant sounds of chirping birds providing a soothing backdrop to their thoughts.

Harper broke the silence with a mischievous glint in her eye, asking, "So, Wiki, any new game releases or fantasy books you're itching to get your hands on?"

Wiki's face lit up, his enthusiasm evident in his voice, "Oh, you bet! There's this new role-playing game coming out next month. It's set in a world filled with magical creatures and ancient quests. It's called *Dungeons and Dragons™*."

Harper laughed, her vibrant spark radiating in her tone as she said, "That sounds exciting, Wiki! How does the game work?"

Wiki gleefully replied, "It's amazing! The entire game revolves around your creativity, there is literally no limit. I can't wait to put our ideas together to create our own elaborate campaigns full of mythical creatures and glorious champions."

Hap, visibly excited for the game, replied, "Oh wow! That really does sound groovy!"

They reached a point where the path opened, revealing the charming sight of Ashenfall Grade School. The red-brick building stood with pride, its windows gleaming in the morning light.

Harper nudged Wiki playfully, suggesting, "Race you to the front door!"

With a burst of laughter, they sprinted ahead, their backpacks bouncing on their shoulders as they competed to be the first to reach the school's entrance. Harper outpaced him and reached the entrance of the school first.

As they caught their breath, Wiki groaned, "I don't know why I even try. You always beat me in a race, I am not very athletic."

Hap giggled, "You might not think you're athletic but you're definitely getting faster."

As they walked through the heavy wooden double doors, the corridors echoed with the sound of shuffling feet, conversations, and the occasional burst of laughter. The two friends knew it was time to go their separate ways and bid each other farewell as they navigated to the lockers they were assigned, marking the start of their typical school day.

Chapter 4

As the bell rang, signaling the end of the school day, Harper and Wiki gathered their belongings and stepped out into the fading daylight. The air was filled with a mix of relief and anticipation, knowing that the school day was over, and it was time to let their imaginations run wild.

Together, they started their walk home, taking their usual path through the woods, reveling in the tranquility of nature. The whispering winds and skittering leaves created a harmonious atmosphere that enveloped them.

Their peaceful stroll was abruptly interrupted when Ethan Cooper and Tyler Nelson, known troublemakers, shouted from a short distance behind, "Hey, look! It's Dragon Nerd and his Fairy Queen."

Their sudden presence startled Harper and Wiki, as they wasted no time boisterously taunting the friends.

Reacting swiftly, Wiki and Harper exchanged quick glances before Hap declared, "Let's ditch these nitwits!"

They both sprinted through the woods, carried by their adrenaline, their feet pounding against the earth. As they dashed forward, Wiki's sharp eyes caught sight of a sparsely traveled path veering off from the main trail. It beckoned to him, its mysterious allure tinged with a hint of familiarity, leading toward a spot his late father had once taken him when he was younger. Feeling an instinctual pull toward this new path, Wiki made a split-second decision and branched off from the main route. Hap, always game for an escapade, followed suit without question.

After several minutes of darting through the dense undergrowth, they finally felt confident that they had left the bullies behind. The forest seemed to hush around them, as if nature itself held its breath for a moment. Pausing to regain their composure, Wiki's ears perked up, attuned to a faint and peculiar sound that seemed to weave through the air.

"Hap, do you hear that noise?" he asked, his voice filled with marvel.

Harper strained her ears, listening intently, but the sound eluded her senses. "I don't hear anything. What does it sound like?" she replied.

"I'm not sure how to describe it. It's faint and it sounds like it's coming from this way," he answered.

Fueled by overwhelming curiosity, he began to follow the source of the sound. Hap, noticing his intrigue, followed suit. As they grew closer to the source, the sound amplified with each step. Venturing forth, Wiki's gaze was drawn to a peculiar glow ahead. He pointed it out to Harper, his voice laced with excitement, "Look, Hap! Do you see that glow up ahead?"

Harper squinted, her eyes straining to perceive what Wiki saw, but the light remained elusive to her. "I don't see anything, Wiki. Are you sure?" she replied, a hint of frustration coloring her words.

Undeterred, they pressed on, Harper took the lead. Her eagerness to understand mounted with each stride.

She turned her head, looking back at Wiki, "Are you sure something is over here? I'm not seeing–,"

As she was saying those words, her foot got caught on an unseen obstacle causing her to stumble forward. She extended her arms out just in time, narrowly avoiding her face hitting a tree root. Hopping to her feet and brushing herself off, she looked down to see what had caused her misstep, her eyes blooming in surprise. There, nestled in the earth, lay a small wooden box.

Wiki hurried over to Hap's side, concern etched on his face, asking, "Are you okay?"

Hap's attention was captivated by the box, her fingers instinctively reaching out to touch its surface. Her bewilderment deepened as she picked it up and brushed it off, inspecting its handmade design. She noticed a tarnished brass hinge, which exhibited the markings of time. The remaining faces were embellished with symbols. One on each of the four sides of the delicate wooden construct, they seemed to pay homage to the elements of earth, wind, water, and fire. Stemming from these intricate emblems were grooves that all traced back to the front.

"What is this, Wiki?" she asked, her voice imbued with confusion.

Wiki, equally puzzled yet filled with an inexplicable sense of excitement, peered over her shoulder.

"I'm not sure Hap but I don't hear that sound anymore," he replied, his gaze fixed on the esoteric box. "And wait! There's the light I saw, coming from those crests."

"I think the lack of oxygen to your brain might have made you even crazier, Wiki. I don't see any light, but I do see beautiful carvings," she jested.

Twisting her torso, she handed him the mysterious wooden container they had stumbled upon.

"Wow! This is beautiful. I wish you could see what I am seeing. The wind crest is infused with a soft grey glow and the swirl is moving fluidly," he described.

As his fingers traced the intricate spiral carved into the glyph etched onto the top, the gentle grey shine pulsed in reaction. The light then wove outwardly through the grooves with a rhythm that varied as it traveled, stopping inches from the symbol.

Startled, he stated, "Whoa! The light moved when I touched it! I think it is asking me to follow it."

Harper, growing more perplexed by the moment, tilted her head and squinted.

"What?! That sounds like you are hallucinating," she said worried, with a furrowed brow.

Wiki chuckled, saying, "I don't think I am hallucinating Hap."

Taking a minute to further study and interpret the strange interaction, he adjusted his grip. Now, holding the left side of the box in his left hand, he placed the thumb and index finger of his right hand around the symbol. Gently urging it to travel along the groove. As he moved it, he could see the light radiating toward the front of the box, further solidifying his interpretation. He noticed as the crest shifted, the light was not behind it, only reaching toward its intended destination.

"Hey! It's working, the light is guiding me to move the swirling crest," Wiki beamed with delight.

Continuing to follow the glowing guide, he rotated his wrist, bringing the symbol around the edge to its final stop. A "Click" echoing from within the box.

"I got it! It is locked in place and won't move," he said.

"Can I give it a shot?" Harper asked, reaching her hand out.

Wiki handed the box over without a second thought, "Of course!"

Harper gripped the box while looking at the left side, saying, "Let's see if I can move this fire one."

In an effort to make it move, she took hold of the inferno symbol and gently nudged it. Unsuccessful in her initial attempt, she applied more force, causing her hand to slip.

Frustrated, she handed the box back to Wiki, saying, "Well, clearly, you've been chosen to open it."

Receiving the box in his left hand, he rotated it, so the water crest was before him. "Did you notice these things glow when you touch them?" Wiki asked.

Harper stated with a sigh, "No. Sadly, I don't see anything glowing."

"Well, that is concerning. Do you think we should be messing with this?" Wiki asked with a trembling voice, haunted by cautionary tales of ancient relics and their unforeseen consequences. The weight of the unknown bore heavily on his hesitant soul.

"We won't know unless we try, Wiki," Hap answered.

"But what if we're not ready for whatever this is? What if it's too much for us to handle?" Winslow questioned as his voice quivered with anxiety.

Harper, picking up on his uneasiness, placed a reassuring hand on his shoulder, her voice filled with gentle encouragement as she said, "We've always faced challenges together, and this is no different. We'll figure it out as we go."

Her words were like a lifeline, anchoring Wiki's wavering resolve. With her support still resonating in his ears, he took a deep breath and steadied his hand. Activating the symbol of waves with the presence of his touch, its guiding light glowed a brilliant blue. Recognizing what he must do next, he navigated it to its final resting place. "Click!"

In rapid succession, he turned the box over, so that the symbol of the mountain was facing him. Again, he repeated the same process, this time following the green luminescence to its predetermined location. "Click!"

"Alright, one more to go!" Winslow said nervously as he passed the box to his right hand, revealing the last crest of flame.

"Oo, this is exciting!" Harper said, her anticipation building.

Wiki, following the reddish orange rays, repeated the process one last time. "Click!"

With the final alignment, the box began to tremble in his grasp, startling him to the point of jumping back in surprise and dropping it to the ground. The forest fell silent once more, their heartbeats echoing in the stillness.

"Why is it shaking like that?" Harper asked.

In an instant, the rumbling ceased. Simultaneously, each spectrum of light shot from its crest back to its starting place, filling the grooves. The vibrance of each color intensified until reaching its peak brightness. The four colors blinked three times rapidly in unison.

Winslow's heart raced as he bent over and extended his arms to retrieve the fumbled box. As he reached out to pick it up, the box suddenly snapped open. It exuded a bright white light causing him to shield his eyes from the incoming assault.

Hap, noticing his reaction, asked, "Is everything okay Wiki?"

"Yeah, everything is fine. That light was just really bright," he said, dropping his guard once the bright light had dissipated.

"I guess not seeing the light isn't such a bad thing," she snickered.

Wiki laughed back before retrieving the now lifeless container and stood back up. Both friends peered inside.

"All that for an empty box?" Harper asked.

Wiki, enthralled by wisps of smokey lettering instinctively read them aloud, "*May this gift enhance your inner light, to vanquish darkness and promote what's right.* ~W.I.K."

As he spoke the words aloud, the hazy tendrils began to transform, blazing with intense heat. Each spoken word caused the letters to sear themselves into the wooden surface as the smoke dispersed, leaving behind permanent, charred impressions. Uttering the final word, a surge of immense energy erupted from deep within his heart, coursing through his entire being.

"Whoa! That really gave me chills," Hap said, her eyes fixed on Wiki.

"Yeah, me too, and I have those same initials." Wiki responded as his gaze moved from Hap back to the wooden box.

"How did you do that?" Harper asked, amazed.

"What do you mean? All I did was read the words," Winslow inquired.

Harper, not fully understanding what she saw, said in a whisper, "Yeah! When you said those words, they just appeared."

Noticing the waning daylight, Wiki stated, "I don't know what is really going on, but we should head home."

The friends set off on their journey back to Winslow's house with the mysterious box in hand.

Chapter 5

Harper joined the Kinney family for dinner, as she often did on weekdays. Her mother tragically passed away during childbirth, leaving a profound void in the lives of both Hap and her father. Her absence was deeply felt, a tender ache that resonated through the years.

Left as a single father, Mr. Jones worked tirelessly to provide for Harper and himself. The demands of his job often kept him late into the evening, striving to secure their financial stability.

Mrs. Kinney would include Harper in many of their family activities to help Mr. Jones. Tonight, Mrs. Kinney had prepared a mouthwatering pot roast for dinner, cooked slowly to perfection. The tender, succulent meat was accompanied by a medley of roasted vegetables, including carrots, potatoes, and onions. The aroma of herbs and spices filled the air, tantalizing their senses and setting their appetites ablaze.

They sat around the table, enjoying the flavors of the delicious meal.

"Mmm, Mrs. Kinney, this roast is amazing!" Harper exclaimed, savoring each bite. "You always know how to make it just right."

Mrs. Kinney beamed with pride as she said, "Thank you, Harper. I'm glad you like it. It's one of our family's favorites. And you know, your dad's lasagna is still the best In town."

Wiki nodded in agreement, he finished chewing before saying, "Yeah, your dad's lasagna is legendary."

Harper chuckled, saying, "Definitely! It has been a while since we had a meal at our place. I'll talk to my dad about it."

With their plates cleared, Harper and Wiki excused themselves, eager to retreat to the sanctuary of Wiki's room. They knew homework awaited them, but their thoughts were consumed by the enigma they had stumbled upon. After putting their plates in the sink, they walked upstairs to Winslow's room.

"Okay, Wiki, let's tackle this math homework," Harper said, eyeing the textbook open in front of them. "We have to solve these problems before my dad comes to pick me up."

Wiki, lying flat on his shaggy carpet, groaned, "I can't concentrate, Hap. My mind keeps wandering back to what happened earlier today."

The moon cast a soft radiance through Wiki's bedroom window as Harper sat cross-legged on the floor, their voices hushed in secrecy as the mysterious box lay open between them.

Hap looked up at Wiki, concern etched on her face as she asked, "Wiki, are you okay? You seem different since you opened the box."

Wiki said with an expression of confusion, "Yeah, I am okay. But Hap, it was... strange. I felt this rush of adrenaline after I read those words. It was like a surge of power passing through me, but I don't understand what it means."

Hap's eyes grew wider and more attentive, her curiosity was re-ignited as she said, "There's definitely something bizarre going on. It has done something to you, but I cannot quite put my finger on it."

Wiki furrowed his brow, asking, "But what does it all mean, Hap? Why did it react to me like that? And what are we supposed to do?" trying to make sense of what they had experienced.

Harper took a deep breath and locked eyes with Wiki before replying, "We can't let these questions go unanswered, Wiki. The library is our best chance to find clues. We can do some research to see if we can find anything about that box," she continued. "With any luck, we might also figure out whose initials those were. Let's start by searching for books on mysterious objects, ancient artifacts, and any information that might help us figure out what is happening."

Wiki nodded, a flicker of excitement lighting up his eyes as he said, "You're right! Maybe we'll find a story or a legend that can help us understand the box and its connection to me."

They decided to keep their discovery a secret for now, not wanting to alarm anyone until they had more information. With a shared insight, they knew they could trust each other to explore the unknown.

As they sat there, contemplating the path ahead, a sense of anticipation enveloped them. They understood that their lives had taken an unexpected turn, and they were on the brink of an extraordinary adventure.

Interrupting their thoughts, Mrs. Kinney called from downstairs, "Harper! Your dad is here!"

Harper quickly grabbed her bookbag as she hollered a response, "On my way down, Mrs. Kinney!" She turned to Wiki, placing a hand on his shoulder as she said, "We will get some answers. I promise."

Wiki stated as he met her gaze with a look of gratitude in his eyes, "Together, Hap. We'll uncover the truth and unravel the mysteries surrounding this box."

With a final wave Harper rushed downstairs, leaving Wiki in his room to continue wondering what was happening to him.

Chapter 6

The following day, after the final school bell rang, the library beckoned them.

"I'm so excited to see what we can find today!" Wiki said while shoving his notebooks into his backpack.

"Yeah! It gives me butterflies just thinking about the possibilities," Hap responded while trying to rush them out of the school building.

Their trip to the library was brief as it resides close to the school. Upon entering the library, they were met with the familiar scent of aged books, lacquered shelves, and hushed whispers. The librarian, Mrs. Jenkins, nodded a greeting as they approached the front desk.

"We're hoping to find some information about an interesting box that we found. What would be the best place to start?" Hap asked quietly.

"Hmm, the best place to start... What kind of box is it?" Mrs. Jenkins probed.

"It's an old wooden box we found in the woods with interesting symbols on it but we're not sure what to make of it," Wiki stated.

"In that case, I suggest that you look in either the History or Anthropology sections as a starting point," Mrs. Jenkins said as she gestured toward their location.

"Thank you! That's why we call you the 'Keeper of Knowledge'," Hap replied as the pair proceeded to the History section.

Mrs. Jenkins smiled with a sense of fulfillment as the two departed. They scoured the shelves, of both sections, flipping through pages and sifting through information, hoping to find any trace of the box, or what Winslow described seeing. Yet, their efforts proved fruitless, leaving the answers they sought shrouded in the mysteries of the unknown.

Sitting at a table in between the shelves and surrounded by old books, Wiki sighed obnoxiously before saying, "Well, this research isn't leading us anywhere. It's getting frustrating. I hoped we would find something about the box in all these books."

Hap nodded as she grabbed a stick of gum from her pocket, before popping it in her mouth she said, "I know,

Wiki. There must be something out there. Maybe we're just looking in the wrong places."

Wiki leaned on the table with his elbows, stating, "You're right. We need to think outside the box."

"That was quite punny," Hap replied with a smile, closing the book she had been flipping through before asking, "For now, do you want to head over to the playground?"

Wiki's face brightened up at the mention of their sanctuary of imagination where time seemed to stand still. The playground, enlivened with swings, slides, and a towering pirate ship structure, had always been their refuge. The place where they could transform into daring adventurers, exploring uncharted territories of their own creation. The sprawling green space inviting them to step into a world where pirates ruled the high seas and treasures awaited discovery.

They returned the books to their rightful places among the shelves and packed up their belongings. Making their way outside, they bid farewell to Mrs. Jenkins. While strolling along the cracked pavement, they reminisced about the countless pirate escapades they had embarked upon. Their footsteps echoing as they approached the world of make-believe and endless possibilities. Their peaceful reverie was immediately shattered when two familiar faces came into view.

Tyler and Ethan sauntered toward them with mischief gleaming in their eyes. Quick to assert their dominance, the bullies snatched up empty cans from a nearby trash bin, their intentions clear. Tyler, lacking finesse, hurled his can with all his might, only for it to fall pathetically short. Ethan, known for his pitching prowess, showcased his skill as he wound up and released the can, its trajectory set on a collision course with Wiki's unsuspecting head.

Time seemed to stand still; the moment frozen in suspense. In a split second, Wiki's instincts took over. His body moved with an agility and grace he had never possessed. He sidestepped the incoming can, its metallic body whizzing past his ear. Harper and Wiki locked eyes, shock reflecting in their wide gazes.

"RUN!" They instinctively shouted in unison, their voices laced with urgency.

Without a moment's hesitation, they sprinted back to the safety of Wiki's house, their hearts pounding in their chests.

As they raced through the streets, Wiki had taken quite a lead when Hap hollered, "Slow down speedy!"

The distance at which he heard her voice caused him to look back. Not realizing how far ahead he was, he came to a stop to wait for her. It was as if the very fabric of their reality had shifted, Wiki had never been able to run faster than Hap, especially not that fast. Once she caught up to him, he began running again but paid closer attention to his pace.

Finally reaching Wiki's street, the two slowed to a jog. Their pace decelerated to a brisk walk as they approached Wiki's yard. As they reached the front door, Hap, breathing heavily, noticed that Wiki wasn't out of breath. They made their way upstairs reaching the refuge of Wiki's room.

Collapsing on the bed, their bodies still trembling with adrenaline, Winslow spoke first, "Phew, it's nice to be home. I wish those two would just leave us alone."

Hap nodded in agreement as she tried to get her breathing under control.

"Hap," Wiki said, his voice filled with uncertainty, "Did you see that? I... I dodged the can. It was like my body moved on its own."

Harper nodded, her voice barely a whisper, "I saw it too, Wiki. You were... different. And I couldn't keep up with your pace. I don't think I've ever seen anyone run that fast and you're not sweating or out of breath."

As they sat up on Wiki's bed, his new abilities pressing on them like an invisible force. The tingling sensation in Wiki's hands intensified, as if tiny electric currents surged through his fingertips, a reminder of the extraordinary power that has awakened within him.

"Hap, this is incredible," Wiki whispered, his voice was barely audible in the hushed room. "I can feel it again, the tingling radiating from my shoulders down to my fingers."

Hap leaned closer, saying, "Wiki, we're in uncharted territory here. These powers, this connection to the box, are beyond our understanding. But we can't ignore it. We have to embrace it and learn to control it."

"What if it's dangerous, Hap?" Wiki's voice quivered, seeking reassurance. "What if I can't control it, and it consumes me?"

Hap reached her arm out, placing a comforting hand on Wiki's trembling shoulder as she affirmed, "We're in this together, Wiki. We'll figure it out. We'll learn to harness this power, to channel it for good. But we need to be cautious. Not everyone will understand what you're going through. Let's keep this a secret, at least for now."

Wiki nodded as he said, "You're right, Hap. We need to keep this to ourselves, at least until we've unraveled its mysteries," his gaze fixed on the thick carpet under him.

Suddenly, a piercing cry shattered the tranquility of the moment.

"HELP!"

The desperate plea rang out, slicing through the air with an urgency that sent shivers down their spines. Wiki and Hap exchanged startled glances, their eyes expanding in alarm. They sprang into action, their legs propelling them with swiftness. They dashed out of the house, their feet pounding against the soft earth, as they followed the source of the distressed call.

The backyard unfolded before them; a familiar landscape transformed by the unexpected turn of events. There, near the burn pit, stood Willow, Wiki's younger sister. Her usually innocent gaze was tinged with fear, her small frame trembling with distress. Old Man Nelson, their neighbor known for his weekly ritual of burning leaves and grass clippings, was nowhere in sight.

"WILLOW, get back!" Wiki's voice erupted with urgency as he yelled, his eyes full of horror.

Time seemed to slow down as Willow's gaze shifted toward Wiki's direction, her foot faltering on the uneven ground. Anxiety washed over Hap as she witnessed her friend's sister teetering toward the perilous flames. Wiki started to panic, wanting his little sister to be okay. His heart started to race as he screamed her name, "WILLOW!"

As he shouted, a plume of smoke erupted from the burn pit just as Willow fell beyond the safety of the stone barrier which surrounded it.

Wiki yelled worriedly, racing to his sister's side, "Willow are you okay?"

As the two friends approached the pit, they heard coughing sounds but struggled to get visual confirmation that she was okay.

"A little help here!" Willow called from beneath the ghastly grey veil. Followed by her little hand extending out in search of assistance.

Wiki, noticing the gesture, immediately reached his hand out to meet hers. "We're right here Willow," he assured, gripping her hand tightly.

Hap stated, following suit, "Give me your other hand."

Holding her hands tightly, they assisted Willow up and out of the pit.

"Are you hurt?" Wiki asked inquisitively while looking for any visible injuries.

"I think I'm okay, but I can't say the same for Ms. Sally. Can you get her and make sure she is okay, please?" Willow said with concern.

Wiki stated, bending down to retrieve the ashen doll, "She has seen better days, that's for sure. Nothing that a wardrobe change, a little blush, and a haircut can't fix." Winslow smiled as he handed the doll to his sister, recommending, "Let's get you inside and cleaned up."

As the three made their way to the house, Wiki asked sternly, "Willow, why were you near that fire?"

"I was trying to get Ms. Sally, who fell in while we were dancing. I looked for Mr. Nelson and I couldn't find him, so I called for help. Then when you came and called my name, it surprised me, and I tripped," Willow answered with tears welling up in her eyes.

"But you almost got burned. That was too dangerous," Hap butted in with concern.

Willow was like a little sister to Harper as well since she didn't have siblings of her own.

Hap's gaze shifted to Wiki, realization in her eyes as she asked, "Wiki, did you... did you yell at the fire?"

Wiki looked at his hands, his voice barely a whisper, stating, "I... I don't know. It was like an instinct, Hap. I saw Willow in danger, and something inside me just... reacted."

The realization washed over Hap, causing her to ask, "Do you think the thing that happened yesterday has anything to do with this? Maybe now you can– "

"HAP!" Wiki interjected; they had agreed this would be a secret until they understood more about what was going on.

Willow looked up at her brother, her eyes expanding with intrigue, asking, "Winslow, you saved me! How did you do that?"

Wiki knelt, wrapping his arms around his sister, his voice filled with love and reassurance as he spoke, "I don't know, Willow. But what matters is that you're safe now. Why don't you go get a snack and play inside for the rest of the day."

"And maybe change your dress if you don't want your Mama asking a bunch of questions," Hap added.

With a small smile, Willow walked into the house with Wiki and Hap following behind at a small distance.

Hap stepped closer, her voice filled with excitement, "Wiki, what was that?"

Wiki's mind raced with possibilities as he said, "I have no idea. I just really didn't want the fire to hurt my sister." Wiki ascended each step carefully as they made their way up the stairs to his bedroom, saying, "Umm by the way, you almost gave it away Hap."

Hap followed him in lock step while gesturing to keep quiet and resisting the urge to respond.

Upon entering his room, she replied, "I am sorry for almost giving away the secret. I need to be better about when I bring it up." She took a seat at his desk, spinning in the chair as she continued, "But we didn't find any answers at the library, this... this is something extraordinary. We have to figure out what's happening to you."

Wiki nodded, saying, "You're right, Hap. We'll keep searching, while also being careful. We need to understand these powers and how to use them responsibly. Maybe we should go back to where we found the box and see if we can find anything?"

Hap gazed off and fumbled with her chin, thinking over what Wiki suggested before replying, "I mean that seems like a great idea to me. What do we have to lose?"

"Arrr, ye scallywags!" Wiki said, transforming his voice into that of a pirate captain with a newfound sense of enthusiasm. "The grand adventure 'o 'Tides of Discovery' sets sail as the bell strikes four, so gather yer loot and be ready to set foot on uncharted shores!"

Harper burst into a hearty laugh as she mockingly snapped her hand against her forehead in a salute, replying, "Aye aye, Cap'n! I be at yer service!" She winked mischievously, playing along.

Equipped with their water flasks, flashlights, and their backpacks, they headed to the front door to embark on their next adventure.

Hap chimed in with a stern tone, "Arrr, our provisions be secured, Cap'n. We be ready to embark on this treacherous voyage!" Giggles escaped their lips, the thrill of their imaginative escapade taking form as they walked outside.

Chapter 7

The sun was casting dappled shadows through the leafy canopy above, creating a mystical ambiance that danced along the forest floor. The pair of friends arrived back at the spot where they found the box to see if they could find any more evidence or clues to help them figure out what Wiki was experiencing.

"This is the place," Hap spouted, her eyes scanning the surroundings.

"The spot where we found the box," Wiki said as he nodded, his gaze focused on the path ahead, "The path doesn't look the same."

The path that was once shimmering with an otherworldly luminosity, seemed ordinary, blending seamlessly with the natural foliage. It was as if the magic had retreated, leaving no trace of its presence.

They moved forward cautiously, stepping onto the path that no longer beckoned with its radiant allure. As they walked deeper into the woods, an unsettling silence enveloped them. Then, a faint sound reached their ears; the distant rustling of leaves and snapping of twigs. It was the unmistakable rhythm of approaching footsteps. Instinctively, they froze, their eyes widening with alarm.

"We need to hide," Hap whispered urgently.

She scanned the area, searching for a suitable place to take cover. Wiki's eyes darted around, and he spotted a cluster of large rocks nestled amidst the thick underbrush.

"Over there," he mouthed silently, pointing toward their potential hiding spot.

They hurriedly made their way to the rocks, their hearts racing, heightening their senses as they crouched behind the natural barricade. Tucked into their hiding spot, the sound of footsteps grew louder, their rhythm drawing nearer.

The forest was quiet, the silence broken only by the faint crackling of twigs beneath heavy boots. Wiki and Hap exchanged worried glances, their breaths shallow and barely audible. Through a small gap between the rocks, they caught a glimpse of the clearing where the box had once been. Harper gripped Winslow's arm as a group of nefarious figures emerged from the thick underbrush.

"Ow! Watch those nails, Hap!" he whispered with a grunt.

Harper looked at Wiki apologetically, mouthing, "Sorry."

The figures were dressed in dark cloaks, their faces obscured by hoods, they moved with purpose. The smallest of them pulled her hood down and approached the clearing. Coming to a halt, she uttered an unintelligible whisper while extending both arms, akin to unfurling wings.

"The Tetrad Vessel was opened here," she said as her eyes, once scanning the scenery, were now still with a distant glimmer as if peering through the veil of reality into something unseen.

Wiki and Hap stayed shrouded behind the rocks, their breaths shallow as they peered through the cracks, trying to hear the whispers of the group before them.

"I can still feel the energy lingering. We must find the one who opened it before they realize what they now possess," the small, robed woman spoke.

Overflowing with contempt, she drew her right hand toward her chest, while her left index finger ascended and traced a deliberate path across her other hand, leaving a rivulet of blood in its wake. Her expression remained composed, unfazed by the act, as if it were a routine motion. She extended her arm. With a calculated grip, she squeezed her hand, coaxing forth additional drops of the sanguine essence. The crimson liquid pooled and intermingled, forming intricate patterns that seemed to pulsate. She raised both hands, now hovering over the gathering pool, and began chanting in a voice barely audible.

Wiki's voice quivered as he whispered, "Are they using blood magic?"

Hap's grip tightened on Wiki's arm as they watched in horror. The robed lady continued her ritualistic chant, her voice growing more fervent. The ground beneath them began to tremble and a swirling vortex of darkness began to materialize, expanding with each passing second. The air crackled with an unsettling intensity. Nervousness, curiosity and a small bit of fear settled in as they remained hidden.

"She is performing some kind of ritual with her blood," Wiki whispered, "I don't like the feeling of this. We need to find out what they're up to."

Harper nodded in agreement, asking, "Is that a portal or something?" her voice filled with a mix of fascination and fear as she saw the dark magic at work.

Wiki nodded as his eyes fixed on the unfolding spectacle, saying, "We'll wait until they're finished. Once they leave, we'll investigate and see if there's anything we can uncover."

As the portal grew larger, its inky tendrils reached toward the sky. Without direction, the group of hooded figures formed a line behind the leader as she finished her chant.

Spinning around, she smirked as she faced the others, her robe catching the wind which gave her a foreboding appearance, "Go. NOW!" she demanded, pointing toward the portal.

One by one, they stepped forward, their bodies engulfed in the haunting sheen. As they entered the portal, their forms wavered and distorted, merging with the mysterious energies.

The friends watched as each member of the group disappeared. Then the portal pulsed with a surge of power, its liveliness like a beating heart, before slowly diminishing in size until it could no longer be seen.

"What did we just watch?" Hap whispered, her voice filled with captivation.

"They just vanished into thin air," Wiki said as his eyes narrowed, trying to comprehend the spectacle before them. "Those people cannot be up to anything good," he said, visibly shaken. "It was like the portal consumed them."

"Now's our chance," Hap said with conviction, "Let's go and see if there's anything left behind."

Cautiously, they emerged from their hiding spot and approached the location of the ephemeral portal. Its energy had dissipated, leaving only residual traces of its presence. They scanned for any clues that might shed light on the group's intentions.

"I am looking but I am not seeing anything here, Wiki," Hap said frustratedly, scanning the area. "We just witnessed something totally out of this world. Something we don't even understand."

Wiki nodded, his eyes gazing into the now empty space where the portal had been as his mind contemplated the myriad of possibilities it could encompass, "You're right, Hap. I don't understand anything that is happening right now. This encounter with the portal and these people has only deepened the mystery surrounding the box." He continued, "We'll keep searching, uncovering every piece of the puzzle until we have the answers we seek. I think for now we should head out of here before anyone else shows up!"

Seized by the moment, they swiftly departed the tranquil clearing. They bounded through the undergrowth as they raced home, their feet kicking up the forest floor.

Chapter 8

After their bellies were satisfied with Mrs. Kinney's home-cooked meal, Wiki and Hap ascended the creaking staircase to his room. The weight of their unfinished homework lingered in the air, but the allure of the magical and mysterious had cast its spell upon them, making it impossible to focus on mundane angles and equations.

Taking a seat on the cozy carpeted floor with their notebooks forgotten, Hap couldn't contain her bubbling excitement.

Her words tumbled out in a rush, "Can you believe what we saw today? Those people in the woods, the mysterious portal, and the very existence of this odd box."

Wiki nodded in agreement, "It's blowing my mind, Hap. That ritual they performed is beyond anything I've ever imagined." He said while his mind continued to grasp the magnitude of what they had encountered.

Leaning closer, Hap's voice dropped to a conspiratorial whisper, "We must figure out the truth about why those people were so desperate to get their hands on that box."

Wiki strained to recall the lady's exact words, before saying, "You're right. She mentioned something about 'The Tetrad Vessel.' I wonder what that could be?"

With a glimmer of excitement in her eyes, Hap leaned in even closer, her voice brimming with enthusiasm, "Hey, Wiki, what if we try something different tomorrow? Instead of going to the library, let's visit Mr. Jennings, the big history fan. He knows all about the legends and mysteries surrounding our town. Maybe he can help us unravel the secrets behind that strange box and the people we saw in the woods."

Wiki's brows scrunched, contemplating Hap's suggestion before replying, "Hmm, that's an interesting idea. My mom told me stories about him and my dad being friends when he was still here. He knows the history of this town more than anyone else. He might have come across something that could help. Do you think he would be willing to share his secrets with a couple of kids like us?"

"That's even if he believes us in the first place!" Hap shrugged, a smile on her face as she continued, "There's only one way to find out, Wiki. We'll never know unless we try. Mr. Jennings has always been kind to us, and he loves sharing stories about the past. I didn't know he was friends with your dad though. That might help us! Maybe if we show him how much we care about this, he'll be willing to guide us in the right direction."

Wiki's voice filled with a tinge of worry, "We gotta be careful, Hap. Those folks we saw, they're into some dark stuff. Who knows what they're capable of?" Entranced by his nightmares coming to life in his mind, he whispered, "Sometimes, I can't help but wonder if this is all just in my head. Maybe I didn't really dodge that can from Ethan, and I'm stuck in some crazy dream."

Even as he said it, he knew it was not true. He could feel something was different inside and he needed to know what. Hap's eyes mirrored his concern, but she remained resolute.

She clasped Wiki's hand firmly, assuring him she said, "I get your doubts, Wiki, but we can't ignore what happened. Those intricate hand carved crests, we both saw those words burn into it, that weird feeling you felt... it's real, I know it. We've stumbled upon something big, something mysterious, and we gotta find out more."

Their conversation was abruptly interrupted by Mrs. Kinney's urgent call from downstairs. "Harper! Your dad's here!"

Hap shot Wiki a quick glance and said, "Meet me at my house tomorrow at nine o'clock in the morning and we'll walk together. Mr. Jennings must know a lot about this stuff. And remember, the lady mentioned 'The Tetrad Vessel.' It's our starting point."

With a sense of urgency, Hap dashed downstairs and disappeared into her father's waiting truck.

Left alone in his room, Wiki stood up to go snuggle in his bed, his mind racing with unanswered questions. "*Why me? Why couldn't Hap see the glow coming from the box? Did I make that fire go out when Willow fell? Who are those people from the woods? Why did they want the box? What was that electrical feeling that moved through me? Why did they cut themselves to use magic...Wait, this means magic is real!*"

The room felt heavy with uncertainty as Wiki wrestled with his thoughts. The idea of using magic, especially if it meant causing harm or shedding blood, made him uneasy. Yet, the idea that magic exists made him feel like his dreams could be coming true. He shook his head, trying to clear his mind, but the questions persisted, swirling like a tempest in his imagination.

Unable to find solace in slumber, Wiki reached for his beloved stack of "X-Men™" comics, hoping to find comfort within their pages. Beast was his favorite superhero. He idolized Beast because they both wore glasses but even more so because of Beast's scientific curiosity and innovative mind. He found inspiration in the way Beast approached understanding mutations and superpowers.

As he immersed himself in the adventures of Beast and the other X-Men™, his eyelids grew heavy, and his thoughts slowly drifted away. With comics scattered around him, the night passed, and the dawn brought a sense of purpose.

Chapter 9

The moment Wiki opened his eyes, he was infused with vibrant excitement. After briefly tidying his room, he went downstairs to face the day. He quickly finished his breakfast, barely tasting the toast and scrambled eggs, his mother had lovingly prepared.

As he tied his laces he called out, "Mom! Today, Hap and I are taking another step forward in unraveling the mysteries of our imaginations."

"Okay honey, that sounds amazing! Stay safe and be home before dinner!" Mrs. Kinney replied laughingly.

With his backpack slung over his shoulder, the wooden box safely tucked away inside, he hurriedly made his way through the familiar streets of their small town. The crisp air carried the scent of dew-kissed grass, and the sound of distant bird songs filled the atmosphere.

He reached Harper's house and without hesitation, turned the doorknob and entered. Hap, who had been waiting in the living room, looked up with a bright smile.

"You're here! Let's not waste another minute. We have a meeting with destiny today, Wiki," she said.

Winslow returned the smile, his eyes shining with hope as he said, "Absolutely, Hap. We need to find answers, and I have a feeling Mr. Jennings knows something, I just hope what he knows helps us."

With synchronized steps, Wiki and Hap made their way through the streets. The morning was alive with the sounds of passing cars, bicycle bells, and snippets of conversations.

"Do you know how your dad knew Mr. Jennings?" Harper asked while jumping over the cracks on the sidewalk.

"I don't know how they met; I've never asked my mom. She has mentioned many times how they would travel to some really cool places. I don't remember all the details," he responded while trying to match her pace.

"Maybe we should ask him while we are there?" She suggested as they turned right onto Mr. Jennings' street.

"That's not a bad idea at all, Hap!" Wiki said as he grinned from ear to ear at the possibility of learning something new about his father.

Arriving at Mr. Jennings' house, Wiki paused for a moment, taking a deep breath to steady his nerves.

"We made it. My stomach is tied in knots, I don't know why I am so nervous," he stammered.

"It's okay, just continue those deep breaths. Once you're ready, we can go knock," she said.

A short moment later, Wiki took the first step, and they made their way up the front porch steps, the boards creaking along the way. The weathered front door stood before him, its paint peeling, bearing the marks of time. Wiki raised his hand and gently knocked, the sound of his knuckles against the wood echoed through the quiet street. After a brief moment, the door opened, revealing Mr. Jennings, a distinguished figure with silver hair and spectacles perched on his nose.

"Hello, Winslow and Harper. To what do I owe this pleasure?" He asked the two friends while standing at the open door, steaming coffee cup in hand.

"Hap and I have some questions for you, do you mind if we come in Mr. Jennings?" Wiki responded.

A gesture with his left hand and his warm smile welcomed them inside, inviting them into a captivating tapestry woven from the threads of the past. Wiki stepped across the threshold, the dimly lit hallway in front of him was adorned with vintage photographs and old newspaper clippings.

"Ah, my young adventurous friends," Mr. Jennings greeted them, his voice carrying a hint of intrigue. "You've come seeking answers, have you?"

Entering Mr. Jennings' cozy study, Wiki and Hap marveled at the shelves lined with books that seemed to hold the weight of decades past. Taking a seat in front of Mr. Jennings' cluttered desk, Wiki and Hap exchanged excited glances.

Wiki's voice trembled as he began, "Mr. Jennings, we've stumbled upon something mysterious; a wooden box with symbols and whispers of 'The Tetrad Vessel.' We need your help to make sense of it all."

Mr. Jennings leaned back in his worn leather chair. He was no stranger to the wild imaginations of adventurous youngsters, but once they said Tetrad Vessel, his interest was piqued.

"What made you come to me for these answers?" He asked while maintaining eye contact with the children.

"Well, you know a lot about history and this town. I figured if anyone would be able to help, it would be you," Wiki answered while fidgeting with the pocket of his jeans.

A knowing smile curled Mr. Jennings' lips as he answered, "I am glad you came to me for help. Sometimes the answers we seek are not handed to us on a silver platter. They lie in unexpected places, awaiting the curious and determined souls who are willing to embark on a journey of exploration."

It was many years ago that someone else came to him with very similar questions. Wiki and Hap exchanged uncertain glances as Mr. Jennings asked, "Did you bring the box with you?"

"Yeah! I've got it," Wiki stated as he began unzipping his backpack, "Right here on top."

He pulled the wooden box out of his backpack and sat it on the desk in front of Mr. Jennings.

Mr. Jennings paused and looked at the artifact before him. "Just like I remember," he said as he appeared to mentally retrace his steps through time. "Many years ago, when your father was not much older than you, he brought the box to me. He was so proud of the name he had given to that old thing." He continued, "He told me he was playing in the woods and felt as if the box called to him, it sounded like a vivid dream. He described the box as having glowing symbols on it. The imagination of children is the stuff of wonder!"

"Wait, you said my dad brought this box to you?" Wiki asked as he momentarily froze in his seat, "I have so many questions and I don't know where to start."

Mr. Jennings nodded his head to confirm as he continued, "He referred to it as The Tetrad Vessel."

An involuntary gasp escaped Hap's mouth before she asked, "So the box is The Tetrad Vessel! Do you know what it means?" gently nudging her elbow to Wiki's side.

"In fact, I do. It is quite clever if you ask me. Have you kids heard about 'Harmonious balance'? It is achieved when the four basic elements come together in perfect synergy," Mr. Jennings answered. Both children nodded in agreement as he continued speaking, "Well, you see, it's as simple as that. 'Tetrad' simply means a set of four things which are connected by a commonality. In this sense, the commonality is 'balance'. In the case of your box, you can see different symbols which appear to be wind, water, fire and earth.

Each of those balances the other. Wind is grounded by earth while fire is tamed by water."

"Oh, yeah? That is super groovy," Hap said while smiling at her friend.

Wiki, still wrapping his head around what Mr. Jennings had described, stated, "I knew you and my dad were friends in the past, but I have never heard stories about this box."

Mr. Jennings smiled in response as he said, "Now that you have your dad's box—rightfully so—I'm sure you'll do your darndest to learn everything about it. For now, I'm afraid I must go tend to the flowers before the heat of the day."

"Thank you, Mr. Jennings!" Wiki said sincerely, "We appreciate your time and help."

Mr. Jennings said in a gentle tone, "You're welcome, I'm glad I could be of help. The truth has a way of revealing itself to those who seek it earnestly. If you have any more questions, I will do my best to help. Good luck on your journey, my young friends."

As Wiki and Hap left Mr. Jennings' study, the weight of their discovery hung heavy in the air. They walked in silence, their steps echoing down the hallway, until they finally stepped outside.

Breaking the silence, Harper spoke up, "So the box is called The Tetrad Vessel and– "

Winslow interrupted, "More importantly, I found this box the same way Mr. Jennings described my dad finding it. That can't be a coincidence. Why was it just out in the woods?"

"I'm not sure Wiki, I think this one answer just opened up a million more questions," Harper responded.

"You're right and yet we still have no idea where to even look for these answers," Winslow said growing visibly more frustrated.

They continued walking through the vibrant streets, the world around them bustling with activity.

"I can't imagine how you must be feeling right now, but I am here to listen if you want to talk," Harper said, hoping to find some way to make her friend feel better but struggling to find the right words.

"I don't know how to feel right now. I just can't believe this was my dad's. Does my mom know anything about this and if she did, why didn't she ever tell me?" Wiki said as he continued to wrap his mind around what he learned.

"If your mom knew and didn't tell you, there had to be a reason," Hap said as they arrived at Wiki's neighborhood.

Wiki answered, his gaze fixed on the distance, "I just don't know if I should ask her about this now, or keep it hidden. I don't know what to do."

His thoughts were consumed by their encounter with Mr. Jennings and wondering if they were truly on the right path. Harper, sensing Wiki's unease, kept her eyes focused ahead. She wanted to be the pillar of support for her best friend, hoping to alleviate his doubts. But deep down, she shared his concerns and didn't know how to answer the question pertaining to his mom.

The wind whispered through the trees, pulling Wiki's attention to a peculiar small sapling on the corner of the street further up the road. Its branches seemed to twist and turn in an intricate pattern, almost beckoning him closer. And then, as if in response to his unwavering gaze, what looked like a face appeared and disappeared just as quickly. He blinked rapidly in disbelief, questioning his own senses.

"Did I just see a face?" he wondered aloud, his voice filled with uncertainty.

Harper paused quickly and turned around, asking, "A face? What do you mean? Where?"

Wiki's heart raced as he struggled to find the right words to describe the surreal encounter. "I... I think I saw a face in the branches of that tree," he replied, his voice filled with disbelief.

Hap peered closely at the tree, trying to figure out what Wiki was talking about before replying, "I don't see it, Wiki. Are you sure?"

Wiki remained fixated on the tree, wondering what tricks his eyes were playing on him. Just as doubt began to cloud his mind, a small giggle reached his ears. It was a sound so pure and innocent that it sent shivers down his spine.

Startled, Wiki pointed toward the tree that left him bewildered with astonishment, yelling, "There! The tree just laughed!"

Harper, unable to hear or see anything out of the ordinary, furrowed her brows with concern as she said, "I don't hear anything, Wiki. Are you sure you're alright?"

Caught in the whirlwind of his own emotions, Wiki struggled to find the right words, he stammered, "I... I don't know, Hap. I think this tree is alive, and it's speaking to me."

Perplexed, Hap searched the area around them. She wanted to understand and support him, but the lack of tangible evidence left her feeling uncertain.

"Uhhh what? I can't hear or see anything, Wiki. But you know, ever since you opened that magical box, strange things have been happening. Maybe it's connected?" she suggested.

The wind picked up slightly, gently ruffling Hap's hair as if to acknowledge her presence.

Wiki nodded, his mind buzzing with possibilities as he said, "You're right, Hap. It could be related. Maybe the box granted me the ability to see and hear things, like ghosts?"

As Harper and Wiki stood there, puzzled and searching for answers, a soft voice broke through the air, pulling Wiki's attention away from the tree.

"I am not a tree or a ghost, silly," it said, sounding like a playful child. Wiki's eyes grew in amazement as he realized he could hear the voice clearly.

"I am The Wind," the voice continued, the face he had seen earlier transforming into a swirling vortex.

Excitement filled Wiki as he turned to Hap and asked, "Did you hear that, Hap? Are you seeing this?"

Concern began to surface on her expression, she responded, "No, I'm not seeing or hearing anything, Wiki," struggling to grasp what was unfolding.

Standing beside him, Harper noticed his eyes intently following something. No matter how hard she tried, she couldn't see what he was seeing. The wind around them subsided for a brief moment, and suddenly, a small gust whipped Harper's ponytail atop her head, causing her hair to cascade over her face. In that moment, a faint giggle reached Wiki's ears again, emanating from the elusive spirit.

Wiki laughed with a mix of awe and delight, "Right here in front of me, it just said, 'I am The Wind'!" he giggled again, "And your hair, it did that too!" Wiki continued watching the wind spirit dance before him, captivated by its enchanting display, he asked, "Why can't my friend see you?"

"Because you are spirit blessed and she is not. So, you can see us, she cannot," the wind spirit replied bluntly.

Wiki's curiosity piqued by the plural pronoun, "Us?" he questioned, his voice tinged with a mix of curiosity and uncertainty.

"Yes, silly! There are many of us. Ya know, the elements?" the spirit replied.

Wiki nodded his head up and down, answering, "Of course I know the elements, I got an A in science."

"Close but not those elements, silly goose. Ya know, the primitive ones; earth, water, fire, and wind," the spirit replied.

"Oh, so there are four of you?" Wiki asked to confirm.

"Yes, and we like to call ourselves The Council. Sounds more official, don't it?" The spirit explained with child-like exuberance. "And we now have you to help us. As for your friend, time will tell if she is trustworthy enough."

At the end of the Wind Spirit's words, its ethereal presence blinked away. Wiki felt a surge of purpose welling up within him, intermingled with a sense of trepidation. He couldn't help but feel a touch overwhelmed.

"It said something about needing to trust you before you can see too," Winslow relayed to Harper, his voice filled with earnestness. "I don't know what it means by that, but I hope they see they can trust you the way I trust you."

Harper's eyes sparkled with gratitude, her voice steady as she responded, "I hope so too, Wiki. I will earn their trust."

"I have no doubt about that, Hap," Wiki responded. "After it said that, it just kind of dissolved with the passing wind. I think it's gone now."

"That sounds amazing, I really wish I could see the same things," Harper said as she glanced up toward the sky noticing the sun's position. "Well, it is getting close to lunchtime, and I still have to pack some stuff."

"What are you packing for?" Wiki inquired as they both began walking home.

"Oh yeah! I forgot to tell you my dad and I are going camping this weekend. I am so excited!" Harper answered as they continued their pace.

"I hope you have fun on your camping trip," Wiki stated.

"Thanks! What are your plans?" she asked.

"My mom is taking us to see Grandma Kinney, but all I'm gonna think about is what happened today," he answered as his mind continued to be consumed by the day's events. "Oh well, I'll try to push back on these intrusive thoughts until we can pick up where we left off on Monday."

"Try to make the best out of seeing your grandma. I'm just glad Monday is the last day of school, before summer.

Then we will have a couple of months to figure this out," Harper said with enthusiasm.

The friends bid each other farewell for the day, each heading home as the weekend began. Harper entered her house, the scent of tacos enveloped her, and she found solace in the familiar embrace of her father's presence. Together, they finished chopping lettuce and tomatoes to put on their tacos, laughter mingling with the sizzle of ground beef and peppers in the pan.

In the quiet of her room later that night, as moonlight filtered through her window, Harper's imagination ran wild. She yearned to unlock the secrets of the wind spirit. With a sense of wonder, she closed her eyes, dreaming of the boundless possibilities that awaited her and Wiki.

Chapter 10

Monday morning arrived and once school ended, Wiki and Hap gathered their backpacks and made their way to the playground.

Hap grinned, her eyes sparkling with mischief as she said, "Last day of school is OVERRR! No more homework, no more tests. We're free!"

Wiki nodded in agreement, excitement evident in his voice, "Finally, we can have a few months of pure adventure."

They stepped onto the playground, feeling the soft cushion of thick plush grass beneath their feet. As they strolled around, they couldn't help but reminisce about their past adventures.

"This feels like one of our epic quests," Hap remarked, her voice filled with enthusiasm.

"Remember the time we fought dragons on this jungle gym?" Wiki chuckled, the memories flooding back, "Very good times!"

While they continued their walk, relishing the freedom of the playground, the sound of obnoxious laughter interrupted their blissful moment.

"Look who it is, the leaders of the nerd squad," Tyler sneered, sharing a triumphant laugh with Ethan.

Rolling her eyes, Hap took a step forward, challenging their taunts as she stated, "At least we're leaders, not just sheep blindly following the herd."

Unable to contain himself, Wiki let out an involuntary snort, which only fueled Ethan and Tyler's anger. They balled their fists, threateningly inching closer to Wiki. Just as tensions began to escalate, a mischievous glimmer caught Wiki's eye. Peering impishly from a muddy patch on the ground, he saw two eyes.

Without hesitation, they provided a reassuring wink before dissolving back into nothing more than uneven, muddy terrain. Wiki blinked rapidly in disbelief trying to get his eyes to refocus.

Simultaneously, an eruption of mud and grass debris was launched from the ground, hurling toward Ethan and Tyler. With impeccable aim, the projectiles soared through the air, finding their intended targets with resounding thuds. The mud missiles made swift deliberate contact.

The first struck Tyler in the left shoulder causing him to cry out from the shock. Next came a large clump which smacked Ethan directly in his chest, knocking him flat on his back and taking his breath away. The last barrage of three smaller clumps pelted Tyler in the stomach causing him to fall to his knees and buckle over with his head resting against the ground.

Stunned and gasping for air, the two bullies found themselves struggling to regain their composure amidst the unexpected assault. As Tyler and Ethan desperately fought to regain their footing, the ground beneath them underwent a remarkable transformation.

What was once solid clay-like earth began to morph into a treacherous sludgy terrain. Thick, brown mud oozed around their shoes, encasing their feet and ankles in a mucky embrace. Their shoes sank further into the mire, making each step a colossal effort as they relentlessly tried to escape the vice-like grip of the clinging mud. With each attempt to extract themselves, the mud clung tenaciously to their legs, pulling them down. Their muscles strained and quivered under the immense resistance, making each movement even more sluggish and laborious; periodic suction sounds filling the air, echoing their struggle. Their faces glistening with mud, evidence of their failed attempts to escape its grasp. Mud-smeared hands pawed at the air, seeking an anchor to pull themselves free.

Amidst the struggle, Wiki's laughter rang out, cutting through the tension like a beacon of amusement. His eyes sparkled with delight as he observed the unfortunate situation before him.

"Looks like karma has a muddy sense of humor!" he exclaimed, while wiping the tears of joy from his face.

Hap couldn't contain her elation either, her laughter reverberated through the air. "Bullseye!" she exclaimed, a gleeful triumph infusing her voice.

Tyler's face contorted with anger and embarrassment, his muddied features twisting in dismay. "You're dead when I get out of here nerd!" he snarled, then he paused to spit out a glob of mud and wiped his mouth with the back of his hand.

Ethan remained silent to refrain from tasting the muck that stuck to him, his wide eyes scanning the area in disarray for the predicament they were facing.

Seizing the moment and not wasting a second to respond, Wiki grasped Hap's hand and gave her a knowing look, indicating that it was time to make their swift escape. "Let's get out of here, Hap!" he exclaimed as he pulled her along with him.

Adrenaline coursed through them as they dashed away from the scene, their laughter trailing behind them like a jubilant melody. In a short time, the two friends arrived at Wiki's front yard, Hap was breathless, and they were both filled with triumphant glee. She leaned against the fence, gasping for breath as her lungs felt starved.

Harper's face wrinkled with confusion as she looked at Wiki and asked, "Hey, what just happened back there? Those muddy projectiles came out of nowhere and knocked Ethan and Tyler down. Did you do that?"

Wiki's eyes lit up as he turned to Hap, eager to share what he saw, he replied, "No, Hap, I didn't do it. I think it was another spirit. Remember when I told you about the wind spirit? Well, I believe a spirit just helped us."

Hap's eyes widened in astonishment, she clarified, "You mean there's another spirit here? That's incredible! But how did it know to help us?"

Wiki shrugged as a playful grin spread across his face, stating, "I'm not entirely sure, I don't know how any of this works." Wiki pretended to wind up and throw an invisible ball as he continued, "Those mud-balls were spot on! It's like the spirit wanted to protect us from Tyler and Ethan." Harper couldn't believe what she was hearing but it was like music to her ears.

"Wow, Wiki, this is amazing! I can't wait to meet the spirits too!" Hap exclaimed.

The two friends exchanged eager glances. Their excitement was interrupted by a familiar voice calling them.

"Ten minutes until supper is ready! Y'all come help Willow set the table," Mrs. Kinney's voice carried through the air, signaling the end of their escapades for now.

Chapter 11

Winslow lay in his bed, his mind swirling with the events that had transpired. The mysteries of the elemental spirits fascinated him, and he couldn't help but wonder which spirit he would encounter next.

As he pondered, a gentle breeze fluttered through his window, causing it to creak open. To his astonishment, the wind spirit materialized on the windowsill, its form swirling and wisping in the air.

"Hi!" Wiki said excited to find out more about what was happening with him.

"Winslow, it is finally time you had a formal introduction," the wind spirit announced with a mischievous grin, while trying to maintain a serious face and a deep voice but instead made them both giggle.

"The other spirits? I get to meet them all!" Wiki said, beaming with enthusiasm and bouncing with joy.

With a playful twirl, the spirit responded, "Yes, silly! They are eager to meet you." The wind spirit glided toward Winslow, hovering above his bed. "Follow me," the wind spirit beckoned, floating toward his bedroom door.

Winslow's eyes widened with apprehension, his voice laced with worry as he said, "I can't just walk out the front door. My Mom would be mad, and I'd be grounded for the rest of my life."

Unfazed, the wind spirit encircled Wiki in a gentle breeze, lifting him off the ground. A sense of weightlessness surrounded him as he looked down, his feet slowly leaving the safety of the floor and then descending once again.

"I will carry you," the spirit assured him with the graceful display.

Winslow's excitement was palpable, making him forget all about the trouble he would be in if he snuck out, as he asked, "Did I just...fly?"

A playful sparkle danced in the spirit's eyes. "Silly Wiki! You can't fly," it replied, encasing Winslow in the wind once more and effortlessly lifting him up from his bedroom floor.

"Whoa! This feels amazing!" Wiki called silently as the spirit guided him out the window, and into the night.

The wind spirit snickered as it gently set Winslow down on the soft ground outside.

"That was incredible," he whispered, his voice filled with awe.

The spirit giggled playfully as it tugged at Winslow's arm, saying, "Just wait! There is more!"

Escorted by the wind spirit, Wiki ventured behind his house and into the familiar woods where he and Hap often spent their time.

As they approached a clearing, the wind spirit whispered, "Don't be alarmed. Remember, they are all excited to meet you!"

The meeting spot was where Hap and Wiki practiced setting up campfires and played in the small creek that meandered through the trees. The spirit barely finished its sentence when a small fire began to blaze in the fire pit, flickering for a few brief moments before vanishing. Winslow peered into the pit, perplexed. There was no wood, no kindling, not even a trace of ash.

"How did that fire... uhm... what just happened?" Wiki stammered; his voice filled with wonder.

Another giggle escaped the wind spirit before it said, "Just keep watching, they are not done yet!"

Before he could respond, a faint gurgling sound rose above the quiet babble of the creek, drawing his eyes to the stream. The water trembled, then began to swell, pushing upward in a spiraling column that defied its natural course. At the crest of the surging geyser, two eyes emerged, encased within a quivering bubble the size of a water balloon, its surface rippling with the motion of the rising current.

The ground beneath his feet rumbled ever so slightly. A pillar of dirt slowly arose from the ground, as the pillar finished its ascension, two emerald eyes became visible. The dirt from the pillar began to merge, shaping a small humanoid creature made of earth; covered in soil, rocks, and moss, resembling a miniature golem.

Winslow couldn't believe his eyes. "Wow! This is the coolest thing I have ever seen. I expected huge spirits that filled the sky," he exclaimed with amazement.

The water spirit responded with a soothing voice that resonated with love and tranquility, "Hello Winslow, we are the Elemental Spirits. This is not our true form, just the form humans can mostly easily comprehend."

Wiki was briefly frozen in shock; all he could muster up was an awkward smile while waving back to the water spirit.

Interrupting their exchange, a fiery orb with a pulsating core spoke sharply, "Can we just give him the book already?" Winslow quickly turned toward the voice, startled by its sudden presence. It was the fire spirit, radiating intense heat and vibrant energy.

Wiki was about to speak up when another column began to emerge from the ground. Reaching its peak, the column of earth began unfurling, revealing a book nestled within its stony embrace.

The earth spirit stomped its feet, commanding authority as it presented the tome to Winslow, stating, "Behold, 'The Spirit Blessed Chronicles.' Within its pages resides the sagas of your predecessors. Delve into its contents; absorb the wisdom it holds."

With intrigue, Winslow accepted the book from the pillar of earth. Its cover was a masterpiece of artistry, immediately capturing his attention. Gold and emerald motifs that coiled around like intricate vines, interwoven to mirror the complex relationship between the Spirit Blessed and the elemental spirits themselves. In that moment, holding the book, Wiki was keenly aware that he possessed something that would unlock unimaginable power.

"The Spirit Blessed is needed when unnatural magics threaten the natural order," the earth spirit declared, its voice resonating with ancient wisdom.

As Winslow absorbed the enormity of his newfound destiny, the wind spirit interrupted, whispering gently, "We should get you back home before your absence is noticed."

"Yeah, you are probably right. It was so cool to finally meet y'all. I can't wait to start reading this!" Wiki exclaimed.

He smiled at the spirits before the wind spirit enveloped him in its ethereal embrace once more, carrying him through the night. They glided back into his room through the window.

With a wink and a chuckle, the wind spirit bid him farewell, "Bye, Wiki!"

"See ya later!" Winslow called back as he crawled in his bed.

Lying there, he tried to process the whirlwind of emotions he was feeling. Sleep seemed impossible as he reflected on the encounter with the elemental spirits, surprised and intrigued by the depth of his connection to the natural world until his dreams finally took over.

Chapter 12

The next morning, Winslow awoke to the soothing sound of raindrops tapping against his windowpane. The stormy weather outside tempted him to stay in bed and indulge in a day of binge-watching his favorite shows.

However, today, held a different purpose for him. He yearned to delve deeper into the mysteries of his spirit blessed abilities and discover the true extent of his powers. The ancient book lay waiting for him on his desk. Holding a wealth of historical knowledge, waiting to be discovered.

After getting out of bed, Winslow eagerly sat down at his desk and picked up the book to inspect it closer. Suddenly, a piece of paper slipped out–floating side to side, before landing softly on his desk. Distracted by the gracefully descending parchment, he sat the book down to his left to further examine the note.

On the front, he was met with handwriting that caught his eye, presumably penned by the previous bearers of this remarkable gift. The text revealed insights and offered invaluable hints for calling upon the elemental forces.

While skimming through, he realized that his physical prowess was not his own; it was the wind spirit enveloping him, carrying him swiftly and gracefully. He discovered that he didn't command fire with mere words or gestures; rather, it was his emotions and willpower that served as conduits, channeling the spirits' energy to aid him in saving his sister.

As the day progressed, the storm eventually gave way to a burst of sunlight. The sight ignited a fire within Winslow's heart, an eagerness to test his newfound abilities.

He knew he would need some help, "I don't know if this is going to work, but it also won't hurt to try," he muttered aloud to himself as he finished changing out of his pajamas. "Wind? Are you there?" Winslow called out in his room, hoping only the wind would hear him and not his mom or his little sister.

Just as he reached for his shoes, the shrill ring of the phone pierced through the air.

"Harper is on the phone for you, Winslow," his mother's voice floated from the kitchen.

Without hesitation, Winslow called back, his voice brimming with urgency, "Can you tell her I'll call her back later? I have something I'm working on." He wasted no time waiting for a response and dashed out of the house.

As he stepped into the backyard, "BOO!" the wind spirit hollered as it appeared right before him, causing him to jump back and release a small yelp. Wind and Winslow broke into laughter.

"What are you doing here?" Winslow asked as he regained his composure.

"What do you mean? You called me!" the spirit responded with a look of confusion.

"Oh! So that did work?" He asked to confirm as he made his way toward the middle of the yard. The spirit nodded its head up and down before Wiki continued, "Well, I called you because I figured you would be the perfect one to help me practice using the wind."

The wind spirit responded quickly, "I can definitely do that!" The spirit fluttered with delight, "Oh this is going to be so much fun! First, we need an open and breezy area and maybe a blanket to sit on."

Winslow looked around and noticed the wet grass from the morning storm, his backyard was about half an acre of cleared land bordered by woods along the edge.

"Check! I think this space covers that. I will run inside and grab something to sit on," he said before making a dash back to the house to grab a picnic blanket from his mom's closet.

"Got it!" He yelled as he ran back toward the wind spirit.

"Perfect! Now find a comfortable spot to sit," Wind instructed.

Winslow laid the picnic blanket down on a fluffy patch of fresh-cut grass and took a seat.

The wind spirit continued its teachings, "To harness the power of any element you should begin with some fundamental practices like breathing exercises. Start by closing your eyes and focus on feeling the wind on your skin."

Winslow closed his eyes, whispering, "This is kind of peaceful."

"As it should be! Keeping your eyes closed, take a deep breath in through your nose. Feel the air filling your lungs. Imagine that air being a gentle breeze, cool and refreshing." It said as it hovered next to him in the grass, practicing along with him. "Very good. Now, as you exhale through your mouth, imagine the breath flowing out from your chest and into the world around you. See it becoming one with the wind."

"Like my breath is the air?" Winslow asked, trying to follow along with the instructions.

"Exactly. You are becoming one with the air. The breeze you feel against your skin is your own breath returning to you. Try it a few more times until it feels natural to you," Wind replied as it floated freely.

Wiki sat in the patch of grass continuing to focus on his breathing and becoming one with the wind.

"I feel the breeze, almost as if the air is responding to me," Winslow said as his focus intensified.

The spirit nodded approvingly, stating, "Now, open your senses to the world around you. Listen to the rustle of leaves, the distant sounds carried by the wind, and the feeling of the air currents brushing your skin. Let these feelings fill your senses."

Wiki kept his eyes closed and lifted his head as if trying to hear farther away before saying, "I hear the leaves and the wind."

The spirit cheered, "Woohoo! That's the first step, the easy one. The next thing we practice will be more difficult."

Winslow sat eagerly awaiting his next set of instructions.

"You still have to master the first step with each element, to do so each spirit will connect with you to show you the ropes," the wind spirit informed him.

"Okay, I think that is an awesome idea! I guess my plan for today is to keep practicing my wind exercise," Winslow said, excitement evident in his smile.

Wind affirmed, saying, "Good plan. With practice, you will be able to attune to the elements much easier. With much practice, you will be permanently attuned to the elements... Practice, practice, practice!"

"Thank you so much. You are very smart for someone who seems so playful," Winslow stated, expressing his gratitude.

The spirit exuded a frolicsome whirlwind as it said, "I'm fun but I have been in this universe longer than this planet has existed, I know some things."

Winslow stood and stretched before he said, "I think I am going to get some food and then get right back to my elemental breathing."

"Good luck, Wiki!" the spirit said as it winked away.

Winslow picked up the blanket he borrowed from his mother and made his way inside the house. He walked in the back door, in the motion of putting the blanket over the back of a chair, he was startled by his mother's voice.

"Excuse me, Sir! What do you think you're doing? You know better, go put that in the dirty laundry where it belongs," Mrs. Kinney said sternly while making grilled cheese sandwiches for lunch.

Wiki grabbed the blanket then turned and faced his mother, "Yes ma'am! I'm sorry. I will do that right now."

He ran down to the basement and tossed the semi-wet blanket in the clothes hamper. His stomach began growling on his way back to the kitchen. He sat down at the dining table, ready to dig in.

"What were you up to out there?" His mother asked as she sat his sandwich on the table in front of him, "I haven't seen you sit that still since you learned to crawl."

Trying to chew quickly and swallow his bite of food before answering, he replied, "I read about this thing called meditation and I wanted to give it a try."

Nodding while washing the pan she used for making lunch, "Okay, and is it working? I have heard some about meditating and trying to be mindful. I liked what I read."

Wiki gulped down his apple juice and smacked his lips, "I don't know yet. That's why I am trying," he answered before he finished the last two bites of his lunch.

He stood up and began cleaning up after himself, saying, "Alright Mom, I am getting back to my meditating."

"Well, good luck and use the same blanket if you plan to sit in the wet grass again," she called out to him as he reached out for the back door's handle.

Stopping abruptly, he replied, "Yes ma'am!" before turning to go fetch the used linen.

Chapter 13

Meanwhile, the Elemental Spirits congregated in a space between dimensions. The wind spirit had brought together Fire, Earth, and Water to discuss the plan for Harper's trial.

Wind spoke first, "We need to decide what trials will be given to the girl. Any ideas on how to test her true intentions?"

The spirits, shimmering in their luminous forms, sat silently as they thought for a moment.

Finally, the earth spirit spoke up, "We must evaluate her connection to the very essence of nature. We could challenge her to rejuvenate a dimension on the brink of withering."

"That is intriguing, but would that be too much for the girl to handle in a short time?" the water spirit, fluid and adaptable, added while trying to conjure more ideas.

"Although, that would test her affinity with nature and also assess her adaptability and resilience," the fire spirit interjected, "Have you forgotten the most important thing? We must examine her inner fortitude, courage and loyalty." Fire continued, "We can transform her dreams into trials where she confronts her deepest fears to protect what she holds most dear."

"Ahhh, dream transformation. That is a wonderful idea, why didn't I think of that? We can challenge her with four separate trials to test for each affinity," the wind spirit exclaimed excitedly, "Using her dreams makes this a lot easier."

As the conversation continued, each of the spirits delved into the specifics of what they would do for each trial. These trials would test Harper's trustworthiness, her dedication to the balance of nature, as well as serve as a crucible in which her true intentions would be revealed. Only by successfully passing all of them would she earn the complete trust of the elemental spirits.

Harper, asleep in her own realm, remained unaware of the extraordinary gathering taking place beyond her dreams. The trials had been conceived and the stage was now set for her journey into the realm of the elemental spirits. Her character would be tested, and her destiny would intertwine with the mystical forces of nature, to see if she was ready to confront dark magic and uphold the natural order.

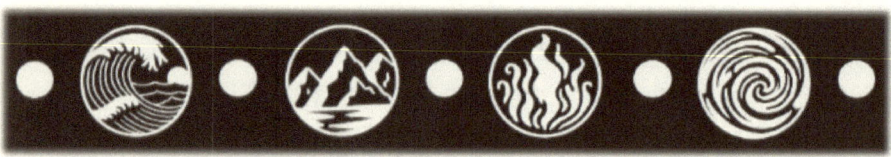

"Now that we have finished discussing the girl, when will we give Winslow the Blessed Artifacts," asked Water.

The fire spirit answered quickly and resolutely, "The artifacts are to be received after he has finished his basic training. Has he even begun?"

The wind spirit snapped its eyes toward Fire, "Actually," the spirit continued, "I have begun training. He called to me asking for help. He has completed the basics of wind, now he will call each of you to train."

The fire spirit seemed to recoil as it stated bluntly, "Well, that can be arranged."

The wind spirit smiled, "I really don't understand why the blessed always call me and not you, Fire," sarcasm staining the words of the spirit.

The fire spirit seethed annoyance and let out a grumble before winking away.

Wind laughed, "I always love driving Fire crazy."

The water spirit wrapped around the wind spirit in a motherly embrace, stating, "Try not to disturb the others, we must all get along together. For that is the true balance of nature," before disappearing from the rest.

The wind spirit and the earth spirit were left together, prompting Wind to ask, "Are you going to yell at me for picking on Fire, too?"

Earth chuckled before replying, "Not in a million years, I live to see these spats. See ya later Windy."

Earth left with a blink; the wind spirit loved the nickname. Wind smiled before heading off to visit Winslow to see how the rest of his practice transpired. Traveling through dimensions, back to the plane of Terra Vitae, the spirit arrived at Winslow's house.

Wind floated outside his bedroom window and tapped, ever so lightly, trying its best not to wake or disturb anyone else in the house. "*Tap, tap, tap.*"

Winslow jumped, frightened by the unexpected knock. Noticing who it was, he made his way to the window. He knew the spirit didn't 'need' to be let in, it was already all around him. It was Wind's way of asking if it could come in.

He unlatched the lock, lifted, and the wind spirit flew in, "Hey! I was not expecting to see you tonight," Wiki exclaimed as he smiled, even though it was an impromptu meeting he was glad the spirit was there. He really enjoyed the conversations he had with Wind.

"How are the wind exercises going?" Wind inquired.

"Really good," Wiki responded, "I am getting so comfortable calling on wind, I'm excited to learn more!"

The spirit glided closer to Wiki, whispering, "That's good, because you're about to train with each of the other elements." It looked deeply into Wiki's eyes, raising an eyebrow, it continued with a serious tone, "And some of them are not as cool as me."

They both burst into laughter. "Shhh," Wiki whispered, "We gotta keep it down before my mom or my sister busts in."

They both took deep breaths to calm their laughter before the spirit added, "You will need to call to each of them as you are ready, the same way you did to me."

Winslow's eyes lit up, saying, "This is so rad, I cannot wait!"

"Before I leave, I also want you to know the next few days Harper will be going through her trials. If she passes them, she will be granted some artifacts to help her assist you on this journey. In the same manor, once you have finished your training on the basics you will be gifted the legendary blessed sword and shield." As Wind said the final words, it then pretended to wield a sword and shield and battle an imaginary adversary.

Wiki giggled as he said, "Are you serious? That is so cool!" He smiled as the spirit made its way toward the window.

"Good night, Wiki," the wind spirit whispered as it departed.

Wiki waved, then he shut and locked the window before snuggling up in bed. Once again, not able to sleep due to the sheer excitement of what the next day would bring.

Chapter 14

The following morning, Wiki hastily washed his hands, making sure they were free of any stickiness before grabbing the phone. His mother had always been strict about cleanliness, especially when it came to the kitchen phone. With clean hands, he dialed Hap's number from memory, his excitement palpable.

"Hello?" Harper's voice greeted him at the other end.

"Hey! I am sorry I forgot to call back yesterday, I have so much to tell you Hap," Winslow responded, his words overflowing with enthusiasm.

"It's okay Wiki, I figured you got grounded or you were busy," Hap chimed in, sharing his excitement.

"Thankfully, I am not grounded. Let's meet at our spot by the creek in an hour," he suggested.

"I will be there," Hap replied before ending the call by hanging the phone back on the receiver.

An hour later, Hap arrived at the creek to find Wiki already there, his attention focused on skipping rocks across the water. As she approached him, she couldn't help but to be astonished.

"Since when have you been able to skip rocks? I've been trying to teach you for years, and you've barely gotten two skips. That rock went all the way across the creek!" Hap exclaimed, amazement in her voice.

Grinning mischievously, Wiki turned to her and responded, "Yeah! Thanks to the elements, I'm pretty much a professional now."

As the two friends shared a laugh, their voices resonated through the serene surroundings of the creek. The soothing sound of water flowing added a melodic backdrop to their conversation.

While they played, Wiki recounted his extraordinary experience of being flown by the wind. Hap's eyes seemed to glass over as she marveled at the thought of flying with the wind and communing with the very forces of nature. The gentle breeze seemed to carry Wiki's words, emphasizing the enchantment of his tale. When he got to the part where he met all the elemental spirits, Hap's face was frozen in astonishment. With each skip of a rock, their spirits soared, the joy evident in their laughter.

After a few minutes, Harper finally asked, "Wait, you mean they actually showed themselves? Here? At our spot?"

Wiki nodded to confirm, a sense of wonder emanating from him as he said, "Yes, Hap! I could see and hear them. They were speaking directly to me. They were pretty much just like you would imagine. Wind was super playful and cheery. Water was soothing and motherly. Earth was this tiny little rock golem looking thing and Fire, well, Fire was … fiery."

They both chuckled.

"Wow, that really is amazing! I wish I was there!" Harper declared.

"Well, you will be meeting them soon too!" Wiki said with a quick wink.

"Huh?" Harper said quizzically, wondering what in tarnation he was talking about.

"They told me you would be going through the trials soon. During that time, I will be training with the elements. They even told me I would be getting a special sword and shield when I finish basic training!" Winslow said, overflowing with energy.

After a short while of continuing to skip rocks, Wiki looked up and noticed the position of the sun.

"We should probably head back toward my place for some lunch," Wiki said softly.

Harper nodded and they threw down the rest of the rocks in their hands and began walking toward Winslow's home.

"This is literally the coolest. We are going to be superheroes that save the world with nature!" Hap beamed, watching her step as they continued their stroll back.

"Yeah, I just wish I knew how my dad was a part of all this. I feel like there is this connection and when we talked to Mr. Jennings, it felt stronger. It seems as though, when we figure out the answer to one question it opens the door to more questions," Wiki stated while looking between Hap and the sky.

"I can't begin to understand that. I just want you to know I am here for you however you need. I will always have your back Wiki!" Hap said as she gave him a reassuring pat.

Winslow smiled, saying, "That is something I never have to question, we will always be a team!"

The pair arrived at the edge of Wiki's yard, "It will be weird not being together these next few days," Hap stated.

Wiki turned toward Hap, he put both hands on her shoulders, looking directly into her eyes. "Yes, it will be," he paused for a moment looking up toward the clouds then back to her. "But then we get to be nature's superheroes!" punching his fist into the air before running toward the swing on the swing set in the Kinney's backyard, yelling, "FOR NATURE!"

He launched himself into the swing on his stomach, like he was flying back and forth through the winds. Harper couldn't help but laugh, then ran to join him.

"Has anyone ever told you how cool you are, Wiki?" Harper asked before launching herself into the swing next to him.

The friends continued to let their imaginations run wild with what their future would bring until their stomachs reminded them why they came back home.

Chapter 15

The elemental spirits decided to test Harper with four trials: The Trial of Earth Rejuvenation, Trial of Resilience, Trial of Inner Fire, and the Trial of Unity. Only by successfully navigating through and triumphing in all four trials would Harper demonstrate her trustworthiness and her unyielding dedication to safeguarding the balance of nature. Hap knew her trials were coming, but she didn't know anything more than that.

As she fell into a slumber she was met with one of her usual dreams, back at the lake with her dad. As she delved into a deeper sleep, her dream began to transform. Her surroundings shifting from the familiar to an otherworldly dreamscape. The transition was so smooth, it left her feeling as if she had entered a different realm.

The landscape around her was desolate and lifeless. The colors muted all around. The atmosphere was heavy with an eerie stillness. She stood there, taking in the environment around her. It was like nothing she had seen before, everywhere she looked was barren. The ground was cracked, with deep, jagged fissures running through the parched soil, revealing the scars of neglect.

Taking in a deep breath she noticed the atmosphere was very heavy. Reminiscent of a world wrapped in the shroud of its own decay, yearning for rejuvenation. Before her, the earth spirit began to manifest as a translucent figure with a green iridescent aura resembling the hue of Earth. The spirit extended a small seed to Harper, speaking no words.

She took the seed from the earth spirit and inspected it. As she did, she sensed a pulse coming from within. It was steady, resonating like a heartbeat that seemed to immediately connect to her own life force, beating in the same rhythm as her own.

When she looked back up to ask the spirit what she should do, it had vanished. Confused, she sat on the cracked earth wondering what this seed was for and why she was stuck in this awful place.

It felt as if hours had passed, growing increasingly frustrated, a glistening teardrop welled up in the corner of her eye. It clung on her lower eyelid for a fraction of a moment, capturing the faintest glimmer of light, before succumbing to gravity. It left a shimmering trail as it traced the curve of her cheek, falling to the seed. As it made contact, something remarkable happened.

The seed immediately absorbed the tear, drawing it inward, proceeding with a gentle pulse of light, that echoed the rhythm she felt in her hand. In that moment she knew she had to nurture this magical seed, to cultivate it with love, and save this land. She attempted to dig into the dry soil with her bare hands, she realized quickly this would not work.

Harper stood up and looked around for something to dig with, when she finally spotted a stone in the shape of an oval with a pointed edge, "This is perfect!" She exclaimed and started digging. She lowered the pulsating seed into the ground and covered it with the soil she removed. She knew this would not be an easy task when she looked up to the sky and there was not a cloud in sight.

"Well, it clearly doesn't rain here," Harper thought aloud.

Hap recalled the seed reacting to her tears, so she sat and attempted to make herself cry. She took a deep breath and tried to think of things that would normally create tears. The one that usually worked was thinking about her mother, whom she never really got to meet. She immediately felt saddened but was unable to cry, most likely because these are feelings she has been processing her whole life.

Frustration set in again, she started to feel defeated. Wiki popped into her mind making her smile softly.

"Wiki would know what to do if he was here with me," she pondered aloud.

Harper's thoughts began to drift to some of their great adventures. Her favorite being the time her father took them both camping for the first time. "*Wiki was so scared that Big Foot would kidnap him while he was sleeping. My dad made the best hamburgers on the grill, and we would always top the night off with s'mores.*" She continued her trip down memory lane visualizing the fluffy, fiery, crunch. It was almost as if she could feel the chocolate melting and the marshmallow oozing.

As she took a bite into her imaginary smore she felt a tear trickle down her cheek. A tear of pure happiness and joy that descended toward the ground, time slowed as she watched the drop, glinting like a crystal, splattered to the fractured earth.

The tear was quickly absorbed. A radiant pulse surged from the break in the soil, throbbing in synchrony to the beat of her heart. The terrain around her began to transform almost instantly, vibrant foliage unfurling in every direction she could see. She felt like she was inside a mesmerizing kaleidoscope. Verdant vegetation erupted from the ground, bursting forth in vibrant hues, with dew glistening on each petal and leaf. The animals, once lifeless, were being reborn into animated existence, their eyes sparkling with the new vitality provided by her recent connection to nature.

She couldn't contain her joy, she jumped up in down while pumping her fists in the air, "Oh yeah, I did it! Oh yeah!"

Hap paused her victory dance when she noticed a small bunny, its soft fur a warm shade of brown that resembled the once desolate land. Its velvety appearance invited her to reach out and pet its dense coat. She bent down and extended out her hand. Before her fingers made contact with the bunny's fur, she jolted awake, leaving the dream realm behind.

"Wow! That was a really weird dream," Harper said as she rubbed her eyes and yawned. She re-snuggled into her comforter and began drifting back into the dream world.

Chapter 16

Congregated within the confines of a dimly lit chamber stood members of The Fang, concealed beneath dark hoods. They devoted themselves to the relentless pursuit of power and control. Their insatiable hunger for that power knew no bounds, and they were prepared to traverse any ethical or moral boundary to achieve their coveted desires. Their veins pulsed with dark blood magic, enhancing their physical and metaphysical capabilities.

At the heart of the room stood the high priestess, Seraphine. A figure of imposing stature with flowing black hair, long pointy nails and a cruel smile. Directly in front of her sat the crimson tainted crystal orb deemed the Blood Crystal, steeped in the ancient rites of sanguimancy. A symphony of scarlet playing out within the glassy orb as each blood droplet pirouettes in a harmonious ballet seemingly intended for her amusement. This powerful display commanded the attention of all nearby.

The high priestess signaled to her direct subordinate, who, upon receiving the cue, struck a large gong three times in sequence. The sound resonated past and squelched the other chamber members where they stood.

As she spoke to address the assembly, her voice carried a distinct authoritarian tone, "Brothers and Sisters, I stand before you inundated with joy. It seems a new spirit blessed has emerged."

The high priestess paused, allowing her words to hang in the air. Gasps and murmurs filled the room, abruptly stopping with a quick gesture from the priestess.

"Fear not! We have been given a rare opportunity. We are stronger now than we have ever been. Let us not dread the spirit blessed any longer. Instead, feed on them like the prey they are!" Seraphine stated before the chamber burst into roars of jubilation.

At the front of the small crowd, an angular-faced woman voiced their collective query, "But have we located the chosen one?"

The priestess responded with confidence, "We have gathered information that has led us to narrow down their whereabouts. But we do not know where in the town the chosen resides."

Curiosity piqued, another member, a tall man emanating an air of cruelty who went by the name of Alistair, spoke up, "And what shall we do once we find him?"

Without hesitation, the priestess snapped back while rolling her eyes, "Simple. We will drain them of their essence and use it to further enhance our own."

Alistair retorted, "Easier said than done. The assistance of the spirits can be quite bothersome."

"Which is why we need to break their bond first! You would be foolish to assume that I don't already have a plan," the high priestess scoffed back.

With a wave of Seraphine's hand, Lilith was summoned to deal with Alistair, as usual.

"First, we will take control of someone from the town so we can further narrow down their whereabouts to identify who it is. We have proven many times how potent the High Priestess's blood control is," Lilith stated as she gestured toward the blood crystal. "Someone who possesses knowledge of the town and can go unnoticed. Then, we will use that information to help break the bond between the blessed and the spirits."

Alistair seized the opportunity to speak in hopes of returning to the priestesses' good side, "Indeed, an intriguing proposition."

Silence enveloped the chamber as each member contemplated the question at hand.

Finally, Silas, a man with a crooked nose broke the stillness, offering a suggestion, "What of the boys who we saw tormenting other children recently, near the library? They are weak-willed and would be easily manipulated, we could mold them into our pawns."

Agreeing with the notion, the priestess nodded pensively, saying, "It is a bold strategy, but it may serve as our best opportunity to precisely locate and capture the spirit blessed."

She faced her congregation again, "Now that we are all in agreement, move forward with tracking down those boys while I start preparing the amulets. Lilith, come with me!" she commanded as she left the chamber.

Chapter 17

Wiki had awakened early this morning to get a jump start on hopefully training with a different element. With his breakfast consumed, he decided to make some peanut butter and jelly sandwiches to take with him on his training journey today. He planned to set up for the day at their favorite spot.

Wiki grabbed his lunch pail and stocked it with the sandwiches he prepared, an apple, and a couple cookies from the cookie jar in the kitchen. He filled his water bottle and was ready to set out for training. He made his way to the front door only to be stopped by his dirty-fingered little sister as she grabbed his arm.

"Eww. Why are your hands so sticky?" Wiki asked as he jerked his arm from her tiny grasp.

"None-ya," she giggled. "Now, where do you think you're going? You promised me we would play!" Willow stomped and crossed her arms over her chest.

Realizing he forgot that little promise, Winslow tried thinking of a way he could get out of this. He knew he needed to keep training if he wanted to be of any help to the elemental spirits.

"I'm sorry Willow, I really have some stuff I need to get done today," he pleaded as Willow began to pout.

"But... But you promised!" she said as she started to sniffle.

"Okay. Well… how about we play whatever you want after dinner tonight. I will be all yours," Wiki suggested with a smile, hoping she would give.

"FINE!" Willow yelled rolling her eyes and storming off.

He knew she wasn't happy with him and maybe one day he could explain why, maybe this was something that his dad had dealt with also. For a moment, his attention shifted to recollections of his father, realizing this he snapped himself back into the moment.

"No time for thinking like that. If I focus on attuning to the elements, I believe I will learn more about my father," he thought to himself.

With those words he set off to commence his training session. He made his way out of the back door.

"*Can't practice in the backyard anymore, Mom might catch on,*" he reasoned as he continued through the backyard.

After about five minutes of winding through the woods, Wiki arrived at the creek. He sat down, closed his eyes, and took long deep breaths, connecting himself to the air around him. Feeling the breeze flow through him on his inhale and drift back out with his exhale. The currents of the wind danced around him; he felt in control. He pushed his arms forward and a burst of wind spewed forth from the palms of his hands. Astonished by the feeling, he quickly opened his eyes. To his surprise nothing seemed different.

"*What was that? I have never felt that before,*" Wiki thought to himself. Disregarding that, he shook his head and stood up to stretch for a few minutes.

Now feeling adequately warmed up, Wiki cleared his throat and called out, "Earth? Uh, I think I'm ready if you are there!"

With no response, he figured that he would continue with his breathing exercises. As he went to inhale again, the ground beneath him began to rumble slightly. Looking around, he searched for the cause. He looked to the right and saw a familiar sight rise from the loose dirt.

"You rang Winslow?" Earth said in a deep, serious tone.

"Yes! Wind told me to call out once I was ready. I'm so excited!" Winslow responded, "How are you doing today, Earth?"

"Feeling a little rocky if you ask me," Earth said with a wink.

Wiki burst into laughter, saying, "That was a good one!"

With a smooth, rolling motion, the miniature golem glided across the ground, leaving a trail of dust in its wake.

Earth asked, "So, you want to learn the basics of earth control?" Without waiting for a response, it continued, "Once fully attuned, there are no limits to what you can create with your imagination."

"I'm ready! What should I do first?" Wiki inquired.

"This may sound silly but take your shoes off. Let your bare feet contact the rocks and soil that make up the Earth," the spirit instructed him.

Looking thoroughly confused, Wiki took his shoes off and wiggled his toes into the loose dirt beneath his feet.

The spirit continued, "Now close your eyes. Notice the solidity of the ground, its strength."

Earth settled down in front of Wiki as he continued with its teachings, "Take deep breaths as Wind guided you to do. Breathe in through your nose, inhaling the earth's essence. Imagine it as rich, grounding energy filling your lungs."

Wiki breathed in deeply; as he was exhaling his face distorted causing him to blurt out, "Oh! I think I can taste the essence; it tastes like dirt."

The earth spirit chuckled as Wiki winced, "Good! That means you are doing something right. Now visualize your breath flowing back into the earth. As if you're returning a part of yourself to the ground."

Nodding his head as he felt a sparking connection to the earth, Wiki responded, "Yes! I can. It feels like the earth is breathing through me."

The earth spirit smiled, stating, "Perfect! You are forming a deep bond with the minerals, metals and rocks that make the soil. It is not just ground beneath your feet; it is an extension of yourself. Keep going and tell me what you feel."

Wiki didn't respond but continued the focused breathing with his eyes loosely shut.

A few moments had passed before Wiki spoke up, "Whoa! It kind of feels like the earth is hugging me right now. I… I don't know how to explain this better than that."

"That is promising. Now, focus harder and let all other sounds fade away. Without tuning your ears, embrace the sounds of the earth. The crunching of gravel, the clinking of small rocks, and the sifting of soil. These are the earth's voices. Let them encase you," the spirit guided.

"I can hear them," Wiki answered as he followed along with the guidance.

Earth continued instructing, "Indeed! The earth is speaking its own language and sharing its wisdom with you.

As you continue this exercise you will decipher all the secrets the earth has to share."

"What should I do next?" Winslow asked the spirit.

"We are going to go a step further. I want you to will the earth to respond to your command. Imagine it shifting and moving beneath you in response to your thoughts," The spirit suggested.

Wiki focused hard, as the image formed, he said, "I see it in my mind," he peaked an eye open to see what was happening.

To his dismay, nothing appeared to be moving under his feet as he pictured.

Feeling frustrated, Wiki stated, "Uh, this is harder than you are making it sound. Nothing is moving. I can still feel my connection to the earth."

Earth comforted him, saying, "It doesn't always happen on your first attempt. Remember the earth is your ally, and you are its steward. As you breathe and focus your intent, allow the ground to heed your call, stay firm."

Listening to the spirit and following his words, Winslow focused again. Reconnecting to the earth and controlling the embrace it returned.

The earth spirit studied him, watching Wiki's arms move up from his side to above his head. As his arms went up, so did tiny pillars of soil. At the pinnacle of the pillars sat tiny pebbles. The earth spirit was impressed, he has never had a spirit blessed achieve manipulation in the first session.

"Wow! Winslow, you have truly amazed me. Open your eyes and look around you," Earth praised.

Wiki followed the instructions, slowly opening his eyes and seeing what he had accomplished. As his eyes refocused from being closed, he noticed the small pillars all around him.

"WOW! Look at that! I did that?" Wiki asked as he stood in full amazement.

"Yes, young one. You did that. You are truly a blessed one. I am excited to see what all you will do with this gift," the spirit said proudly. "You are beginning to grasp the art of earth manipulation. You will notice that some techniques taught to you for calling elements are very similar to each other. Focused breathing and connecting yourself to the element is always the first step in controlling it." Earth continued, "Each of the other spirits will take you a step further in your training, pushing you to your full potential. As your connection to the earth deepens, you'll be able to shape it with greater precision as is true for each of the elements. Finally, remember that patience and respect for each element are essential on this journey."

Wiki looked at Earth in awe, stating, "That means I can use the same steps in manipulating wind? I have already been practicing connecting to the air, now I can use this to practice calling on air and earth!"

With a deep fatherly chuckle, Earth responded, "Yes, that is exactly it. That is a grand plan! Have a great day Winslow."

The spirit sunk into the soil and disappeared as Wiki pushed forward with his practice after pausing to enjoy his lunch he brought with him.

Chapter 18

"Thonk! Thonk!" echoed through the air as Harper hurled her tennis ball against the brick structure of the garage.

"*I wonder what Wiki is doing right now,*" she thought to herself, "*If he is training, he is probably at mission control by the creek. Mission time!*"

She gathered her tennis ball and glove and tossed it near the front door before grabbing her bicycle that was laying in the driveway. She peddled vigorously toward Wiki's house. Once she arrived, she dumped her bike in the front of the house then ran through the yard toward the woods.

Upon reaching the forest entrance, she eased her pace, taking a moment to catch her breath as she made her way down the well-trodden path Wiki and herself had formed throughout the years. The sun had started its descent, casting shadows throughout the forest's floor.

"Slap!" Rang through the air as she swatted at pesky mosquitoes, landing a killing blow. "Eww," she called out seeing the bug guts left on her arm before brushing them away.

As Harper approached the creek, she could hear sounds of rocks hitting the ground over and over, "Thump, thump, thump."

"Hey Wiki! Whatcha doing out here?" she asked as she stepped out into the creek's clearing.

"Hap! Hi! Uh, I am trying to manipulate earth and wind," he responded, dropping his concentration.

"How long have you been out here?" she questioned, making her way to his side.

"Pretty much all day," he replied with a short chuckle, "Right this moment, I am trying to get these dirt missiles to hit my target on that tree."

He pointed over at the tree in question, baring a small 'X' carved into the trunk.

"Ah, X marks the spot I see," Harper giggled before stepping over to grab a tiny pebble and threw it at the marked tree.

"Bullseye!" she yelled, as the rock connected with the center of the target.

Winslow smiled, saying, "Hey no fair. You have always had an impeccable aim since you started softball a few years ago."

Hap winked at him, stating confidently, "You know my plans, I'm going to grow up and pitch no-hitters just like Nolan Ryan did!"

Wiki smirked as he jested, "You know I will be in the dugout cheering you on! If they let me in there." They both giggled.

Harper threw another small pebble at the tree trunk, "Okay Wiki, you've got this! Try again!"

Shaking off the nerves now that he had an audience, "Yeah, I can do this!" he said as he shifted his concentration back to his connection with earth.

He began raising his hands and three pillars of dirt rose before him. Hap, flabbergasted, remained silent with her mouth ajar. Winslow began to shift his concentration to wind, closing his eyes once again and focusing on his breathing. He slowly raised his arms with his palms facing outward. Upon inhaling, the back of his hand gravitated toward his chest. Now ready, he opened his eyes to home in on his target. In a fluid singular motion, he exhaled as he thrusted his arms forward sending a shockwave of wind bursting from his palms. The sheer force of the explosive wind display snapped the pillars. Causing the pieces to become tiny earthen projectiles, striking the marked tree in unison.

"Thwap! Thwap! Thonk!"

"Wooohooo!" Wiki and Harper yelled as they both jumped in joy over his accomplishment.

"I did it!" Wiki said, feeling slightly exhausted.

"Incredible! I knew you could do it! I just didn't know it would look so cool!" Harper exclaimed while raising her hand for a high five.

Wiki, noticing the gesture responded and their hands slapped together.

"I just didn't know if I could Hap," he said.

Hap rolled her eyes, "I don't know why you doubt yourself. The more practice you get, the better you will be. Same thing happened with my pitching."

"You are totally right. Practice always makes perfect." Wiki responded with a soft smile.

"Are you hungry yet? I'm starving!" Harper asked while rubbing her stomach.

Wiki attempted to mimic a British accent, but it came out awkward and exaggerated as he said, "I too, am feeling a bit peckish."

Not being able to contain their laughter, the friends made brief eye contact before erupting into a contagious giggle at Wiki's failed impersonation. Then, the two friends headed back to Winslow's house to gorge on some delicious food.

Chapter 19

Arriving home, Harper began her mundane routine of getting ready for bed. She washed her face, flossed, and brushed her teeth. Once done with her upkeep, she made her way from the bathroom to her bedroom. Retrieving her hairbrush from her desk where she always kept it, she brushed her hair and grabbed a hair tie, putting it up to ensure it maintained its neat and tidy state.

Once done, she plopped down on her bed and grabbed a novel from her nightstand. As she got lost in the grand visions of adventure, her mind was overrun with all the infinite possibilities of what awaited her and Wiki. After a short while, the exhaustion of the day crept up on her, causing her eye lids to get heavier. Slowly, she drifted into her own world as she crossed the barrier between the real and the imaginative.

Harper found herself frolicking through the woods, making her way to the familiar creek.

She called out, "Wiki! Where are you?" searching for any sign of her friend.

Realizing that Wiki wasn't around, she decided to skip rocks to pass the time, waiting on her friend. In search of the perfect skipping rock, she scanned the edge of the creek. Shortly after, she identified a pebble with a flat side that was almost the size of her palm.

"This is it! I wonder if I can break my record with this one?" she said aloud to herself.

Reaching down to pick up the skimming stone, she noticed the creek began moving in ways she had never seen before. The water at the edge of the creek, where she stood, was swirling in a vortex. Stunned, she momentarily forgot about the rock. She gave all her attention to the turbulence of the water in front of her.

Perplexed she thought, "*I wonder what is making this happen?*"

Almost immediately, the water began to rise from the center of the swirling maelstrom causing her to take a step back. The liquid shifted and transformed until finally settling into a somewhat movable, yet static state. The form, familiar yet hard to see clearly, resembled the silhouette of an elderly woman. Intrigued, Hap moved closer in proximity to better inspect the anomaly. She leaned her head forward and squinted in curiosity.

Thinking out loud again Hap wondered, *"What in tarnation is happening here?"*

As she approached, eyes began to form on the silhouette as it spoke to her, saying, "Hello Harper," in a soft tone.

The unexpected voice caused Harper to jump back, a bit startled.

"Water spirit? Is that you?" Hap questioned as the spirit finished materializing.

"Yes, it is I," the water spirit replied without much inflection.

"Far out!" Harper exclaimed while being mesmerized by the flowing spectacle before her.

"I have come to test you. Be forewarned, this test is not for the weak. Are you ready to sink or swim?" the spirit asked soothingly.

Nervously smiling, Harper responded, "Ready as I'll ever be!"

Without a moment's notice, the once elderly silhouette began to balloon in size until it encircled Hap within its core. Harper, swirling amongst the ebbs and flows of the fluid orb around her, struggled to see beyond the aqua veil. The once tall, broad trees and thick, hearty foliage were distorting at all angles. The current's speed slowly increased, causing her to become disoriented, unable to identify the dissolving landscape in the distance. Soon after succumbing to the confusion, the currents began to slow down until finally everything seemed to stand still.

Frozen in the moment, Harper felt a sense of serenity, immediately followed by a sudden drop in her stomach and the sounds of the watery sphere crashing down around her.

"Thump!" Rang out as she landed on the seat of a dinghy.

Confused, she began to hear the familiar voice of the water spirit, "Harper, all you must do is make it to the island."

Noticing the land in the distance, Harper stated with confidence, "That doesn't look so hard."

Without hesitation, she lowered the sail and secured it, beginning her trial. The sea around her was calm except for the wake created by the boat. Sprits of water splashed her face as the vessel pushed forth through the vast body of water.

With the sailboat picking up speed, Harper yelled out, "Woo! This is awesome!"

After two hours had seemingly passed, Harper noticed the feeling of the sun beating down on her. Looking up in anticipation of how much progress she had made, the smile on her face quickly turned into a look of concern as she realized she wasn't any closer to the island than when she started. In fact, she wondered if she was further from the island.

Shaking off these nonsensical ideas, she continued her journey. Re-centering her concentration on the task at hand, making it a point to remain more vigilant of her surroundings. About thirty more minutes had passed as she began to see dark clouds rolling in on her position.

Without any time to react, the once calm water now thrashed violently with no rhyme or reason. Harper braced for the impending chaos. As the thrashing waves became worse, the storm settled overhead. Harper feared she underestimated this trial. With a thunderous crackle, a streak of light came forth, striking the base of the mast.

"Boom!" rang out, followed by the sizzling hiss of electricity and the sharp, splintering sound of wood cracking.

Instinctively, she raised her hands to protect her face. Magically, the storm dissipated in a matter of seconds. Harper, realizing it was safe to put her hands down, looked up to see what damage had been done. She saw the devastation of the mast and quickly scanned for the remainder of it. Only to realize that the sail and the rest of the mast were beyond her reach, floating further away.

Pushing through, she stated, "Well, I guess the rest I have to do by hand," as she glanced down to retrieve the oars of the boat and began rowing.

What felt like an hour had passed, her muscles were beginning to cramp, and sweat was dripping profusely from her brow.

She stopped rowing to ponder for a moment, "*What is happening? I'm sure now that I am getting further from the island… Hm…, well I tried going forward, maybe I should try going backward? What do I have to lose?*"

Harper pressed on, rowing backward. After quite some time, her arms weighed heavily with exhaustion.

Taking a moment to rest her aching muscles, she set down the oars to wipe the sweat from her face and tried to focus in on the distant land.

"I can't really tell if it's closer yet, guess I gotta just keep going," she stated aloud as she shrugged her shoulders.

She picked the oars back up and continued rowing backward, hoping this was the right choice. A few more hours had passed, and she was aching throughout her body.

She wearily looked up to catch a glimpse of the island, saying, "Ha! I am getting closer. I can do this!"

With her newfound adrenaline coursing through her, she rowed vigorously. Now that she was getting closer to the island, she began to make out some of the tiny details on the land. She started to see jagged rocks encircling the land. She could see the water crashing into them, realizing the danger they imposed. Upon this realization, she turned her head around to see what was behind her.

Her eyes widened in bewilderment, thinking, "*Huh? How is the island behind me?*"

Questioning herself, she turned her head to confirm the island had just been right in front of her. Her mouth dropped in awe; the island was gone. It was now behind her.

Taking a few seconds to register what was going on, she thought aloud, "I think I know what is happening now, this has all just been a big mirror! I was intentionally misled."

Understanding what was going on now, she turned herself around on the boat to be able to finish rowing forward to the island. Just when she thought she was in the clear, the turbulent waters sent the small sailboat crashing into the jagged rocks, sending Hap overboard and destroying the boat.

The waves knocked her from side to side, she knew what she needed to do but the water churning and frothing made it increasingly difficult to see where she needed to go to reach the island. She began her freestyle stroke, arm over arm she swam.

After what seemed like an eternity, she reached the nearshore zone of the island and the rough waters subsided. Exhausted and worn out from all the physical exertions, she flipped to her back and continued the rest of her swim in a backstroke. Feeling the coarse sand brush against her hand during her stroke, she turned and crawled the rest of the way onto the beach and collapsed.

"I finally made it," she said in a barely audible voice before surrendering to her exhaustion and falling into a deeper, uneventful slumber.

Chapter 20

The flickering light of dimly lit candles cast dancing shadows upon the ritual chamber's walls as the members worked. Their surroundings engulfed in an eerie atmosphere as they embarked upon a series of dark rituals, propelled by the potent force of blood magic coursing through them. The air itself seemed to grow heavy with the weight of malevolence as they channeled their collective powers.

The Fang stood in a circle, their eyes gleaming with an unholy light, their bodies bathed in a spectral aura. As the binding ritual progressed, their powers surged, like a tempestuous storm gathering strength.

With meticulous precision, they completed the final incantation, "Through veils of mist and darkness deep, 'Mentis Domitor' shall ever keep. In whispers low and secrets old, 'Vinculum Obscurum' tightly hold." Their voices harmonized in a chilling chorus that resonated throughout.

As the last syllable hung in the air, a burst of energy surged through the room, swirling around them like a violent cyclone. Then, with a resounding crescendo, the energy coalesced into two amulets, pulsating with a malevolent glow.

Seraphine's eyes gleamed with satisfaction as she stepped forward. She bit down on her index finger, allowing her life force to surface in a slow drip. Extending her slender hand, she closed her bloodied fingers around the amulets, their cold, intricate surfaces pressing into her palm. Her essence began seeping into the artifacts, engulfing them as their designs began to pulse with an unholy vitality.

As the final drops of ichor fused with the amulets, a wave of potency radiated outward from the artifacts. She looked down at them in her unfurled palm, a wicked smile curling on her lips as she reveled in the knowledge that they would grant her dominion over the unfortunate souls foolish or desperate enough to wear them.

Seraphine turned her piercing gaze upon her fellow Fang, her voice echoing as she demanded, "Go now! You have two hours to bring them to me. DO NOT BE LATE!" Her words were a command that brooked no dissent.

Alistair pointed to five members, and they set out to complete their high priestess's bidding with swift obedience. They ventured into the night as shadowy figures blending seamlessly with the darkness as they sought out their targets and captured them.

Finally, Ethan and Tyler were brought before Seraphine, their faces etched with fear. The room in which they now stood was unlike anything they had ever seen; its oppressiveness was unsettling. They cast bewildered glances at each other, their minds racing to comprehend how they even ended up in this nightmarish place.

Seraphine regarded them with an icy gaze as her words dripped with a chilling certainty, she intoned, "You stand before The Fang. You have been chosen for a purpose. A destiny entwined with our desires."

Ethan and Tyler exchanged uneasy glances, their confusion giving way to a growing sense of trepidation. They struggled to make sense of the situation, but the overwhelming aura of power and danger emanating from the high priestess stifled any protests or attempts to flee.

"W... What?? What is The Fang?" Ethan asked, stammering over his words.

The priestess spoke in an alluring tone completely ignoring the question proposed, "Boys, I am here to offer a trade. I can offer you power if you can complete a simple task for me."

Ethan and Tyler's expressions switched to one of intrigue and eagerness to ascertain.

Letting his curiosity win over his fear, Tyler inquired, "How can we do that?"

From the depths of her pocket, Seraphine retrieved the two small amulets as she explained, "These amulets harness the essence of our magic. By wearing it, you shall possess unrivaled strength, agility, and power."

Ethan questioned cautiously, "Did you just say magic? That must mean there is a catch?"

The priestess chuckled, her voice dripping with wry amusement as she answered, "Yes, we said magic. My young friends, all we require is your commitment to employ your powers in assisting us with locating someone who possesses something very important to us. It is a small box with four symbols on it; representing the four elements." The priestess continued as Ethan and Tyler exchanged glances, "Other than that, just have fun with your new gift!"

Seraphine winked and gave the boys a moment to contemplate her offer. The allure of such extraordinary power proved insurmountable, and both boys accepted an amulet, placing it delicately around their necks.

The instant the amulets contacted their skin, a surge of energy jolted through their bodies, imbuing them with a profound sense of invincibility. Their blood seemed to quicken its pace, overflowing with vitality.

The priestess's smile widened, and her eyes gleamed with triumph as she relished in the knowledge that her plan was set into motion with every step meticulously calculated to ensure the downfall of the spirit blessed.

Seraphine's commanding voice reverberated through the dim chamber as she declared, "Your first task is clear," her eyes glistened with a sinister twinkle as she continued, "Locate the box." She turned her attention to a subordinate on her right that was standing behind the boys, "Now take these boys back home!"

The Fang member reached out both of his arms and grabbed a shoulder of each boy, saying firmly, "Come with me."

The boys obediently followed and the three retreated from the priestess's presence. Their forms blended seamlessly into the enveloping darkness. The room fell into a moment of silence, the members awaiting the next demand.

Seraphine turned to her fellow cohorts, declaring, "We stand united." She paused to let her eyes meet those of her comrades with an unwavering resolve before she continued, "The acquisition of these pawns grants us possession of weapons with immense power. The blessed one will soon comprehend the gravity of their predicament."

A disturbing chorus of murmurs filled the room, a symphony of agreement that underscored the collective understanding of the imminent threat they posed to the blessed. The Fang members exchanged knowing glances, their shared anticipation simmering beneath the surface of their darkened expressions.

"We shall unleash chaos upon them," one of the members voiced a hiss, its tone dripping with malice.

"And they will crumble beneath the weight of our power," added another, their words laced with sadistic satisfaction.

Seraphine surveyed her devoted followers, "Our victory is assured," she proclaimed, "We hold the keys to their undoing. Soon, the blessed one and those pawns will bear witness to their own demise."

With a collective nod, the members dispersed. The wheels of their insidious plot were set into motion, their success hinged upon the intertwined threads of manipulation, darkness, and the unyielding grip of blood magic.

The priestess, standing at the heart of their malevolent web, cast a final glance toward the shadowy depths where the bullies had vanished. Her smile was wicked, and her eyes gleamed with vicious delight.

Chapter 21

Excited for the day, Wiki sprung from his bed and raced through his morning routine. On his way to the door, he grabbed his backpack. After wishing his mom farewell, he departed for the day. As soon as he closed the door behind him, he began skipping to the rhythmic beat of excitement in his heart, with a broad smile on his face.

"Today is a good day," he beamed as he continued skipping until he reached the opening of the forest.

Then, slowing to a walk, he looked around with a new admiration for everything around him. The whispering of the wind carried soft secrets through the leaves. The fluttering of bird wings beat a delicate rhythm overhead. The sounds of the trees' expansive roots communicating underneath him in an ancient language. All the sounds harmonized in a peaceful cadence. These fresh senses, now awakened since beginning his attunement training, gave him a look into nature. Those things he once took for granted, he now appreciated like never before.

Reaching his destination, Wiki began his warmup meditation. He closed his eyes to absorb the sensations and connect with the earthen elements around him. Once he could feel the bond, he envisioned bricks of stone rising from the ground. The earth began to rumble with a subtle vibration momentarily, then halted.

Opening his eyes, he looked around to see if what he was trying to do had worked. To his amazement, there were eleven perfect building blocks surrounding him.

"Epic!" he thought aloud.

Wasting no time, he closed his eyes again, communing with the swirling breezes around him. Feeling the attachment, he opened his eyes and focused on one of the stones. Like a conductor among an orchestra of stone, he gestured up, around, and down. Meticulously he moved and stacked each block to form two symmetrical towers, placing the final puzzle piece atop, bridging the two.

Feeling accomplished, Wiki stood up and stretched, in preparation for his lesson with the fire spirit. With his body now limber he summoned the attention of Fire.

"Fire! I'm ready to face the flames," he smirked, amused at his own humor.

Glancing around for any sign of his call being answered, he heard the faint snapping of a twig in the distance. Pulling his attention, he scanned the area for the source and saw nothing. At that moment, he felt warmth followed by an intense heat coming from behind him. He spun around making eye contact with the fire spirit.

"Winslow, you called?" the spirit responded irritably.

Not paying attention to the spirit's tone of annoyance, Wiki answered, "Yes! I can't wait to start training with you!"

Rolling its eyes, the spirit moved from the firepit to stand on Wiki's side. As he moved Winslow noticed there was no aftermath of Fire's presence; no smoke, no embers, no trace at all.

Astounded, Wiki thought to himself, *"Unbelievable!"* choosing not to voice it aloud to avoid sparking the spirit's perceived frustration.

"Are you sure you're ready?" Fire asked.

"Absolutely!" Wiki nodded with eagerness.

Immediately, the fire spirit raised a hand of flame and gestured with a snap, resulting in a fire that roared from the pit, radiating immense heat.

"Much like your other trainings, attune to it," he said bluntly, giving no further explanation.

"Oh... Okay," Wiki stammered as he nervously inched closer to the blazing fire to find a good place to sit.

He situated himself on the ground and closed his eyes. Guiding his mind and recalling the lessons he had learned, he let the heat surround him. He took a deep breath, the aroma of smoke and ash assaulted his nostrils, causing him to cough and briefly lose his concentration. Aware of this, he re-centered himself by tuning out all sounds other than the crackles and pops produced by the fire until he felt he was one with the element.

"Follow my lead," the fire spirit began, "Raise your right hand, palm to the sky. Envision the palm of your hand in your mind. From the center of your palm, feel the heat radiating outward until you see in your mind's eye, the fire dancing in your hand."

Keeping his eyes closed and heeding Fire's guidance, Wiki visualized a small flame raging from his hand.

"When you believe you are ready, open your eyes," the fire spirit instructed.

Wiki opened his eyes and to his dismay, there was no evidence of anything out of the ordinary.

"Did I… do it?" Wiki asked inquisitively.

"No, nothing happened," Fire said directly while shaking its head left and right.

"It felt like I was the fire. I could see the flame's furiosity in my palm. What am I doing wrong?" Winslow asked with the voice of defeat.

"You said furiosity? Do you know what the essence of fire is?" the spirit asked.

"Anger, rage, and destruction?" Wiki answered unsurely as he shrugged his shoulders.

"That's all wrong!" retorted the fire spirit, it continued, "While fire can be associated with all the things you mentioned, fire is much more than that. Fire is passion. It cooks your food, keeps you warm at night, and removes the old to make way for the new. The anger and rage you alluded to comes from a place of passion. The destruction is but a storm before the calm; it is necessary for restoration. Stop viewing it in such a simplistic way and try again."

Wiki, with a different perspective, began again. He closed his eyes, focused his breathing and repeated the gesture fire guided him with previously. He centered his thoughts on a time he was happy around the fire, like that time last winter when his mom made a fire in the backyard for family time.

"Mom was telling ghost stories while Willow and I cozied up near the heat to keep us toasty."

The warm loving thoughts ignited the heat deep within his core. Feeling more assured about his connection, he opened his eyes to see a tiny flame passionately dancing in his palm. His eyes grew wide as he witnessed his achievement before him.

Proudly, the fire spirit stated, "It seems you understand now. Continue improving on this every day and you will make great strides." After giving the final instruction, the fire spirit vanished leaving a plume of smoke and a sizzling sound behind.

Chapter 22

Ethan's phone rang, and he swiftly answered, "Hello?"

"Ethan? You want to hang out today?" Tyler's voice came through the other end of the phone.

"Yeah, come over to my place. I've been feeling strange since... You know. Have you noticed it too?" Ethan replied.

"Yeah man, it's what I was hoping we could talk about. I'll head over now," Tyler said.

"Alright superstar, hurry it up, I ain't got all day!" Ethan quipped before hanging up the phone.

Tyler quickly slipped on his shoes and raced out the door, his soles echoed against the pavement as he made his way to his friend's house. Ethan's residence stood grand and imposing, a testament to his family's wealth. Luxurious furnishings decorated the spacious rooms. The loft, where they often spent their time, was a haven for their shared interests. The walls were adorned with posters featuring Hank Aaron, Pong, and Speed Racer. Surrounded by empty soda cans and candy wrappers, they settled into the room.

Breaking the silence, Tyler asked, "Did you see how fast I ran the plates when I hit that homerun? These powers are amazing!"

Ethan nodded, his expression mirroring Tyler's sentiments as he added, "Yeah! It's crazy, I'm pitching way faster than I ever have before and I'm not even trying!"

"Maybe we should go see what else we can do?" Tyler asked as he attempted to sink a wad of paper into a small basketball net attached to the door.

Ethan jumped up and grabbed his shoes as he said, "Heck yeah! I was bored anyway. Let's head to the courts," not waiting for an answer, he began tying his laces before he grabbed his basketball.

"Sure, why not," Tyler murmured with resignation, realizing his friend made a demand and not a suggestion.

Excited to test their limits, the boys left Ethan's house and began their walk.

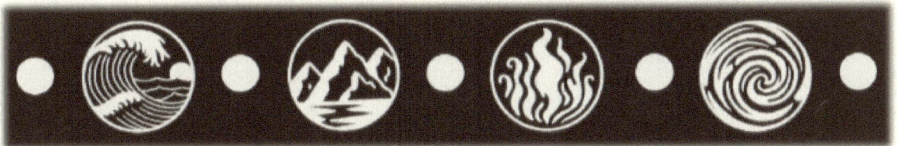

Meanwhile, Wiki and Hap decided to embrace their inner child today and met up at the playground. Giggling uncontrollably and completely caught up in the moment, they competed to see who could swing the highest. Out of Wiki's peripheral view, he saw Ethan and Tyler at a distance.

Pausing his laughter, he said, "Oh man, the jerks are incoming. Maybe we should head out?"

"Yeah, let's get outta here!" Harper agreed.

As they swung forward, they eyed the ground, calculating the perfect moment.

Wiki counted aloud, "One, two, three!"

They released their grips in unison and jumped, a rush of adrenaline coursing through them as they soared and landed gracefully on the soft grass.

As the bullies passed by, the sudden burst of motion from the playground captured Tyler's attention.

Nudging Ethan's arm then pointing out Winslow and Harper, Tyler jested, "Hey, look! It's the dweebs. Want to go mess with them?"

"Yeah!" Ethan said to his friend before he yelled out, "Where do y'all think you're going?" taunting Wiki and Hap.

Hearing the tormentors, Harper took off running in a full sprint, calling back, "Come on Wiki!"

Winslow wasted no time grabbing his backpack and catching up to match her pace.

"They think they can get away from us this time!" Tyler laughed before both boys bounded in unnatural strides after their prey.

Wiki looked back, checking if they were in the clear, and noticed the bullies were rapidly gaining on them. It was as if Winslow and Harper weren't even moving.

"Hurry Hap! They are gaining on us… Uh, really quickly!" Wiki stated worriedly as he turned his attention back to his front to see where they were heading.

They could both hear the tyrannical footsteps advancing. Not even a moment later, Ethan hurled the basketball toward Winslow and Harper, sending it whizzing with tremendous force. The ball struck Wiki in the bottom of his bookbag. The powerful impact caused Winslow to lose his balance and tumble through the grass; his backpack falling open and spilling its contents. The antiquated box rolled to a stop and immediately caught the eye of Ethan.

He reached down and grabbed it, stating, "Tyler! Do you think this is what those people wanted?" as he noticed the symbols as described by the high priestess.

Harper, coming to the defense of her best friend, declared, "That doesn't belong to you!" before winding back her hand and throwing a haymaker toward Ethan's blindside.

Instantly, Ethan caught her punch without looking. He turned to Harper, his eyes blood red, his voice intertwining with Seraphine's, taking on a dual-tone quality as he said, "Begone, you insignificant creature."

With a flick of his wrist, Ethan sent Harper flying. She landed next to Wiki, who was still laying on the ground after his tumble.

"Hap! Are you okay?" Winslow asked as he began pulling himself up.

"Yeah, I'm fine, but his eyes were glowing red, and he sounded really weird," she answered while standing up and brushing herself off.

Desperate to regain the link between him and his father, Wiki extended his hand. Without realizing it, his overwhelming emotions commanded the wind, and a roaring gust came from behind Tyler, rushing with immense power toward Winslow's hand. The troublemakers were unfazed. In unison, the boys sidestepped the gust and turned their gaze to Winslow.

"So, you are the one I have been looking for. You're just a mere child," The dual-tone voice scoffed eerily from Ethan's mouth in a synchronized fashion that was unnaturally precise, each word perfectly matched in timing and intonation.

"Give it back!" Wiki yelled out, reaching for the box again.

"Oh? This piece of junk?" Seraphine taunted through Ethan using the control of the amulet. "You can have it. It's useless to me anyway." Unfazed by the pain, Ethan's shoulder dislocated as Seraphine flung the wooden container with all Ethan's might toward Wiki's face in a superhuman effort.

With little time to react, Wiki flinched and covered his head. At the same moment, the ground split open with a thunderous roar, scattering rocks and soil in all directions. A colossal arm of clay and stone emerged from the crack and caught the ancient artifact right before it contacted Winslow's face. With the box in hand, a familiar golem began rising from the fracture. Once fully emerged, the once enormous hand quickly returned to its proportionate size.

Earth glanced at Wiki and Hap, stating, "I need you both to get back so that I can handle this."

The golem handed Winslow the box. As the spirit turned its attention back to the boys, rippling waves of earth moved Winslow and Harper to a safe distance.

"The games are over," the earth spirit bellowed before releasing a stomp that caused ten-foot rock walls to shoot forth from the ground on each side of the puppets.

The spirit clapped, causing the towering walls to begin grinding inward with a menacing speed. Seraphine quickly noticed the imminent threat the enormous obstacles posed and pulled the strings of her marionettes with synchronized grace, causing them to leap backward. Each one arched through the air in opposite directions, clearing the nearest walls with ease and landing gracefully just beyond the rapidly closing barriers.

"Silly earthen fool. I'm not that easily thwarted," Seraphine mocked.

Earth began to chuckle as it said, "Seems you're the foolish one."

Trying to comprehend what the spirit was insinuating, the high priestess looked down through both sets of the boys' eyes. She noticed their feet were encased in thick clay, hindering their escape. As the realization sank in, muddy tendrils swirled around, encasing each of the boys before hardening and rendering them immovable.

Seraphine destroyed her connection to the amulets, knowing that her pawns had no moves left. The immense power drained from the boys immediately, leaving them in an unconscious state as Wiki and Hap made their way back to Earth's side.

"Wow! That rocked!" Harper winked, raising her arm to the golem for a high-five.

Complying with the gesture, Earth matched her motion as it responded, "That was a good one, I knew I liked you Harper."

"You are just like I dreamed!" Hap stated in awe.

"That's because I was in your dream. You did very well in my trial," the golem said. Turning its attention to Wiki, Earth explained, "Our magic will reshape their memory, turning it into nothing more than a nightmare, and we will guide them safely back."

"But what about Ethan's shoulder? Will he be, okay?" Winslow asked.

"The boy will be just fine. He made his bed and now he must lie in it. They would not have been in this situation had they not accepted such a dark power in the first place," the spirit said as it wrapped Tyler and Ethan in individual cocoons of earthen soil before pulling them beneath the surface.

"Farewell young ones," Earth said before melting into the ground and disappearing.

Left behind, Wiki and Hap exchanged exhausted, yet relieved looks.

"Yeah, I don't think I've ever wanted a nap this badly," Harper joked.

Winslow responded with a weary laugh, then said, "Let's head back to my house, I know my mom is already worried we never came home to check in. Dealing with bullies under the influence of magic won't be a good excuse for her."

The friends laughed as they hurriedly grabbed their belongings and raced back to Wiki's house, ready for the lecture they were about to receive.

Chapter 23

Outside the confines of time and space, in a realm of celestial beauty surrounded by ethereal structures and landscapes demonstrating unfathomable, perfect harmony in its purest form, lay a world untouchable by the hand of corruption. The four elemental spirits gathered, their presence emanating a sense of ancient wisdom.

"I am so happy with how Wiki and Hap are progressing." Wind said while bouncing around all the other spirits, it continued, "The boy has shown remarkable promise in his attunement training."

The earth spirit nodded in agreement, its golem form a perpetual-cycle of moving rocks and spinning gravel.

"True. The blessed from the past have taken much longer to grasp the basics," it rumbled.

The fire spirit crackled with extreme energy, as it hovered over the ground, saying, "The boy has shown a deep connection to all living things around him. He has the innate ability to not only hear, but to feel their communication, a precursor to vibrational signaling. As for the girl, even without power, she has proven herself to be an impressive fighter. Together, they have the potential to take their place amongst our greatest warriors."

The water spirit spoke up, its form flowing like a tranquil river. "United, they form a formidable force that can aid us in preserving the natural equilibrium."

Their conversation was interrupted by a sudden sense of unease that washed over the group. They exchanged tense glances, each of them feeling the unmistakable, creeping sensation. They knew what it meant, the Corrupted ones are up to something.

"We need to act swiftly," the wind spirit said, its voice filled with urgency.

"They are becoming more bothersome by the minute. We can no longer afford to ignore their presence," the earth spirit agreed as it balled its fists tightly.

The fire spirit's flames intensified momentarily by the passing frustration clearly evident in its tone, "It seems our job is never done."

The water spirit shook its head gently, saying, "No, and it never will be. Earth, can you commune with our oldest allies?"

"I can do that," the earth spirit responded.

Without a single movement from the golem, reality itself seemed to bend and yield to the spirit's power. The space before it shimmered, as if the very fabric of existence was being torn apart. A rift began to form, its edges glowing with a majestic light that danced in hues of green and gold, colors of the earth's essence.

"Once I am finished speaking with our friends, I will report back here, and then we can meet with the young ones." Earth stated before stepping through the portal.

The spirit arrived in the Terra Vitae realm within a vast forest on the planet Earth, to establish communication with the Plantarii, the plant-related beings. With a low rumble, the earth spirit coiled itself into a dense sphere of soil and descended into the ground, its form merging seamlessly with the surface of the planet. Its energy flowed through the subterranean veins, traveling deep into the core where the lifeblood of the world pulsed with ancient, rhythmic power.

Reaching the heart of the planet, the earth spirit extended its consciousness, intertwining with the core's radiant energy. The planet responded, its nucleus glowing brighter as it resonated with the spirit's presence. Through this profound connection, the spirit could feel the heartbeat of Earth, a steady, life-giving thrum echoing.

Transmitting waves of natural energy, the earth spirit spoke directly to the Plantarii, "Noble friends, the shadows of the past have stirred once more, and their intentions are unclear. I call upon you to cautiously observe and report any signs of our old adversary. Your vigilance is crucial as your timely insights will be our greatest asset in thwarting their plans."

This call resonated with the Plantarii, awakening their long dormant consciousness. The primal beings, from the tallest trees to the smallest mushrooms, felt the spirit's message vibrating through their roots and mycelia.

"Esteemed protector, your request has enlivened us. We, the Plantarii, will watch, listen, and protect," They replied collectively.

"We are forever grateful for your unwavering dedication," the earth spirit thanked them before returning home.

Chapter 24

Harper, still exhausted from her encounter with Ethan and Tyler, lay in bed with her eyes shut. Her mind raced back and forth between the last day's events.

Getting caught in a singular moment, Hap thought to herself, "*How did Ethan even see my punch? He was looking away from me… It doesn't make any sense.*"

She was unable to reason about the confrontation and slowly lost an appetite for resolution. The familiar sensations of the bed dissolved, being replaced by the creaking of wooden planks beneath her feet. The soft rustle of the sheets transformed into the whisper of the wind and the distant call of seagulls. A sudden rush of cool, salty air brushed against her face, mingling with the warmth of the sun.

Opening her eyes, now wide and clear, she found herself standing on the bow of a grand pirate ship, the vast ocean stretching out in all directions. Atop her head sat a tricorn hat with a jaunty feather in its brim. A black leather coat with gold embroidery wrapped around her slightly wrinkled crisp white shirt, tucked into high-waisted trousers matching the appearance of the coat.

With one foot upon the bulwark and the other grounded on the deck, she pulled the cutlass from its sheath and hoisted it in the air, in a forward chopping motion, "Give 'er all she's got, lads! Full sail ahead mateys!" she commanded.

Echoing Hap's order, "Rawk! Full sail ahead!" her parrot squawked. Its mangy and unkept appearance with bedraggled feathers, sat upon her shoulder, mimicking her sentiment.

"Aye aye, Cap'n!" the crew complied unanimously.

Taking their rightful positions, five members of the crew hoisted the sails. The wind began to pick up, whipping Harper's hair. Looking through her monocular, she noticed splintered masts jutting from the horizon at odd angles.

Excited by the prospect before them, Hap bellowed, "Avast, ye scallywags! Trim the sails and be quick about it or I'll have ye swabbing the decks till dawn!"

Without hesitation, the crew adjusted the sails, filling them with the wind, causing a satisfying snap as Harper continued. "Listen up ye bilge rats, prepare yerselves to plunder the wreck ahead!"

"Rawk, bilge rats, rawk," the bird mirrored.

"Alright, foul feather duster, that's enough outta ye," Harper snipped while keeping her eyes on the surrounding area. Approaching the wreck, "Drop anchor, ye scurvy dogs!" she decreed, "Let no booty slip thru our fingers!"

Obeying the command, the crew descended into the murky depths, exploring the partially sunken remains. Harper, awaiting a report from them, paced back and forth on the starboard quarter of the vessel.

"Cap'n, ye won't believe it!" a crew member said as they lifted a weathered chest onto the ship.

"What be the spoils that lie inside?" Hap asked, slamming the butt of her cutlass into the rusted, worn lock.

The lid creaked open, revealing gold doubloons and gems galore. Nestled in the middle, lay a pearlescent crystal skull.

"At last, we've found the Imperium Crown! With it, we'll rule the seas!" Harper exclaimed.

"Rawk. You Cap'n, you'll rule the seas," her feathered mate cawed, "Control of all, be yers! Rawk."

Ignoring the suggestion, Hap began to daydream of the grand things she could achieve with such a powerful artifact before snapping back to reality, demanding, "Take it to me quarters at once!"

Grinning deviously, two members crept toward the treasure from opposite sides, their movements purposeful and synchronized like predators closing in on prey. They grasped the chest by its ornate, weathered handles, the ancient metal groaning faintly under the strain, and vanished into the shadows below deck. Harper, noticing the subtle flicker of unease on her crew's faces, felt a knot of tension coil in her stomach. Something wasn't right. Her senses sharpened as she remained poised, her gaze darting between the retreating figures and the rest of the room.

"Now!" The remaining four crew members drew their sabers with a flash of steel, their eyes glinting with betrayal as they lunged forward. "Get 'er!"

Hap, meeting their challenge with a smirk, deftly raised her blade to parry the first strike, the clash of steel ringing out like a war drum. With a swift pivot, she drove a sharp kick into her attacker's chest, sending him reeling backward, his weapon tumbling from his grasp and skidding across the deck. From her right, her first mate barreled forward, his eyes blazing as he unleashed a furious overhead swing. Harper shifted her stance, countering with a precise strike of her pommel that connected with a resounding crack, sending him sprawling to the deck in a dazed heap.

Behind her, a sharp voice barked, "Gotcha now!" as a deckhand lunged, his blade slicing through the air with lethal intent.

Hap twisted instinctively, the blade grazing perilously close as she rolled forward to evade it. Dust and splinters scattered under her weight as she sprang to her feet with feline agility.

A sly wink accompanied her mocking retort, "Ye missed me!"

Seizing a rope swaying from the foremast, she launched herself off the starboard railing, soaring through the air. The rope twisted and curled around the mast like a living serpent, entangling the remaining two adversaries in its unyielding grip before she swiftly disarmed them.

With the immediate threat neutralized, her focus shifted to the last pair, who had vanished with the treasure. Moving with silent determination, she slipped into her quarters and found them hunched over the bounty, their greed plain as day. Without hesitation, she incapacitated them with precise strikes, leaving no room for resistance.

Hauling all the subdued crew members to the bow, she lashed them together with expert knots, ensuring none could wriggle free. The ropes creaked as they shifted uncomfortably, each one eyeing her warily, unsure of her next move.

"What 'm I gonna do wit' dese scallywags?" she muttered, her gaze drifting over the subdued crew, their defiant scowls meeting her calculating stare.

"Ye could make 'em walk the plank!" squawked the parrot perched on her shoulder, its feathers bristling with anticipation.

"No, no. They've been a decent crew till now," Harper replied, her voice laced with reluctant forgiveness.

"Rawk. Wit' yer shiny new toy, ye could command 'em without question," the bird suggested, its beady eyes glinting with mischief.

"That don't sit right wit' me," she declared, shaking her head. "What's the point in havin' puppets who can't think fer themselves?"

"Ye be no fun," the parrot groused, flapping its wings in mock frustration.

"Aha! I've got it!" Harper exclaimed, a sly grin spreading across her face.

Grabbing a bucket of seawater, she emptied it over the rails of the ship before flipping it over and placing it down as a stool. Stepping atop, Hap commanded the attention of her restrained crewmates.

"Listen up! This here's the problem," she said, hoisting the bejeweled skull high. Its intricate carvings gleamed ominously in the dim light. "I've decided to get rid o' it."

She raised her arm to throw it when the bird squawked sharply. "Think carefully. That there holds unstoppable power."

Harper rolled her eyes dramatically before hurling the skull skyward. It spun, glittering in the fading light, before vanishing into the horizon.

"Rawk! Ye fool!" the bird screeched, its wings flapping in outrage.

"Enough outta ye!" Harper snapped, grabbing the parrot and tossing it after the skull. The bird squawked indignantly, flailing as it disappeared into the distance.

Turning back to the crew, Harper crossed her arms and smirked. "As fer the rest o' ye, I'm splittin' the loot evenly—on one condition: yer undyin' loyalty."

The crew hesitated for a moment before erupting into cheers, their voices ringing in unison, "Aye aye, Cap'n!"

As the chorus of loyalty settled, a gale-force wind swept in from the west, roaring across the deck and forcing Harper to clutch her hat tightly to her head. Her coat billowed wildly, and she braced herself against the force, tucking her chin into her chest. When the tempest finally eased, she straightened, releasing her hat and letting her eyes scan the now eerily still surroundings.

Before her, where the wind had howled moments earlier, a figure began to materialize. The being, sculpted entirely of swirling winds and faint traces of mist, took on the form of a homunculus. Its body was an ever-shifting tapestry of storm clouds and eddies, each movement a reflection of the boundless tempest it embodied. The creature seemed both solid and intangible, its form ceaselessly undulating like a raging storm barely held in check.

The entity puffed out its chest and spoke in a resonant voice that carried power. "Harper, you have done well."

Though its words were solemn, a faint flicker of mischief played at the edges of its tone. Wind chuckled internally, trying to maintain an air of gravity. Harper stood rooted in place, the weight of the wind spirit's presence silencing any immediate response.

Without waiting for her to speak, the humanoid form began to dissipate. Its edges curled and billowed outward, blending seamlessly into the passing breeze. The figure unraveled like smoke caught in a gentle draft, its form swirling softly around her before vanishing entirely.

Chapter 25

Rendezvousing at their cherished hideaway with the intention of training together, Hap launched into her tale, her voice animated. "And then, my own crew started a mutiny! It was insane!"

"Wow! I bet you put them in their place," Wiki replied, a chuckle escaping him.

"You bet I did!" Harper said, flexing her bicep with a triumphant grin. "Then, I'm pretty confident I was visited by the wind spirit, but I'm not entirely sure."

"What did it look like?" Winslow asked, his brow lifting with curiosity.

"The best way I can describe it is… kind of like a human shape, but smaller than normal. It was made of tightly curling, super fierce wind. Pretty scary, if you ask me," she explained, her tone shifting to awe.

"That doesn't sound like Wind to me," he said, shrugging nonchalantly.

"Anyway," he began, changing the subject, "I have something I wanted to try. Can you grab a handful of those pebbles and maybe some sticks?"

"Uh, sure. What do you want me to do with them?" she asked, crouching to scoop up the requested items.

"Okay, hear me out. I need you to practice your pitches and throw them at me. Let's start with one at a time and maybe… softly." He laughed, a mischievous glint in his eye.

"I get where you're going. You want to practice your defenses," she said, catching on quickly.

"Exactly! I gotta focus–" Winslow began, only to be cut off by a sudden "Thump!" as a tiny stone smacked his upper arm. "Ow! Hey! I wasn't ready yet!" he exclaimed, mockingly rubbing the spot where the pebble hit.

"Just testing you," Harper replied with a wink, her grin devious.

Their laughter filled the clearing before Wiki composed himself again. "Give me a minute to focus. When I say 'ready,' then bring it on."

Hap nodded, her face alight with playfulness as she stood quietly, waiting for her cue.

Moments later, Wiki felt the connection settle within him, his stance firm. "Ready!" he called, his voice steady with resolve.

With a grin, Harper dropped her hand, launching the small rock in a smooth underhand motion. The pebble arced through the air toward Wiki, he raised his hand and attempted to summon a precise jet of air. The gust veered slightly off-target, and as the rock continued its trajectory, he quickly sidestepped, narrowly avoiding a hit to his knee.

"Dang it, I missed! Throw another one!" Wiki shouted; his tone full of frustration.

"Alrighty!" Harper responded, aiming more carefully this time.

She swung her arm low and released another small rock with a flick of her wrist. It sailed toward him with slightly more speed.

Wiki tracked the apex of the incoming projectile, timing his response. He pushed forward another gust of air, this one closer to the mark but still off by a fraction. The pebble barreled forward, leaving him no time to dodge. Pivoting sharply, he turned his shoulder to absorb the impact, wincing slightly but laughing it off.

"Aww man, so close! I thought I had that one. Let's try again," he said.

"You bet!" Harper replied, quickly selecting another pebble.

She sent it flying with a flick, this time smaller and faster. The pebble zipped through the air, catching Wiki off guard.

"Thwap!"

"Ow! That one hit me right in the forehead!" Wiki groaned, rubbing the spot as a sheepish smile crept across his face.

Harper burst into laughter. "Sorry about that! I didn't think I threw it so hard."

"It's fine, but you definitely caught me by surprise," he replied, chuckling as he waved off her concern. "Let's try something different this time. Give me a moment to get ready."

Harper nodded, tossing a pebble back and forth between her hands to pass the time. "Any time now," she murmured, her tone teasing.

"Okay, all set!" Wiki declared. "This time, send more at once."

With a mischievous glint in her eye, Harper crouched down and scooped up a handful of pebbles and dirt clumps. "You asked for it!" she said, unleashing a chaotic spray in a wide arc. The projectiles scattered through the air like a swarm of tiny missiles.

Winslow planted his feet and raised both hands in unison. The ground trembled briefly before a makeshift dirt barricade erupted in front of him, intercepting the incoming debris with a muted thud. Dust settled around them as the last of the pebbles fell harmlessly to the ground.

"Now that's what I'm talking about," Wiki said with a grin, lowering his hands as the dirt barrier crumbled back to the earth.

"Whoa! Nice," Harper said encouragingly, brushing the dirt from her palms.

"It worked!" Wiki cheered, his enthusiasm bubbling over. "That was so much easier than trying to stop it with wind. Guess I need to work on my accuracy, though."

Hap strode over, clapping him on the back with mock solemnity. "You definitely need better aim. But don't worry, I've got an idea that'll help."

With a spring in her step, she hurried to a weathered tree stump nearby, gathering pinecones scattered across the ground as she went. Placing them in neat rows atop the stump, she turned back to Wiki.

"How about trying to hit something that isn't flying straight at your face?" she teased.

"Great idea!" Wiki replied, his tone eager as he focused on the targets.

Concentration etched into his features; he attempted to channel his energy more precisely. One by one, he aimed gusts of air at the pinecones, managing to knock a few off but missing others. After several tries, he noticed Harper's attention wandering, her expression shifting from amusement to mild boredom.

"Hey, wanna switch this up?" Wiki asked, breaking her reverie.

"Switch it up how?" Harper's curiosity reignited, her eyes sparkling.

"Well," Winslow began, grinning as an idea formed, "What if I tossed you up in the air? With a bit of timing, you might be able to jump even higher!"

"That sounds awesome! Let's do it!" Hap exclaimed, bouncing on her toes in anticipation.

Wiki took a moment to steady himself, planting his feet firmly as he prepared. "Alright, on the count of three, I'll give it a go. Ready?"

"Ready!" Harper called back, her grin widening.

"One, two, three!" Wiki motioned with a sweeping underhand gesture, his connection with the earth sparking to life. The ground beneath Harper shifted subtly, then surged upward with a controlled burst of energy, lifting her clean off her feet. She landed lightly, a laugh spilling from her lips.

"Okay, I didn't even jump that time. Let's do it again—I'll be ready this time!" she said, her voice brimming with excitement.

Wiki nodded, his confidence growing. "Alright, here we go. On three again."

As Winslow motioned, the earth propelled Harper upward, and she jumped in tandem, soaring higher than before. At the height of her ascent, a realization struck her like a thunderclap.

"Oh no, I didn't plan for the landing!" she yelped, her arms flailing as she plummeted back to the ground. She hit the gravelly surface with a thud, scraping her knee.

"Hap! Are you okay?" Wiki cried, rushing to her side, guilt etched across his face.

Brushing off the dirt and flashing a grin, Harper waved him off. "It's just a scratch, nothing to worry about. Did you see how high I got, though?"

"Yeah, and it was terrifying," Winslow replied, shaking his head.

Before either could say more, the distant sound of rushing water began to rise, capturing their attention. Both turned toward the creek, watching as the tranquil flow transformed into an animated current. The ripples converged at a single point, swirling faster and faster until a figure began to emerge. The water rose, shimmering and translucent, shaping itself into a humanoid form. Its limbs flowed like liquid tendrils, constantly shifting and reforming, creating a mesmerizing, ever-changing silhouette.

"Winslow, I have come to begin your training," the figure spoke, its voice a harmonious blend of flowing water and serene power.

Wiki and Hap stood rooted in awe, the weight of the moment sinking in as they faced the water spirit's fluid, commanding presence.

"I was planning to call out to you tomorrow," Winslow said, his voice filled with surprise.

"Due to unforeseen circumstances, we needed to conclude your basic training sooner," the spirit replied with calm authority.

"Oh, okay!" Wiki responded eagerly, a joyful compliance lighting up his face.

Glancing at Harper's scraped knee, the spirit's gaze softened. "Come here, child," it said gently.

Harper hesitated briefly, then approached the edge of the creek, her injured leg favoring her steps.

"Remove your shoe and place the foot of your injured leg into the water," the spirit instructed.

Hap winced as the cold water enveloped her foot. "Oo, that's freezing!" she exclaimed.

Ignoring her remark, the water spirit turned to Wiki. "Watch closely, Winslow. This will be your task in time."

With a graceful motion, the water rose from the creek, spiraling upward around Harper's leg. It formed intricate, fluid patterns around the injured area, each swirl glowing faintly. Harper's pain ebbed with every pass of the water, replaced by a soothing warmth that spread through her limb. Wiki's eyes widened as the scrape visibly mended before him.

"Yes, Wiki," the spirit said, noticing his amazement. "The elements can heal all, but only when you are fully attuned. Let's begin with something simpler."

"Remove your shoes and join me by the water," the spirit continued. Winslow obeyed, stepping to the edge of the creek, anticipation flickering in his eyes.

"Extend your hand and open your senses. Don't be alarmed; this will sting a little," the spirit warned. In a swift motion, it formed a fine icicle in its liquid hand and pricked Wiki's index finger.

"Ow!" Wiki flinched, shaking his hand slightly.

The spirit gave him a moment to compose himself. "Now, close your eyes. Listen to the soothing sounds of the creek–the gentle lapping, the rhythmic ripples. As you breathe in, feel the dense, cool air filling your lungs and let it settle within you."

Following the guidance, Winslow spoke softly. "I feel a tingling in my feet... it almost tickles."

"Good," the spirit said approvingly. "Let that sensation saturate your skin, flowing through you. Imagine it merging with your essence."

Wiki focused intently. The water seemed not just beneath his feet but coursing through him, a rhythmic pulse weaving into his very being. "It feels... peaceful and refreshing," he murmured.

"Now," the spirit instructed, "guide the water to wash away the pain."

The creek's water flowed over Winslow's finger, its constant cycling soothing the tiny wound. Within moments, the throbbing ceased.

"The pain is gone!" Wiki exclaimed, his excitement bubbling over.

"Well done," the spirit said warmly. "To heal, you must first understand what is broken. In time, you will learn to connect deeply with others' pain and repair it from within."

Struck by the profound words, Winslow and Harper remained silent, their expressions filled with awe.

"With that, I must take my leave," the spirit said, its form beginning to dissolve. Tendrils of water unraveled gracefully, merging back into the creek until nothing remained but its gentle babble.

"That was incredible!" Hap exclaimed, her exuberance breaking the silence.

"It felt surreal," Wiki agreed, glancing down at his now-healed finger. "But now my clothes are soaked."

"Yeah, it's starting to get late," Harper noted. "Maybe we should head back soon."

"Or..." Wiki suggested with a grin, "I can get a fire going to dry us off. That way, my mom won't ask any awkward questions."

"Good idea! Plus, it gives us more time to hang out!" Harper said with a wide grin.

They gathered branches, snapping the larger ones into manageable pieces, and arranged them in a teepee formation. Winslow summoned a small flame in his palm, marveling at the warmth and energy. Carefully, he directed it to the pyre, igniting it with a graceful flick.

As the fire crackled, they sat side by side, the orange glow casting playful shadows on their faces. Laughter and jokes filled the clearing, their camaraderie growing stronger as the sun dipped below the horizon. When night finally settled in, they extinguished the fire and made their way back to Wiki's house, just in time for dinner.

Chapter 26

As the sun dipped lower in the sky, it cast elongated shadows across the swelling dunes and the rocky outcrops that punctuated the horizon. The Plantarii, having identified the source of the corrupted disturbance, collectively vibrated their roots with a deep, resonant thrum to beckon the Earth spirit's attention. The air in the sweltering desert shimmered with waves of heat. Sparse vegetation clung to life amidst the harsh landscape. Answering their call, the familiar stone sentinel took form near a gathering of scattered boulders, where a refreshing microhabitat lay, teeming with hardy succulents, resilient desert grasses, and small, colorful cacti thriving in the cool, shaded crevices.

"I heard you, old friends," leaning closer to the desert plants, its stony fingers gently brushing against the weathered leaves and fragile stems. "What news do you bring?" Earth questioned.

"In our quest, we encountered barriers," murmured the Plantarii through its collective mind, its essence intertwined with the sunbaked earth. "A web of enchantments cloaks their intentions, obscuring our insights." The Earth spirit sat quietly, absorbing the information.

The Plantarii continued, "While we could not discern their precise location or specifics regarding their intentions, we did ascertain that they are not far from this location. Through our watchful eye, we have noticed an increase in residual energy from dark magic practices, telling us that they have become progressively more active in a short time, which causes concern."

Soaking it in and pondering for a moment, the spirit responded, expressing gratitude, "Thank you for providing this helpful information. The Corrupted's influence has spread fiercely of late, and I am concerned for the Blessed One's safety. Please keep a vigilant watch over him and his companion." The Plantarii agreed, their muted whispers seemed to echo their silent promise of protection.

"Maintain your guard and stay safe," The Earth spirit said, before tearing a rip in the fabric of reality and returning home to relay the information it had received.

Arriving in the elemental enclave, Earth summons the other spirits by internalizing its want for the other elements to convene. Feeling its call, each of the spirits returned within a matter of minutes.

"Brethren, I have received word from the Plantarii." Earth said, informing them of the new knowledge, "Our timeline has shortened, with the impending threat, it is crucial that we finalize our testing and proceed with the ceremony."

"Agreed, Let's get on with it!" Fire said, full of vitality.

"Wait!" Water interjected, "Have you all decided what to gift the girl? I have already chosen to provide her with a bow."

"I've chosen gauntlets," Earth remarked.

"From me, she will get a whip, both a weapon and a utility," Fire announced decisively.

"I'm gonna give her the gift of speed, agility, and BOUNCEYNESS!" Wind proclaimed while visibly shaking with excitement.

"Are we all squared away then?" Fire asked bluntly.

Sequentially, the spirits nodded in agreement, Wind, a gentle swirl; Water, a smooth slosh; Earth, a subtle shift. The collective motion of the spirits conveyed a silent but powerful unity, an unspoken bond that underscored their shared purpose.

"With that settled, let the games begin!" Fire asserted, its voice crackling with intensity.

With a swift and decisive motion, it scorched a fissure in reality itself. The air sizzled as the fracture widened, revealing a portal to Terra Vitae. Without hesitation, Fire stepped through the portal, its form engulfed in a brilliant blaze as it departed to fulfill its task. The portal closed behind it, leaving only a faint, lingering heat in the air.

Chapter 27

Harper, in a deep slumber and unaware of the strange and perilous journey that awaited her in the realm of dreams, found herself in a spacious hall. It was decorated with colorful streamers, balloons, and a large banner that hung from the ceiling, proclaiming "Happy Birthday Harper!" She felt a surge of joy and excitement as she recognized the familiar faces of her father and friends, who greeted her with hugs and smiles. They led her outside, to a table laden with cake and presents and sang "Happy Birthday" in unison. Harper blew out the candles and made a wish, feeling happy and loved. Opening her eyes, she turned to find solace in Wiki's reassuring smile.

"What did you wish for, Hap?" Wiki asked curiously.

"You know I can't tell you that! Otherwise, it won't come true," Harper responded, nudging his arm.

"I know, I know… Hey! Did you notice the cotton candy? I've been eyeing it since I got here," he suggested, pointing over to the machine.

"Yeah, I've been wanting some, but I don't want to go near that creepy clown manning the station," she recoiled at the sight of the red nosed, rainbow haired monster.

"He doesn't look creepy, Hap," Winslow chuckled, "It is just a normal clown, but I don't mind grabbing some for both of us!" He offered as he stood up.

"Yeah! That would be great! Thanks," she said, truly grateful that she didn't have to get close to the bozo.

She directed her attention to her cousin, who wanted to know how her softball games were going, enjoying the conversation as time slipped away. Realizing Wiki should be back by now, she began to look around for him. He wasn't at the cotton candy stand.

As panic began to set in, her search intensified. Scanning the distant surroundings, she caught a glimpse of her pal being carried away by another clown with a sinister grin and garish makeup. Wiki's limp body hung out of a multicolored, polka dotted knapsack. The sight made her uneasy and she realized that she needed to act quickly. Jumping up from her seat at the table, she dashed off after the menacing figure which had her dearest friend.

"Hey, wait!" she yelled.

"Honk-honk!" Stopping her in her tracks, three more clowns encircled her. One taunting her with a balloon animal; one trying to paint her face with a moldy paintbrush; one honking an annoying horn in her face. She pushed past them to continue her pursuit. In the distance she could see the clown with Wiki, disappearing into the thick foliage.

As she crossed the threshold into the woods, her surroundings began to shift. The once bright skies dimmed as dark clouds rolled in and an eerie fog began to settle. A sudden weight and clinking caused her to stumble. Glancing down in shock, she noticed her attire had transformed. Gone were the festive clothes from the birthday party. Instead, she found herself clad in gleaming knight's armor, each piece intricately detailed and surprisingly well-fitted. In her hand, she clutched a hefty sword with a polished blade.

"Whoa," she said, bewildered by the transformation as she admired her new armament.

The birds were no longer chirping, the once vibrant melodies had fallen silent. Instead, only the eerie sounds of skittering could be heard all around her. The soft, unsettling rustle of tiny feet moving swiftly across the ground and through the underbrush filled the air. The silence of the avian wildlife heightened the tension, making the scampering seem louder and more ominous in the stillness.

"I really hope that isn't what I think it is." She thought to herself, as she shuddered at the idea of her greatest fear, eight-legged nightmares.

Torn between the urge to rescue her friend and her desire to return to the happy familiarity of her loved ones, she pressed on. Each step felt heavier with the weight of uncertainty and fear. In the distance, she could barely hear Wiki calling for help, the plea echoing softly through the vegetation. The sound was muffled but unmistakable. Determined, she steeled herself and continued deeper into the unknown.

"Hap, help! I can't see where I am, and I can't move." Wiki pleaded.

"I'm coming Wiki! Where are you?" Hap asked with concern lacing her voice.

"Over here," Wiki continued to use his voice to guide her.

As Harper continued to follow the sounds of her cherished friend. Shadowy tendrils escaping around a large oak tree caught her attention. As she adjusted to get a better look, she immediately recognized two sets of four glinting eyes peering at her from the darkness. As the realization set in that her deepest fears may have come to life, her stomach sank. In that moment, a large segmented, chitinous appendage covered in fine sensory hairs, crept out from the shadows.

"Nope!" Harper exclaimed before succumbing to her fear and taking off in the opposite direction.

"Hap, please! I'm scared." Wiki echoed.

Harper, hearing his cries for help, froze in place. She began analyzing the situation. "*That thing was massive, but I need to help Wiki*." She thought to herself.

Knowing she was his only hope gave her a reinvigorated sense of bravery. She turned back toward the location of the large arachnid and her lifelong friend.

"Hap!" Wiki cried.

With confirmation that she was heading in the right direction, she kicked her pace into high gear.

"I'm coming Wiki!" Harper decreed as she pressed forward.

Jumping over a toppled tree, she was met by two yellow and black spiders, each as large as she was. Recoiling in mild terror, she readied her sturdy blade. The spiderlings reared back on their hind legs, their fangs glistening threateningly. Harper took a deep breath and rolled forward just as both of the spiders lunged at her. The creatures' strikes missed her by inches as they collided with each other. Seizing the brief opening created by their mishap, Harper sprinted forward. As she rushed away from them, the spiders shot nets of silk, each one narrowly missing her with a whistling whoosh. Harper weaved through the deadly threads with agility, her eyes locked on her path ahead. She could feel the rush of air from the silk nets as they passed by her, but she did not falter.

"That was close, but no time to waste, gotta find Wiki." She thought aloud, continuing her momentum.

As she pressed deeper, gossamer strands twinkled in the faint sunlight that peeked through the grey clouds. Stopping short of being ensnared, she wielded her sword to sever an intricately woven web.

"Wiki, I'm almost there!" Hap declared barreling onward.

Darting through the brush, skillfully avoiding the remainder of the silken traps, she rounded the base of an exceptionally large tree which towered over her. The roots, gnarled and ancient, formed a natural archway at the entrance of a gaping cave that burrowed deep beneath the trunk. Pausing for a moment, Harper caught her breath and assessed the petrifying entryway. The cave's mouth seemed to beckon her with an ominous whisper. She tightened her grip on her blade and cautiously stepped forward.

"Wiki, are you in there?" Harper inquired.

"Hap, I'm worried. I can't see anything." Wiki exclaimed.

Upon entering the lair, she observed silken spheres sparkling with a delicate, pearlescent sheen. The remarkably large egg sacs reflected the immense size of their creator. Each sac pulsated faintly from the life growing within, filled with hundreds, perhaps thousands, of tiny, developing spiderlings. Out of the corner of her eye, she caught a glimpse of a set of eight larger, patterned eyes, shimmering from the darkness above, sending chills coursing through her body. Refusing to acknowledge the encroaching danger, she quickly rushed over to Wiki's side.

"I've got you, Wiki," she said as she sliced open the tomb of strands encasing him.

"Thank you!" Wiki said while coughing.

"Save your thanks until we get out of here," she said hurriedly.

A distinct hissing whisper filled the air, sending a shiver down Harper's spine. She looked up just in time to see the colossal brood mother descending rapidly from the hollow trunk. The creature was immense, its glossy black exoskeleton reflecting the dim light that filtered through from above. Its multiple eyes glinted with predatory intelligence, and its legs moved with eerie precision.

As it descended, the brood mother's hiss grew louder, reverberating through the cave. Harper's heart pounded in her chest, but she stood her ground, her blade ready for the impending confrontation. The brood mother landed with a thud, shaking the ground beneath Harper's feet, and loomed over her, blocking the entrance to the cave.

Second guessing her ability to take on such a behemoth, Hap strategized, while visibly frazzled, "We need to get out of here. There's no way we can beat this thing."

"Agreed! Maybe we could create a distraction or something," Winslow proposed.

"Great idea, Wiki! Leave it to me," Harper said reassuringly.

In a confident motion, she relinquished her weapon, throwing it to the other side of the cavern. It bounced off the wall with a reverberating thud and landed on the floor with a sharp "Clink." Immediately, the brood mother scurried toward the noise, her many legs moving swiftly to investigate the disturbance.

Seizing this crucial moment, Harper darted forward, grabbing Wiki's hand with a firm grip. With urgency, she guided him away from the looming danger, weaving through the massive roots and toward the safety of the forest beyond. The sound of the brood mother's movement faded behind them as they ran, each step taking them further from the perilous cavern and closer to freedom. With sounds of the spiderlings' skittering amplifying, they pushed harder to make their escape.

"We're almost there! Just a little bit further," Hap encouraged.

"They sound like they are gaining on us," Wiki said shakily.

Emerging from the forest, Harper jolted awake. Her heart raced as she found herself drenched in sweat, the vividness of the dream lingering in her mind. She took deep, calming breaths, trying to steady herself. The familiar surroundings of her room brought a sense of relief, and she wiped the sweat from her brow, grateful to be safe.

"*Oh, thank goodness. It was just a dream… I never want to experience that again.*" She thought to herself before dozing back off, to a more peaceful rest.

Chapter 28

The next morning, Wiki was awakened by a gentle breeze that caressed his face. He opened his eyes and saw the Wind spirit hovering above him, its translucent form scintillating in the sunlight. It smiled at him and whispered in his ear.

"Good morning sleepyhead! I need you to do something for me. Get Harper and meet me at your spot by the creek. We have important matters to discuss. Don't dilly-dally, this is urgent." The spirit voiced, before wisping through the open window from which it had arrived.

Wiki shot out of bed, feeling a surge of excitement and curiosity. He quickly got dressed, informed his mom of his plans to go play, grabbed his backpack and a banana, then ran to Harper's house. Knowing that he was arriving earlier than normal he hoped the Joneses were awake.

"Harper, it's me, Wiki. Are you up?" he said as he knocked on the door. He heard some movement inside, then Mr. Jones opened the door with steaming coffee in his mug.

"Good morning, Winslow. What's all the excitement for?" Mr. Jones asked while gesturing for Wiki to come inside. As they entered the foyer, Hap's dad called up the stairs, "Harper! Winslow is here to see you," he turned to Wiki waiting for his response.

"Oh, nothing too huge. We just have a big adventure planned to take down the neighboring kingdom," Wiki said as he made his way to the kitchen, taking a seat to wait for Harper.

"That sounds exhilarating," Mr. Jones stated as he prepared his thermos for the half day of work ahead, "Y'all make sure to stay out of trouble."

"You know we will, Dad!" Harper stated gleefully as she hopped down the stairs and smiled when she saw Winslow.

"Wiki, hey. What's going on?" Hap asked, rubbing the sleep from her eyes.

"Come on, we have to hurry. That evil kingdom is encroaching on our villages," he jested, hoping she caught on to his shenanigans.

Harper, taking the hint, grabbed her backpack and kissed her dad on the cheek.

"Make sure you are back by noon, lunch and a movie!" Mr. Jones reminded her.

"I can't wait, see ya later, Dad! I hope you have a good day!" she called back as the friends departed the house. Turning to face Wiki, she asked, "So, why the rush?"

"Wind visited me and asked us to meet at the creek. It said it was urgent," he replied.

As they made their way to mission control, Harper filled Wiki in on the details of her terrifying dream.

Coming into view of their spot, they noticed Earth and Water sitting next to Fire, who was keeping the blazing pit ignited.

"Hey everyone! Where is Wind?" Wiki said inquisitively, waving to the spirits.

As it manifested itself, the winds picked up quickly, blowing the kid's hair around their faces, "I am here!" Wind lowered its voice, in an attempt to achieve a deeper, more ominous tone. The turbulent form puffed out its chest and snapped its fists to its hips, like a superhero pose.

After being startled briefly, Wiki realized what was happening and chuckled, "Why do you look like that?" he asked.

"I was just trying to be serious for the trials," Wind said before transforming in front of the two children, from a surging tempestuous form into its whimsical natured avatar, "I thought it was fitting for Hap to see me the way she did in her dream before revealing my preferred form," Wind responded as its voice returned to its more playful, childlike tone. "Today, we have a special treat for both of you!" Wind said cheerfully.

"Exciting!" Harper said quivering with eagerness.

"Cool! What is it?" Wiki chimed in, equally enthusiastic.

"Today is indeed a day to be excited, you both have done well in your trials and training," Earth spoke up as it shifted its way toward the friends. "First things first, let's set the ambiance," it stated before raising its pebble-strewn arms skyward.

As it did, the ground began to tremble and shift. A massive dome of earth rose around the gathered friends and spirits alike, encircling them in a convex shell. Small pyres began to form, creating a natural path down the middle.

With a sudden spark, the fire spirit animated the pyres. Flames danced to life, casting a warm, flickering glow that illuminated the dome. The path they formed was lined with golden light, guiding the eye toward the center.

Wind fluttered throughout the shell, carrying the invigorating aroma of a mountain meadow. The subtle fragrance of wildflowers mingled with the fresh, clean scent of pine, creating a soothing and refreshing atmosphere.

The water spirit, graceful and fluid, streamed its arms in elegant, swirling motions. The water from the creek responded to the spirit's call, cascading up the inner walls of the dome in hypnotic patterns. The liquid shimmered with a pearlescent shine, refracting the light from the pyres into a sparkling display that filled the dome with a magical aura. As the dome's walls glistened, the water spirit directed its attention to the path between the pyres. With another twirl of its wrist, it conjured a runner of water that flowed deliberately down the aisle. The water moved with a life of its own, sparkling under the light and creating a visual symphony of motion and brilliance.

At the end of this watery path, the earth spirit conjured a throne from the ground. It rose majestically, crafted from the same earthen materials as the dome but imbued with an aura of regality. The throne stood as the centerpiece of the mesmerizing display of elemental magic, each spirit contributing to a harmonious creation that transformed the simple clearing into a sanctuary of wonder, a perfect blend of natural beauty and supernatural artistry.

"Now that's much better, a hall fit for the warriors you are," Earth stated as it stood proudly. "Winslow, we will begin with you," Earth gestured toward the throne.

Wiki, taking the cue, approached the seat. As he sat down, he was filled with a mixture of excitement and nervousness for what was to come. The spirits gathered in front of Wiki, leaving room for Harper to see what was unfolding. With no gestures from the spirits, water began to puddle up on the ground before him. Wisps of fire danced atop the surface causing a ripple, defying nature's usual laws. The wind picked up, swirling around the flames, feeding it with oxygen–causing it to blaze brighter and more fiercely.

Without additional instruction, the elements began to seep into the ground. The water was absorbed first, followed by the fire and wind, which left trails of smoke and steam as they melded with the dirt. Wiki watched in awe, from the very spot where the elements had converged, a sword and shield emerged.

"Winslow," the spirits spoke in unison, "these artifacts are crafted from our combined essence. The sword and shield before you can embody any element and any shape of your choosing."

The sword's blade sparkled with the brilliance of fiery embers, while its hilt was enhanced with intricate patterns reminiscent of flowing water. The shield, sturdy and robust, had veins of molten rock running through it, and a faint breeze seemed to swirl around its edges. Collectively, they exuded a potent aura, a testament to the harmonious combination of the elements that forged them.

"Harmony's Edge," the Earth spirit continued, "can cleave through any obstacle, its blade adaptable to the strength of stone or the agility of wind."

"Harmony's Guard," the Fire spirit added, "can withstand the wildest flames and fiercest tidal waves, its surface shifting to protect you against any threat."

Winslow stood up and stepped forward, reverently reaching out to take the sword and shield. As his hands grasped the hilt of the sword and the handle of the shield, he felt a surge of power and connection to the elements. "This feels like the day I found the Tetrad Vessel and read those words," Wiki said as he took in the sight of his new gear, "Uh, how am I supposed to carry all this around all the time?" he inquired.

"Hold your horses buddy, we are getting to that part," Wind jested as it swirled around in its normal playful manner, "Ya know that feeling you're feeling? That is elemental attunement, silly."

"These artifacts are not just mere weapons, they are a part of you," the Water spirit said, flowing toward Winslow. "Very similar to your training, close your eyes. Rather than paying attention to a particular element to connect with it, this time exhale and pay attention to that energy exiting through your lungs."

Following the instructions, he closed his eyes and took a deep breath before exhaling. On his breath out he felt the pent-up energy begin to subside.

Harper sat in amazement as ethereal strands extended from both instruments in a dazzling display of enchantment, as the fibers absorbed into Wiki's body. He repeated the steps until it was no longer noticeable.

"Now open your eyes, Winslow," the Water spirit guided.

Doing so, he looked at his clenched fists where the weapons were once grasped. Dumbfounded, Wiki asked, "Where did they go?" He looked around as if they had been teleported somewhere nearby.

"Silly Wiki, she just told you they were within you," Wind interjected before bouncing back around the other elemental spirits.

"Wind is correct, your new gifts are within your very being," Water stated.

"So, how do I get them back?" Wiki asked.

"That is easy, choose a hand and raise it, palm facing up," the water spirit instructed.

Winslow, choosing his right hand, presented his palm. With the water spirit's gentle touch, his skin began to tingle and warm. Slowly, symbols started to take shape on his palm, the marks appearing simultaneously. The compass rose-shaped design featured the wind crest to the north, with water to the east, earth to the south, and fire to the west, exactly as he had seen on The Tetrad Vessel.

"Whoa, I got tattoos? That's awesome!" Wiki questioned with enthusiasm.

"They are not tattoos. They are known as 'The Mark of the Blessed,' which only the Spirit Blessed and their companions have the ability to see. Since the symbols are created from our essence, you only need to clench your fist to feel our connection. Go ahead and try it now," Water continued its guidance.

Wiki, curious to see how it all worked, followed the instructions again. Raising his newly marked fist and clenching tightly. As he did, a bright illumination pulsated from inside his curled hand. The same rush of energy, yet mild by comparison, he felt when wielding the artifacts for the first time.

"It's that feeling again!" he exclaimed as the tingling warmth emitted throughout his body.

"Now, bring the artifacts to the center of your attention," Water instructed.

Winslow envisioned the intricate details of each weapon, bringing them to life in his hands. Delicate blue, brown, white, and orange filaments of misty illumination poured forth from his chest, ebbing, flowing, and branching apart until they converged. The tendrils wove together, solidifying into the shape of the sword in his right hand and the shield in his left.

Astonished by the transformation that took place before his very eyes, he exclaimed, "Wow! This is amazing. I can't believe I just did that."

"Finally, imagine them safely stowed away," Water said mellowly.

Continuing to follow instruction, he imagined them safely stored away in a treasure chest on a pirate ship. Smiling at his own thought, the weapons dissipated, the vibrant strands unraveled and flowed back into him. Wiki's smile grew wider as he looked around at everyone in the celebratory dome.

"Woohoo!" Wiki cheered as he pumped his fist into the air.

"You've done well Winslow, there will be much time to revel in your accomplishments. For now, we need to move on to you, Harper. Winslow, please remain where you are and resummon Harmony's Edge," Fire stated as it motioned Hap toward the throne.

Harper anxiously approached and took a seat, smiling proudly at her best friend.

Wiki smiled in return. He clenched his right hand firmly and visualized the sword, almost immediately, it took its glorious shape.

Wind spoke up, breezing over to Wiki's side, "I'll be presiding over this part," rotating its pointer finger in the air, clearly directing him to turn around.

Wiki, understanding the gesture, turned to face the throne where Hap sat.

"Harper, close your eyes. This part requires a bit of trust," Wind said with a wink.

Hap closed her eyes without a moment of hesitation. As she did, her smile expanded into a broad grin.

"Wiki, step forward and place the blade of Harmony's Edge upon each shoulder followed by Hap's head. Then, repeat the following: With the blessing of the elemental spirits, awaken and rise to your potential," Wind directed.

Wiki stepped forward and carefully raised the sword, setting the flat of the blade gently on each of her shoulders, before touching the top of her head. He echoed the mantra, "With the blessing of the elemental spirits, awaken and rise to your potential."

As the final words were spoken, a warm, tingling sensation spread from each of the sword's points of contact, coursing through her body like a river of energy, exuding a comforting heat, like basking in the sun's rays. Opening her eyes, Harper and Winslow made eye contact, this moment will be one they will never forget, and their joy was evident.

Winslow, with a delighted smirk, said, "I've always wanted to knight someone," as he lowered the sword to his side, waiting for the next instruction.

Harper, hopping up from the throne, jested, "Man, I feel good! It's more intense than eating a whole bag of candy," as she drew her fists up to her chest, clenching them tightly as an overwhelming sense of adrenaline washed over her.

"Wiki, you may put away your blade and take a few steps back, your part is done for now," the wind spirit said before the other spirits joined at its side.

Wiki did as he was told and took a stance behind the elemental spirits, excited to see what they had in store for his best friend.

The fire spirit began, "Harper, your courage against your darkest fears was inspirational. I give you my blessing and this token to aid the Blessed," as it finished speaking it extended its flaming hand, a surge of heat and light emanated from its core. As it opened its hand, the Firebrand was revealed. Its handle was cooled and solidified molten lava, providing texture to ensure a firm grip. The whip itself took shape as a living serpent of flame. The body of the whip was a continuous, undulating ribbon of fire, its colors shifting from deep crimson at the base to bright, searing orange and yellow at the tip.

Harper reached out to take the whip, enthralled by its beauty. As she grasped it, she felt a pulse of power flowing from her grip on Firebrand, moving throughout her body.

"Whoa! This is so cool, thank you," she said in a starstruck manner, entranced by the sight before her.

"No need for thanks, young companion. You have earned it. Now, recall the instructions given to Winslow, take a moment to release that energy," the Fire spirit said, giving her that opportunity.

Harper closed her eyes and concentrated on dispelling the energy. With each exhalation, she felt the energy slowly draining away. Opening her eyes, she caught a glimpse of the whip's last orange tendril vanishing into her chest.

Without giving her much time to take in what happened, the Earth spirit interjected, "Your ability to emotionally connect with the world around you is truly awe-inspiring. I give you my blessing and this token to aid the Blessed," The spirit placed its small, sturdy hands over its chest, where a soft, pulsating glow began to emanate. Slowly, it drew its hands apart, revealing a cavity in its chest that shimmered with a deep, earthen light. From within this luminescent core, the earth spirit pulled forth a pair of gauntlets. They were exquisite, each crafted in dark obsidian with intricate veins of gold and silver winding through, like the roots of an ancient tree. The surface was smooth and highly polished with a glass-like sheen.

As Hap slipped her hands into the gauntlets, she felt the warm, tingling sensation amplify again. The gauntlets adjusted, form-fitting perfectly to her hands and forearms, as she flexed her fingers.

"They've molded to my hands like a second skin, and the inside is silky smooth," she said, astonished by the unbelievable display.

"The Earthshapers will serve you well as you aid Winslow. As you did with the whip, please relinquish them for now," Earth guided, and Harper repeated the process.

As they disappeared, Water spoke in a nurturing tone, "Harper, in my trial, I was profoundly moved by your display of perseverance, which showed no limits and truly highlights your drive. I give you my blessing and this token to aid the Blessed," The water spirit placed one fluid hand atop the other.

A soft, murmuring sound filled the air as it slowly drew its hands apart. From the top hand, a miniature waterfall began to flow, cascading down to the bottom. The water streamed with a serene grace, shimmering like liquid crystal in the light. It began to part, revealing a magnificent bow, its structure was fluid yet solid.

The body of the bow was a deep, translucent blue, with delicate patterns that captured the movement of waves. Veins of lighter blue and white ran through it, resembling seafoam and cascading waterfalls. The bowstring, formed from strands of water that had solidified into a flexible yet strong icy material, glistened like morning dew.

"This is Tidecaller," the water spirit's voice echoed softly, "Born from the depths of my heart and the serenity of the rivers, it carries the power to command the tides and summon the strength of the seas. With it, you can channel the fluidity and adaptability of water, as well as its unyielding force."

As Harper grasped Tidecaller, the familiar surge of energy spread through her fingers and up her arm. The bow felt perfectly balanced, as if it were an extension of her own body.

"It's so beautiful," Hap gasped.

"It is very beautiful, just remember although water is nurturing it is also considered the most destructive force," the water spirit added, "As you did with Firebrand and the Earthshapers, tuck the Tidecaller away for now."

Harper did as she was instructed, putting away the bow for the time being.

Mimicking the sound of clearing ones throat, "Ahem. Finally, it's my turn," the wind spirit exasperated, "Of course we saved the best for last," the spirit chuckled before taking a more serious tone. "Hap, during my trial, you proved your purity both internally and externally, showing that outside influences do not compromise your sense of self. I give you my blessing and this token to aid the Blessed."

Pausing for a moment, "Phew, I'm glad the serious stuff is over. Now watch this!" Wind winked.

In an instant, the air in front of Harper began to circulate and condense, taking the form of a miniature cyclone. The tiny windstorm raged on for a brief moment before stopping. The once thrashing, turbulent winds became still, as if frozen in place. Layer by layer, cloudy wisps peeled away and faded, revealing a pair of boots. They were made from supple leather, that had a sleek and aerodynamic design, gleaming with a pearlescent luster. It was decorated with delicate engravings, depicting swirling patterns reminiscent of wind currents. The intricate details seemed to come alive when caught in the light, creating an illusion of movement.

Harper eagerly slipped on the boots, "Wow, they're so light!" she exclaimed, taking a few experimental steps. "I can already feel the wind guiding my movements and I kind of feel… bouncier!"

Wind, immediately picking up on the words Harper chose, "YES! BOUNCEYNESS!" the spirit exclaimed raising both hands to the sky, praising Harper for understanding. "See guys," Wind stated, while nudging the fire spirit, "I told you she would get it," the spirit turned back to Harper, "Okay, as you did with the other gifts, it's time to put these away," the spirit instructed, and Harper listened.

"This next part, has not been done before," the water spirit said, "Choose a hand for your mark."

Harper, building with anticipation, presented her left hand with her palm facing up. The water spirit performed the same ritual, as it complemented her, "You are special. Your connection to Wiki is unbridled. We have never had a companion pass all four trials and awaken alongside their Blessed One. Because of this, you are also receiving, 'The

Mark of the Blessed,'" Water continued, leaving behind the same design, "Now, try to use your mark to call your gifts and then recall them."

Harper, super excited to get the bouncy boots back, recalled the advice given to Wiki on calling his weapons. She began to imagine the moment she had equipped each of the artifacts, she clenched her fist tightly, concentrating her thoughts. As she did, colorful tendrils began to emerge from her; white vines forming the Windwalkers, brown forming the Earthshapers, orange forming the Firebrand in her left hand, and blue forming the Tidecaller in her right. With all items activated, the rush of energy felt immense, coursing through her at each point of contact her skin made with the artifacts and meeting at her core.

"I feel so alive!" checking herself out, "And, I… kind of look like a real-life superhero," Hap giggled, giddy with excitement, before beginning to recall them as instructed, "Okay, where to put them… Where to pu–Aha!" she called out before fibers outstretched from the artifacts and disappeared into her chest. "I know it's not a tattoo because its way cooler, but it makes me feel like I have one now. Wiki, did you feel like this too?" she asked with a hint of a smirk.

"I'm pretty sure that's how I've felt since I read the words in that box," Winslow answered with a huge grin.

Breaking up the conversation, Fire commanded, "Alright, I need your attention!" The spirit paused, giving a brief moment for the sound to hush. "Heed these words; If you forsake your true purpose, such acts will lead to their disappearance, for these gifts are meant to serve the greater good and maintain equilibrium." The spirit gave pause again, letting the children soak in the words before asking, "Do you have any questions?"

"Oh yeah, I have one. Wind, why doesn't everyone call you Air?" Harper spoke up quickly, as if it had been weighing on her mind.

"Oh, I got this," Wind chimed in, "I don't want to be called air, because air is boring and wind..." it said as it twirled up higher into the air, "Well wind is... wind-msical!" the spirit swirled its way back down.

Both children giggled, their laughter filling the air with a lighthearted melody. The sound was infectious, spreading a sense of joy and innocence as they shared a moment of pure happiness.

Earth, finding a break in the chatter, spoke up, "With all of this said, you both need to train now. We do not have time today because we know that you need to get going, Harper. Tomorrow, we start at nine o'clock on the dot, meet back here and do not be late."

"How did you know I had somewhere to go?" Harper asked, genuinely confused.

The water spirit answered, "To ensure your safety until you're ready, we have been keeping an eye on both of you. Be off now, before it gets too late."

As those words were uttered, the beautiful display used for the ceremony returned to its natural state among the forest. Winslow and Harper waved at the elemental spirits as they departed, walking to the forest's boundary and parting ways to their respective houses.

Chapter 29

Later that day, after dinner, Winslow locked himself away in his room so that he could keep practicing what he had gone through with the spirits. Sitting at his desk, he raised his right hand slightly and turned it over to further inspect the marking he had received.

"*I wonder… no… well, maybe… time to fly,*" he said as he thought to himself, before scooting back from the desk to give himself enough space. Clasping his palm and feeling the surge of energy, he pictured a platform of air beneath his chair that gently lifted him off the ground. With a subtle upward gesture, he felt himself begin to lift slowly, the chair rising.

For a moment, he hovered there, feeling the exhilarating sensation of being suspended in the air, giving him a new perspective of the familiar space. Taking a deep breath and slowly lowering his hand, he tried to guide the air platform back down.

As he began to descend, the chair wobbled unsteadily, causing him to lose his focus. In an instant, the chair fell unevenly, sending both it and Winslow sprawling to the floor with a loud crash. The commotion echoed throughout the house, and a moment later, there was a knock on his door.

"Winslow are you okay?" his mom called out, concern evident in her voice.

Quickly scrambling to his feet, setting the chair upright, Wiki called back, "No need to worry, Mom, I'm fine. I just tripped over my chair."

There was a brief pause, then a sigh of relief, "Alright, just be careful," she replied before walking away.

Winslow exhaled, thinking to himself, "*Phew, that was close. Maybe I just try something that won't cause a ruckus.*"

With that in mind, he again glanced down to his new marking and clenched his fist before picturing them in his mind's eye. Instantly taking form in his hands, Harmony's Edge and Harmony's Guard shone gallantly. Holding the shield defensively, he swung the sword in a short swift arc, followed by a long swipe in the opposite direction.

"Wow, these things are practically weightless," he said, impressed by the blade and bulwark.

Pulling the sword back to his waist, he raised the shield and thrusted it forward, careful not to bump or break anything in the room. After a few more minutes of swordplay, he decided to put the instruments away and practice channeling each element for the rest of the evening.

Meanwhile, in the sun-scorched expanse of the Sonoran Desert lies a hidden underground lair, a sanctuary shrouded in secrecy and shadow. The subterranean refuge is carved deep into the bedrock, insulated from the relentless heat and sandstorms above.

Protected by dark concealment magic, the lair's entrance is a narrow, winding staircase, hewn from the stone itself, leading down into the cool, dimly lit depths. The fortress consists of three expansive floors. The top level is the chamber of assembly, the second contains the living quarters, and the third houses the ritual room.

Seraphine wound her way down the staircase with the Blood Crystal tethered to her side by magical forces. Flickering torches mounted on the walls cast eerie, dancing shadows, further adding to the stark atmosphere.

Opening the iron bound door to the living area, she looked around the poorly illuminated corridor for her disciple. The space consisted of a long hallway that stretched out, to her left was the barracks, on her right was the bathroom and kitchen. At the end of the hall, a large communal area with heavy wooden tables and chairs sat. Behind that were shelves lined with scrolls and books containing their forbidden knowledge, acquired over many centuries.

Seraphine beckoned, her voice echoing throughout the enormous cavity, "Alistair!" while she continued to search for his whereabouts. Jumping up quickly, Alistair leaned out from the barracks door, answering her call.

"Yes, High Priestess. I am here," he reported while rushing over to her, fearful of triggering her wrath.

"Make your way downstairs promptly," she commanded, before quickly turning and walking away, "We have matters to discuss." Seraphine continued to the ritual room.

Entering the deepest layer of their sanctuary she was met with the scent of burning incense hanging thick in the air, mingling with a faint, metallic tang that hinted at their darker deeds.

At the center of the chamber was a massive crescent stone altar, cut from a single slab of onyx, the glossy surface mirrored the flickering torchlight, creating an illusion of depth and movement. The altar bore the dark stains of dried blood, glowing runes carved deep into the stone creating a sinister crimson hue. Shallow channels traced the edges, designed to guide the sacrificial blood to a hollowed basin at the heart. Intricate symbols, chiseled deep into the floor, surrounding it in a complex pattern of arcane power.

Bookshelves lined the walls, crammed with ancient tomes and ritualistic artifacts.

Seraphine, arriving at Lilith's side at the altar, asked, "Have the provisions been secured? Alistair is on his way and there is no time to waste. We must get this done in two days' time; failure is not an option."

"Yes, High Priestess. We have the mirror, dagger, nightshade, and grimoire, among the other supplies you specifically requested," Lilith answered quickly.

"Good, now we just need Alistair to fulfill his part," Seraphine said, her distaste for Alistair seeping from her tone.

As if on cue, Alistair entered the ritual room and hastily made his way over to Seraphine and Lilith, who were standing before the crescent shaped centerpiece.

"High Priestess, how may I be of service?" Alistair queried nervously with sweat beading up on his brow.

"I need you to take ten acolytes to the Ashenfall Cemetery to retrieve the personal belongings of each grave. This matter is time-sensitive and must be completed within twenty-four hours. Failure will not be tolerated," Seraphine demanded. Pausing briefly, she scowled more intensely at him and added, "It would be in your best interest to remain unnoticed or risk jeopardizing your own safety," she threatened. Gesturing with a flick of her wrist, "Go now!"

"Yes, Master," Alistair replied, before confidently marching off to get ready for his mission.

Alistair made his way back to the living quarters to assemble his team. Once he had selected his recruits, each chosen delicately for the task at hand, they proceeded to the ritual room. He began the intricate process of summoning a portal. The rift pulsated into existence, and they stepped forward to begin their work.

Chapter 30

To ensure they were not late, Wiki and Hap arrived ten minutes early to their spot. Thick, grey clouds drifted lazily across the sky, muting the bright summer light and casting a gentle shade over the landscape. A chilly breeze blew a welcome respite from the usual heat, providing a refreshing touch to the air.

"Glad my dad told me to grab my jacket this morning," Harper said, walking closer to the creek.

"You're silly, it's not even cold. It feels great," Winslow said as he laughed with his friend.

The spirits emerged, and Wind spoke up, "Howdy! Ready to get started?" The spirit swirled in front of Winslow and Harper.

Slightly startled, Winslow responded eagerly, "You bet I am!"

Harper interjected, "Yeah, me too! This is gonna be so groovy," she couldn't contain her smile.

"Hap! Come with me," Wind called out as it glided its way to the other side of the creek with Harper trailing behind.

"Winslow, I will begin by asking you to summon some training dummies for us to use today. Here is one for reference," Earth said, nodding its head toward the right. Instantly, a four-foot-tall figure made of clay rose from the dirt, holding a stone shield. "Your turn," Earth gestured to Wiki.

Activating his mark, Winslow gestured his right hand upward firmly. He tried to replicate the practice doll, imagining the clay beneath the soil rising. Slowly, the ground began to shift and mold. A crude shape emerged, as he focused harder, it refined itself, gaining more distinct features. The torso formed first, followed by the head and limbs, until a rough but recognizable training dummy stood before him, lacking the shield.

"Try again," Earth stated directly, its voice steady and unwavering.

Determined to get it right, Wiki crafted yet another dummy. To his delight, the stone shield was present.

"I did it!" Winslow said happily, his face lighting up with a triumphant smile.

"Great job little one," Earth said, audibly grinning, "Now, equip only Harmony's Edge."

Thinking about his trusty blade caused it to materialize in his right hand, bringing Wiki a sense of confidence and readiness.

"Good," Fire interrupted, "Now, grip the sword firmly, but not too tight. Let it be an extension of your arm. Remember, control and precision are more important than strength." Motioning to the dummy, the spirit continued, "Start with a basic strike, aim for the torso."

Winslow, raising his sword, slashed horizontally from right to left, slicing through the tip of the shield without touching the dummy's core.

"I said, the torso, try again. Slow down a little bit and work on your precision," Fire directed.

Taking a deep breath, Wiki narrowed his eyes, making the torso his focal point. Thrusting his sword forward, he connected squarely with the exposed part of the dummy's torso, piercing through without resistance.

"Much better," Fire commended, continuing, "This time, I want a fluid strike connecting with the head, followed by the left arm."

Winslow continued his offensive training with Fire, as Wind and Harper were running laps in the clearing.

"I'm so fast! I could run all the bases in no time if I had these during my games," Harper said humorously, letting out a slight chuckle.

"Alright, let's try something else," Wind suggested as it slowed its pace down from Harper's. The spirit hovered gracefully beside Hap, "Imagine the air beneath your feet solidifying into stairs, each step supporting your weight as you ascend."

Harper nodded, taking a deep breath, fixing her gaze on an imaginary path ascending into the sky. She bent her knees slightly and then leaped upward. To her amazement, her foot landed on a solid, invisible platform of air, holding her weight securely. Encouraged by this success, she pushed off from the platform and leaped to the next one, feeling the wind form a new step beneath her. With each jump Hap's confidence grew. Continuing upwards, she created a series of steps that allowed her to ascend deftly.

As Hap neared the base of the treetop, a murder of crows cawed and took flight, startling her. In that instant, the solid air platform beneath her feet vanished. She gasped as she began to fall, the wind rushed past her, causing a surge of panic to take hold.

Before Harper could react, the wind spirit acted swiftly by thickening the air around her. A gentle but firm current of wind enveloped her, slowing her descent and cradling her like an invisible safety net.

Hap's feet touched the ground softly, the wind holding her steady before gently dissipating. She stood there, heart pounding, eyes wide with a mixture of relief and lingering fear. The wind spirit hovered beside her; its eyes filled with concern.

"Are you alright?" Wind asked in a soothing voice.

Harper nodded, taking a deep breath to steady herself. "Yes, I'm fine. Thank you for saving my life!"

"Remember, the wind will always support you. Trust in it, and you will soar as high as your heart desires," Wind encouraged as it levitated upwards in a spiraling motion. As it came back down Wind added, "All you need is a clear image in your mind of what you want, the boots will do the rest."

Wind continued guiding Harper on the Windwalkers as Fire worked with Winslow on channeling the different elements through Harmony's Edge.

"Let's start with fire," Fire instructed, "Imbue the sword using your connection."

Wiki focused, feeling the heat surge through his veins, rushing toward his hand and into the weapon. Brilliant blue flames erupted from the sword's edge, radiating immense heat.

Unfazed, he took a calculated swing, arcing the sword diagonally through the air, imagining the flames extending outward in a broad fan. Massive streams of blue and orange fire poured forth from the blade, engulfing both training dummies in their path, leaving them charred and smoldering. The air crackled with energy, and the acrid scent of burnt material filled his nostrils.

"Fantastic! I knew you were promising," Fire announced, drawing attention to the spectacle.

Earth clapped, chiming in, "Impressive, not many advance this quickly. Now, show me what you can do with the earth. You may also want new targets."

"Yeah, that is a good idea," Winslow agreed, nodding his head.

"Well then, make them," Fire interjected, its voice sharp and commanding.

Gathering the image of the training doll in his mind, the ground listened to his unspoken instructions. To his surprise, the pieces of the old dummies sunk into the earth as two more emerged.

"Did that just happen purely from my imagination?" he thought to himself, noticing a gesture was not needed.

Wiki refocused while adjusting his footing. He thought about the unyielding element enveloping his instrument. Suddenly, the energy within him became dense and powerful, like bedrock. Harmony's Edge darkened in color, emanating a deep, brown glow.

In a fluid motion, he drew the sword across to his left side before slashing across in a backstroke motion. Stone, arrow-like projectiles burst forth from the blade's path, as if the very earth itself had been weaponized and launched toward the target with unrelenting intent.

"*Whoosh! Thud! Thonk!*" rang out.

"Good job," Earth commended, before giving some wisdom, "Just remember, if you can imagine it, you can do it!" he exclaimed.

Before Wiki had time to respond, Wind hollered encouragingly from across the creek, "My turn! I want to see what you can do with wind, Wiki!" Turning its attention back to Hap quickly, the wind spirit said, "Hold on, I gotta see this."

"You heard Wind," Fire urged, its tone firm.

Wiki reset the dummies and readied his stance, adjusting to a two-handed grip. The feeling within him lightened, becoming as intangible as a breeze. Harmony's Edge was now encased in a mantle of restless wind, with spirals of condensed air curling around the blade, forming translucent ribbons.

He hoisted it into the air above his head. Slashing downward, the blade cut through the air, generating a miniature cyclone that sliced through the training dummies, destroying them and throwing debris in its wake.

"Whoa, you really showed those dummies," Wind said jokingly, a hint of humor in its voice, as it enjoyed its wordplay before turning its attention back to Harper.

Water's voice rippled through the air, "Impressive, Winslow. Now let us see how your talents fare with water. Show me what you can do."

"I'll give it a shot," Wiki stated, sweat beading on his forehead.

Winslow reset the dummies once more. Then, he lowered the sword by his side as he envisioned the fluid, adaptive nature of water. The energy within him shifted, cooling and flowing like a stream. Immediately, the sword projected that feeling, cloaking it in a swirling veil of liquid. Jabbing the sword forward in a sharp motion, he lunged, sending a condensed high-speed torrent of water crashing into the targets, crumbling them.

"Maybe we should give him a real challenge," Fire stated while gesturing to Earth to capture its attention.

"What do you have in mind, Sparky?" Earth said with an auditory smirk.

"You know I don't like that nickname," Fire retorted, before making a suggestion, "Perhaps a moving target."

"Ah, good idea," Earth agreed, before clicking together pebbles, in a snapping motion.

Just then, the two war-torn dummies dissolved into the dirt, as two more emerged. This time, they were twice as large and boasted club-like dirt weapons in their right hands, along with stone shields in their left.

"That's perfect," Fire said, "Now, do the thing."

With another snap from Earth, the lifeless dummies moved into a defensive stance.

"Wow, cool!" Wiki exclaimed.

"You won't say that in a moment," Fire laughed, knowing what was to come.

"Winslow, you may want to consider calling your guard and standing at the ready," Earth suggested.

Shifting its mentorship, Fire directed, "Harper, I think it's time for you to change focus. Come over here."

Harper, hearing her name, perked up and obliged. Using the boots she was now faintly familiar with, she leapt over in two strides.

"Hey, Pebbles! Can I get another one of those stationary toys over here?" Fire requested.

"Fine, but don't call me that," Earth grumbled, gesturing once more to comply.

"You started it," Fire replied with a chuckle before turning its attention to Harper, "Bring forth Firebrand so that we can get started."

Harper imagined the intricate details of Firebrand's hilt, causing it to take form in her left hand.

"The first thing you need to understand is that the whip is an extension of your arm. You need to be both confident and relaxed to control it effectively," Fire guided.

Harper took a deep breath to calm her nerves. In response to her ease, the whip uncoiled and fell to the ground with a soft, sizzling thud.

"Oo, that's hot!" Harper exclaimed, seeing the sear on the ground where the molten tip touched the earth.

"Grab the lash of the whip," Fire directed while gesturing toward the flaming tail.

Hesitating for a moment, Harper reluctantly reached out and clasped the molten lash. Shocked, she responded, "It didn't burn me!"

"Precisely, your new gifts will not hurt you. The more you trust in them, the more they will respond to your will," Fire coached, "Now, strike the target in front of you."

Hap gripped the hilt firmly, feeling the weight of Firebrand in her hand. She drew her arm back slowly, the length of the whip trailing behind her in a smooth arc. Locking her eyes onto the target, she swung her arm forward channeling all her strength into the motion, causing the tail to whip out with a speed she couldn't control.

Instead of the sharp crack she envisioned, the lash wrapped around the target in a haphazard twist. She let out an exasperated sigh, her shoulders slumping in disheartenment.

"That was a good try. Seeing as you're wrapped up, it's probably important to learn to retract Firebrand," Fire encouraged, "You don't need to use force, imagine the flame loosening its grip, and coming back to you using a gentle recalling motion with your wrist."

Complying, Harper moved her wrist in a smooth beckoning gesture. Obeying her mental command, the living flame lash responded, slithering off the dummy and returning to her hand in a controlled, fluid motion.

"It's all about your connection with the whip. It follows your intent. Let's give it another shot. You're getting there," Fire motivated.

Narrowing her eyes to focus her intention, she repeated the motion, heeding the advice of her instructor. Drawing her arm back, she fluidly brought it forward. As the flame tendril lashed out, she anticipated it making contact with the dummy. In that instant, she flicked her wrist, causing a wave of energy to build up and flow through the whip. It released with a loud, "Crack," sending sparks and embers shooting forth from the tip of the fiery tentacle.

"Well done," Fire praised, adding, "Now, when you crack the whip, you're not just throwing it out. You need to use your whole arm, starting from your shoulder, down through your elbow, and finally your wrist. It's a flowing motion, like casting a fishing line."

"My dad takes me fishing all the time. I got this," Harper replied with a newfound confidence.

Hap adjusted her stance and reconfigured her grip on the handle before trying again. With a deep breath, she raised the whip. On her exhalation, she cast it, timing the crack perfectly as she flicked it once more. This time the whip struck the doll in the chest. From the point of impact, flames exploded forth with such force that it decimated the target. All that remained were smoldering clumps of dirt and stone.

"Fantastic! I knew you would be a quick study," Fire congratulated with pride in its voice.

"Yes, very good, Harper," Water interjected. Looking toward Earth and Winslow, it called out, "Earth!" The spirit paused until it had the attention of the stone golem. "May we please have two training dolls?"

Nodding, Earth complied with the request, snapping its pebbles. Once the dummies appeared, Earth returned its attention to Winslow.

"Harper, tuck away Firebrand and bring out Tidecaller," Wind instructed with a soothing tone.

Pausing for a moment, Hap began to imagine the Firebrand being stowed as Tidecaller was called to her opposite hand. Orange and blue tendrils streamed in and out of her core simultaneously. The weapons took form and dissipated in synchrony. Pleased with the ease of the transition, Harper looked up to the water spirit, smiling, waiting for the next instruction.

"Very nice. It appears that your practice at home is paying off," Water praised. Not giving Harper time to respond, the spirit continued, "Let's start with a proper stance, your feet should be shoulder-width apart, body facing perpendicular to the target." Listening, Harper adjusted her footing. "Good. Now, relax," Water urged motherly, its words seeming to caress Hap in a gentle embrace.

Soothed by Water's voice, Harper visibly relaxed and assumed a comfortable, yet sturdy position. "Um, this may be a silly question, but where are my arrows?" Hap inquired.

"You must learn how to conjure your arrows," Water answered, "Raise the bow and embrace the energy flowing from you into Tidecaller, let it become a part of you." The spirit mentored on, "Now, draw the string." Harper followed along.

"Wow! That was easy," Hap exclaimed, releasing and applying more tension to the drawstring, familiarizing herself with it.

"Understand this is not about physical strength, it is about channeling your will," Water guided soothingly, "Next, clear your mind and picture the projectile you desire."

Forming the image in her mind, the arrow began to manifest from where her left pointer finger and thumb held the string, extending past the arrow rest. A slender, crystal-clear stem glistened with fluid ripples. The watery arrowhead was sharp, refracting light into a spectrum of colors. The fletching consisted of elongated water droplets, perfectly symmetrical and quivering with potential energy.

"You did very well, the details are beautiful," Water awed, truly impressed. "Finally, pour your will into the arrow, control its path with your intent. Fully envision the arrow striking the target," the spirit instructed.

As Harper released the arrow, the string hummed with power. The water projectile moved with an effortless grace, leaving a trail of sparkling particles that traced its journey. It flew straight, striking the dummy in the left shoulder with a splash, piercing through the doll before fully dissolving.

"Nice aim, again please," Water requested.

Harper raised Tidecaller and drew the string, focusing her intent she formed and released her arrow. As it rapidly approached its target, a wall of water shot forth from the ground. Absorbing the arrow's momentum and throwing it away gently.

"You must keep in mind your enemy's defenses. Get more creative," Water suggested. "Picture the path you want the arrow to take; imagine it bending around obstacles, finding its way to the target. Feel the connection between your thoughts and the water arrow, infuse it with your intention."

Harper imagined the arrow arcing around the training dummy and striking it from the back. Releasing the string, the hum whispered in her ears as the arrow soared, curving exactly as she planned and striking the target from behind, with a satisfying splash.

"Woohoo! That was awesome," Harper cheered, "Wiki! I'm an archer!"

"I can't wait to see your new skills," Winslow hollered back unable to give his full attention, focused instead on the puppets before him.

"Keep those feet grounded, Winslow. Watch your opponent's movements," Earth instructed as Wiki battled on. One of the dummies swung its club in a wide arc, Earth continued, "Anticipate the attack. Feel the shield's energy and guide it, put your faith in its ability to protect you."

Winslow lifted Harmony's guard just in time. As the club struck, the shield flared to life; earth solidifying to absorb the impact, water rippling to disperse the force, fire searing the club to deflect, and wind swirling to redirect the blow.

The spirit nodded approvingly, "Good. Now, counterattack. Use the elements within the shield to push them off balance."

Taking a moment to clear his mind and refocus his intentions, he took a few deep breaths. He focused on spewing a gust of wind forward to repel the attacker, but before he could finish his train of thought the other dummy attacked from his left.

Almost instinctively, he adjusted his footing and swung the shield, warding off the incoming blow. The force of the impact was stronger than Wiki expected, knocking him off balance. Hyperfixated on recovering, his now-distracted mind muddled his mental imagery, preventing him from clearly conveying his intent to Harmony's Guard.

Realizing the barrier to his success, he distanced himself from the two opponents by leaping backward, planting his feet firmly. Without the added pressure of an onslaught, he stilled his focus, raising his shield and thrusting forward, releasing a fierce, howling blast of air. The offensive wind strike soared toward the puppets with such force that it pushed them backward, shearing off fragments of their frames.

"Okay, I just have to work on doing that while also being attacked with clubs," Winslow said, chuckling nervously.

"It will come with time, trust, and self-assurance," Earth reinforced, before adding, "Keeping that positive mindset will be of great benefit to you, in your learning journey and beyond." Turning its attention toward the water spirit, asking, "Do you think that you could be of more help in teaching Winslow to trust in his own abilities?" Water nodded as it made its way over.

Earth rolled over to where Harper was actively practicing with Tidecaller. "The time has come to *shape* your destiny," the earth spirit winked jestingly, before requesting, "Please put away the bow for now and summon the Earthshapers."

Hap obliged, relinquishing Tidecaller and equipping the gauntlets. The shiny gloves took form, as she clasped her hands and wiggled her fingers, responding to the feel of the exoskeletons.

"Good. Now, what is your favorite melee weapon?" Earth inquired.

Harper, thinking for a moment, responded, "I've always fancied the look of pirate swords."

"Recall one very specific one, and vividly picture it in your mind, seeing every intricate detail from the hilt to the tip of the blade," Earth guided.

"Got it!" Harper announced as a cutlass materialized in her grip, forming from the gauntlet.

The handle was a masterpiece of craftsmanship, embedded with rich sapphires and vibrant emeralds. Its blade was razor sharp and flawlessly honed, its edge was decorated with intricate floral etchings. She marveled for a moment at the mesmerizing weapon.

"Yeah, this is definitely fit for a pirate king!" she declared, hoisting the sword skyward.

"You have quite the imagination, it's very detailed," Earth commended, taking in the artistry.

"Thank you," she blushingly replied with a curtsy. Raising her sword-bearing left hand, she swiped, slashed, and thrust, amping herself up. "This is so light and easy to move. Can I hit the dummy now?"

"Go ahead, take a stab at it," Earth said lightheartedly.

Harper, ecstatic to use the sword, yelled out, "Take this ye scallywags!"

She advanced, cleaving the cutlass, cleanly slicing through the clay-stone doll. She withdrew the blade, leaving a pristine, seamless cut.

"Very good, I knew you would shine here," Earth applauded Hap, "Though, you should loosen your grip slightly. Too tight, and you'll tire quickly; too loose, and you'll lose control. As with your other gifts, they are merely an extension of you and your will."

Harper listened intently, nodding as she soaked in the information.

Earth continued, "Now that you feel comfortable summoning with your main hand, use your off hand to bring forth a shield."

Imagining the infinite possibilities, Harper singled in on a particular visualization. Golden strands materialized from the gauntlet encasing her right hand, flowing outward and weaving together in a rapid, almost organic process. The strands intertwined, solidifying into a small but formidable buckler that radiated both beauty and power.

At the heart of the buckler was a raised boss, showcasing an intricate emblem of a lion's head. The lion, sculpted from the same golden strands, bared its teeth in a display of ferocity. Its eyes, set with gleaming rubies, glowed with a fierce red light, adding a touch of menace to its regal visage.

"Somehow, that is even more impressive than the sword," Earth chimed in, admiring the craftsmanship. "Now that you have been introduced to each of your gifts, it is time to put them to use," the spirit said before snapping, summoning two animated dummies for Harper.

"Winslow, you look exhausted. Why don't you take a break and watch Harper?" Earth wisely suggested.

"A break sounds nice, I could use one of those right about now," Wiki concurred, visibly tired. Putting away his artifacts, he and the water spirit migrated over to the sidelines of the theatrical display.

"Sweet, I'm ready for this!" Hap exclaimed as she took a fighting stance, sword at the ready with her shield up to guard.

Without any warning, the clay animations lurched forward with surprising speed. With a swift motion, she sidestepped the first one's swing, her cutlass slicing through the air with rapid, precise side-to-side movements, dicing it into pieces. Without missing a beat, she raised her buckler to deflect a strike from the second. Pivoting on her heel, she brought her sword around in a sharp arc, cleaving through the second dummy, leaving it in two.

"Well, that looked a bit too easy," Earth stated, adding, "Don't limit yourself, use the gifts together," it snapped its fingers, bringing four more, larger, dolls to life.

The animated puppets came up fast, catching Harper off guard. At the last second, she caught movement in her peripheral vision, quickly blocking and riposting.

Raising her right foot, she kicked off of an invisible wall, summoned from her imagination. Somersaulting backward, she exchanged weapons; the cutlass and buckler dematerializing back into the Earthshapers as Tidecaller came forth.

Landing gracefully, she took aim and released four arrows of liquidy ice, each freezing their target and locking them in place. Immediately, she raised her left hand, summoning Firebrand, before lashing the whip, creating a fiery explosion. The fireball struck with such force that it shattered the ice before it could melt, destroying the puppets, leaving only puddles of water and remnants of charred clay-stone-like debris.

Everyone burst into cheers at the immaculate display. Harper, sweating profusely, bent over with her hands on her knees, trying to catch her breath.

"I can't believe that worked!" Hap panted.

"Wow, that was amazing, Hap!" Winslow cheered enthusiastically, his eyes wide with admiration.

"Woo! That was spectacular, Harper," Wind exclaimed, as Fire and Water's applause echoed through the space, a harmonious blend of crackling flames and gentle splashes.

"Very impressive," Fire added, its voice carrying a warm approving tone.

"Yes, indeed," Water stated, its tone calm and affirming.

"Truly inspiring, young one," The Earth spirit said before pausing for a second. "Excuse me, but I do need to leave. Our friends have news," Earth informed everyone, continuing before melting into the ground and departing, "I will see you back here tomorrow, Winslow and Harper."

"Well, that's our cue," Wind chimed in, "I think you both have worked hard enough today and deserve a hearty meal."

"We didn't mean to keep you past lunch, but I expect you both here at the same time tomorrow morning," Fire stated bluntly. The elemental spirits gestured goodbye before departing as well.

Harper and Winslow sat by the creek, to give Hap a chance to catch her breath. They leaned back on their hands, their legs stretched out in front of them, enjoying the cool, damp earth beneath their fingers.

"Hey, I meant to ask you this, but where do you store your weapons?" Wiki inquired.

"Do you even have to ask?" Harper answered before suggesting, "Okay at the count of three, we will both say it. Ready, one…two…three,"

In unison, they both called out, "Treasure chest!" As each other's answers registered, they laughed uncontrollably.

"I knew it!" Wiki shouted.

"I told you, you didn't even have to ask," Harper jested, as her stomach gurglingly let out a ferocious growl.

"That sounds like our cue to head back and eat," Winslow chuckled, as the two friends gathered their belongings and started their walk back to Wiki's house.

Chapter 31

Wiki, Hap, and Willow gathered in the cozy living room of the Kinneys' home. The walls were enhanced with vibrant floral-printed wallpaper, and a shaggy carpet sprawled across the floor. Winslow's late father's beloved record player sat on a wooden side table, a testament to their family's deep love for music. The room resonated with the sounds of timeless classics, as their extensive record collection showcased legendary albums from Pink Floyd to Stevie Wonder and many more.

Laughter echoed through the air as Willow's enthusiastic dance attempt ended in a comical tumble to the ground, eliciting joyous amusement from the friends. Hap lowered the volume of the music as she grabbed Monopoly®.

"Who is up for a game?" Harper questioned.

"Me! Me! Me!" Willow exclaimed as she raised her right hand.

"Yeah, that sounds fun! I can set up the board," Winslow offered as Harper brought the board game over to the coffee table.

Taking their places around the table, Willow quickly grabbed the top hat figurine as Wiki proposed the first question while setting up the board, "Okay, who wants to be the banker this round?"

Willow, her lip pouting slightly, pleaded, "Can I do it? I never get to be the banker."

With a nod and a smile, Wiki agreed, "Alright, Willow, you can be the banker. I'll take the thimble." Turning his attention to his friend, he asked, "And Hap, what piece do you want?"

Harper contemplated her choice before replying, "I prefer the top hat, but I will take the doggie this time and let Willow have it."

"Thank you, Hap!" Willow said excitedly.

As the game commenced, the trio immersed themselves in the captivating world of Monopoly®.

"Willow, you can go first since you're the youngest," Winslow suggested.

Willow grabbed the dice and began her turn, followed by Hap, then Wiki. They continued their turns, moving their pieces and buying properties as they landed on them. A few turns later, Harper rolled a four that landed her on Park Place.

Hap couldn't contain her enthusiasm, exclaiming, "Yes! I want to buy it!"

Wiki, wearing a quizzical expression, interjected, "Hold on there, Hap. You know it'll cost you most of your money, right?"

Harper shrugged her shoulders, "Did you not see that I am about to pass 'GO'." She handed Willow the money, who in turn gave her the property card. She smirked mischievously, remarking, "What I know, is that you both will owe me a fortune when you land on it once I have houses!"

"If you get houses," Willow quipped, as she organized her money in front of her.

Laughter and excitement filled the room as Wiki, Hap, and Willow continued their intense Monopoly® game. Their faces radiated joy as they eagerly maneuvered their game pieces, engaged in banter, and playful taunts.

Wiki grinned, warning, "Watch out! I'm coming for Boardwalk!"

He glanced at the dice in his hand, heart pounding with anticipation. A roll of three was all he needed to wrest it from Hap's grasp. As the dice left his hand, time seemed to slow. They tumbled across the board, Winslow's eyes fixed on them with a mix of hope and anxiety. Unfortunately, instead of the desired three, the dice finally settled on snake eyes, a pair of ones. Winslow's heart sank as he realized his fate. He was now faced with the unwelcome reality of paying $75 for landing on Luxury Tax.

"Nooooo!" Winslow called out in defeat before handing the money over to the banker.

Their playful banter elicited laughter, infusing the room with a lighthearted spirit. Luck was not on Wiki's side this game after an additional series of disastrous rolls, putting him in dire financial straits. Each progressing turn seemed to bring new misfortune as he landed on costly properties, chance cards demanding hefty payments, and his own mortgaged assets providing no respite. With most of his properties now under mortgage and his cash reserves dwindling, the final blow came when he rolled and landed on B&O Railroad.

Willow couldn't contain her delight as she revealed, "That, big brother, is my railroad you landed on." Her smile concealed a devilish grin, as she relished the opportunity to bankrupt her brother.

Concerned, Hap asked, "Do you have enough cash, Wiki?"

Winslow shook his head, his expression filled with resignation. "No, I only have $10, and my properties are all mortgaged. Looks like I'm out of this one, now it's just you two."

Curiosity piqued, Hap inquired, "How did you manage to collect all four railroads so quickly, Willow?"

Blowing a bubble with her gum, Willow replied confidently, "Because I'm the best, duh! Hap, you're next, prepare for bankruptcy!"

Walking into the living room to tidy up before bed, Mrs. Kinney declared, "Y'all need to wrap that up. It's getting late and Mr. Jones will be here any minute to pick up Harper." As she was putting records back, she added, "Also, there is a festival in town, and I was thinking we could all go."

"Yes! I want to get my face painted like a butterfly," Willow chimed in.

"I want to ride the Ferris Wheel," Winslow added.

"All I want is funnel cakes and a turkey leg," Harper said, dreaming of all the yummy snacks festivals bring.

"I'm sure we will be able to do all those things and maybe a bit more!" Mrs. Kinney replied. "Now clean up that game," she insisted.

"Okay, since Wiki is already out, let's count what we have to see who won," Harper suggested.

The decisive moment arrived. Both girls counted their money, their faces a mix of hope and nerves.

Hap, as she calculated her wealth, exclaimed, "Wow, I am so rich! This could finally be my chance!"

Willow, checking her properties, whispered, "It all comes down to this final count."

Wiki, ever the gracious competitor, joined in anticipation, eagerly awaiting the outcome. "Let's see who reigns supreme. The moment of truth has arrived!"

A momentary silence enveloped the room as Harper and Willow tallied up their totals before the winner was revealed.

Breaking the silence, Harper said, "I've totaled my properties and cash, I've got $4,000. What about you, Willow?"

Winslow stepped up to help his sister determine her total value. "Let's see, you have $1,200 in cash, $2,800 in properties, and $600 in your houses and hotels. That gives you a total of $4,600," he stated, breaking down his analysis. "You won, Willow!" Wiki announced.

Willow leaped up, pumping her fist in victory. "Yes! I did it! I've won!"

Hap clapped enthusiastically, her applause brimming with genuine admiration as she high-fived Willow.

"Congratulations! You played an incredible game and I almost had you beat. Well-deserved victory!" Harper, displaying her sportsmanship, acknowledged Willow's triumph. "Well done! You outfoxed us all. You're the Monopoly® master!"

The room buzzed with the thrill of the game's climactic conclusion, a crescendo of emotions reaching their peak. Flush with exhilaration, the friends gathered around the table after cleaning up the board game and grabbing refreshments. They clinked their glasses of apple juice together in celebration, toasting to the memorable game while waiting for Hap's dad to arrive.

Chapter 32

Under the pale, silvery light of a waning moon, the Ashenfall Cemetery lay shrouded in an eerie silence. Ancient oak trees stood sentinel, their gnarled branches casting twisted shadows on the ground. A thick mist curled around the tombstones, weaving through the graveyard like a ghostly serpent.

The Fang had been working since the night before, marking graves and casting protective spells. By the first light of dawn, they paused to lie in wait, ensuring their presence went unnoticed by the townspeople. As the second night unfolded, they returned to complete their grim task. Alistair, with ten acolytes in tow, proceeded to the nearest grave.

"Pay close attention, we need to get this right and we need to get this done, tonight!" Alistair commanded.

With practiced ease, Alistair began to chant in a guttural, ancient language that seemed to thrum with dark energy. The words "Da mihi rem pretiosam" reverberated through the night. His eyes, glinting with a sinister red hue, glowed brighter as he focused his power. Slowly, a golden bracelet from the deceased, lifted gently into the air from the grave, obeying his words.

"Go fetch me the rest," Alistair demanded, raising a hand and shooing his disciples, signaling them to begin their work.

Cloaked in shadows, they moved with purpose and precision. Each member carried a ceremonial dagger to enhance their abilities, the blades were etched with arcane symbols that caused them to pulse with ominous crimson light. The members approached the marked graves with reverence, not out of respect for the dead, but because they needed to carefully retrieve the fragile personal items buried within. These cherished relics, imbued with sentimental significance, were crucial for their dark ritual and had to be handled with the utmost delicacy to preserve their potency.

The acolytes' eyes glowed brighter as they focused their power, and slowly, the personal effects of the deceased began to rise from the soil. Rings, lockets, and other cherished possessions were meticulously handled and carefully placed in leather pouches, which they carried with them. The personal effects, imbued with the memories and essence of the deceased, were vital components in their nefarious plan. The graves remained undisturbed, the earth settling back into place as if nothing had been taken.

As they worked, a rustling sound broke the silence. The Fang members froze, their eyes darting toward the source. Emerging from the shadows was the graveyard keeper, a stout man with a lantern in hand. His eyes widened as he took in the scene before him, the glow of his lantern revealing the cloaked figures.

"Who are you? What are you doing here?" he demanded, his voice trembling with a mix of fear and anger.

Alistair stepped forward, his eyes locking onto the keeper's. With a swift motion, he raised his left hand to his temple and murmured an incantation. The keeper's eyes glazed over as if an invisible force had gripped his mind. He tried to resist, but the dark magic was too powerful.

"Somnus," Alistair commanded, and the keeper collapsed to the ground, unconscious but unharmed.

The disciples resumed their work, Alistair keeping a watchful eye on the inert form of the keeper. When the last item had been claimed, Alistair approached the keeper and knelt beside him. He placed a hand slightly above the keeper's forehead before speaking.

"Oblitus," he whispered, his voice barely audible.

The magic seeped into the keeper's mind, erasing all memory of the night's events. Satisfied, Alistair stood and motioned for the other members to follow.

With their task accomplished, they melted into the shadows, leaving the cemetery as it was found, a place of undisturbed rest; or so it seemed.

Upon their departure, the Plantarii contacted the earth spirit to relay their findings, as requested during their brief meeting earlier that day.

The Plantarii reported to Earth once the spirit arrived, "While protective spells prevented us from seeing their direct actions, our patience always prevails. Once they left and their protections weakened, we recognized that personal belongings of each grave were taken. Having seen similar behavior in the past, we knew that this information would be of vital importance."

"Indeed, this is concerning. With this information we will prepare accordingly. Thank you for your observational prowess, old friends," Earth stated, showing its gratitude. Continuing, "I shall notify the others, so I must be off." Earth snapped its pebbly fingers, tearing a slit into the fabric of reality, before stepping through and vanishing.

Chapter 33

"Imagine a figure in your mind, a personification of life," the water spirit guided, its voice a soothing murmur. Tiny droplets of water floated around the spirit, catching the light and casting rainbows in the air.

Water paused, allowing Wiki a moment to delve into his imagination. "Now, give it specific characteristics. Is it a courageous warrior, standing tall and resolute with armor gleaming under the sun? Or perhaps a nurturing protector, gentle and compassionate, its aura radiating warmth and safety?"

A vivid image of a warrior-like character began to take shape in Winslow's mind, conjured from his Saturday morning cartoon routine with Willow.

The water spirit's presence was like a guiding hand, gently nudging his thoughts into clarity, its tone imbued with ancient wisdom. "Once you have the picture, the next step is to impress that into the object. To do so, imagine yourself as the object, embodying its texture, its weight, its essence. Allow your persona to flow into it, like water seeping into every crevice of a stone."

Wiki's focus intensified, feeling the transformation as his consciousness melded with the figure.

"Feel the bond between your persona and the object solidify, like roots anchoring a tree to the earth," the spirit's voice grew softer, yet more compelling. "Until they are no longer separate."

Water paused again, giving Winslow the chance to concentrate. The clay golem before him started to stir, quivering slightly. Slowly, the vibrations intensified, the clay figure's arm, clutching a club, twitched experimentally. The once rigid surface rippled as the arm flexed and the fingers around the hilt tightened, testing its grip. The shield-bearing arm followed suit, rising slightly, then it settled into a more defensive stance. The figure's head tilted, seemingly scanning the surroundings with newfound awareness.

"Well done, Winslow," Water stated, "Now, simply command it with your mind and since it is of your creation, it will obey."

Wiki, thinking about needing a sparring partner, readied Harmony's Edge and Guard. The training puppet followed suit raising its shield and advancing, taking the order.

"That was awesome!" Wiki exclaimed as he lowered his weapons, dropping his guard and shifting his focus.

Simultaneously, the sparring partner stopped advancing as if it was waiting to resume training.

Winslow asked, "What's next?"

"I get to show you something funky," Wind interjected. "Go ahead and put away your Guard for now so that we can simplify the next lesson by focusing on Edge, but it is applicable to both." The spirit hovered in front of Winslow as he waited. "Your weapons can take on any shape you require. I'm sure you are noticing the pattern in how these things work, it's all your imagination. You see the sword but let that image go, see it as a mighty hammer of justice that can smash stuff!" the wind spirit said with enthusiasm as it mimicked a smashing gesture with its wispy hands.

Grasping Wind's excitement for smashing stuff, Wiki began to imagine the hammer. As he did, Harmony's Edge transformed. Hazy, white tendrils surrounded the sword's blade and dissipated, leaving a two-foot-long war hammer in his right grip.

The hammer's massive, double-sided head was forged from polished steel. Each side featured a flat, broad striking surface designed to deliver devastating blows. Its handle was made of a rich dark oak with a smooth finish, wrapped with bands of supple black leather, providing additional grip. At the base, a finely polished pommel cap of solid steel served as a testament to the beauty of simplicity.

"Oo! That's pretty but make it bigger…" Wind said as it stretched its cloudy limbs out wide.

Following the friendly demand, Winslow gripped Edge with both hands, enlarging the image in his mind two-fold, as the weapon grew in response.

Perplexed by the realization that the transformation had no impact, Wiki asked, "How can it weigh the same?"

Wind answered in a less-playful tone, "Harmony's Edge and Guard may have appeared as a sword and shield, but they are much more than that. They are crafted from the perfect harmony of the elements. This is why they have virtually no weight, regardless of the size. They can alter their forms at will and are able to emerge, as well as infuse with, the elements."

While gesturing toward Winslow and Harper, Earth interjected, "I believe this would be a good time for some sparring between you two."

Hap, warming up with the Windwalkers, ran over to Wiki's side. "Let's do it! I am ready for some action," she said eagerly.

In response, Winslow jumped backward, distancing himself and taking a defensive stance with a two-handed grip on the massive hammer. Harper, wasting no time, raised her left arm as Firebrand formed in her hand. She flicked her wrist and sent the flaming tail lashing out toward Wiki in a blazing intensity. He leapt back further, avoiding the searing coil of the whip. As Firebrand's lash cracked, it sent tiny embers and sparks sputtering outward, falling short of him.

"Harper don't hold back. Winslow will be fine," Fire yelled out over the commotion of the battle.

Heeding Fire's words, Hap cast the lash forward again, flicking her wrist at the opportune moment. Winslow jumped back once more, thinking that the distance would keep him safe. Torrential waves of flames shot forth from the end of the lash, heading straight for Wiki. With no shield in hand, he extended the hammer outward defensively as the flames engulfed him. Harper's eyes widened at the sight of her best friend wrapped in fire. Before she could rush over, the flames subsided, leaving Winslow confused.

Checking himself for burns, Wiki exclaimed, "I thought I was a goner."

"You are Blessed. The elements, free from corruption, are here to help you, not injure you," Water confirmed. "Harper, it is a bit different for you. The artifacts you wield pose no danger to yourself. Additionally, since Winslow has no desire to do you harm, his attacks will not inflict any damage."

Harper readied her stance to continue as her stomach let out a deep growl.

"Dang, I heard that from here," Winslow called out.

"Keep sparring, lunch is soon," Fire stated bluntly, gesturing to the children to continue.

Both friends stood ready. Harper, leveraging the Windwalkers, shot to the left with a burst of wind. Winslow, deciding to change his equipment, transformed Edge into a spear and brought forth his Guard while tracking her movement. Hap nocked an arrow in Tidecaller and released it toward Wiki.

In response, he raised his shield just in time to absorb the impact of the watery arrow. Riposting without delay, Winslow imbued Edge with earth, sending rocky spikes toward her. Quickly thinking, Hap jumped onto a platform of air to dodge the incoming projectiles.

After successfully dodging, she proceeded to make a series of platforms as she stepped up into the air. She flicked and snapped Firebrand directly under her footing, as the whip cracked, the flames roared from the lash. She backflipped off the platform, using Windwalkers to create a downward gale that spiraled the flames to the ground, creating a flaming cylindrical cyclone barreling toward Winslow.

Wiki slammed Guard on the ground, as it made contact with the earth, water surged up from the soil. The liquid rose in a swift, spiraling motion, weaving into a seamless, protective bubble around him. As the fiery tubular whirlwind slammed into the protective barrier it caused the flames to sizzle, fizzle, and steam. The surface rippled with the force of the impact but held strong. After the flames subsided, Winslow wasted no time. With a swift motion, he commanded the watery bubble to launch a battalion of gleaming, liquid arrows.

Harper used the Earthshapers to form bucklers in each hand. Gauging the timing, she used them to block the onslaught of incoming projectiles. Having dealt with the threat coming directly at her, she noticed in her peripheral that two more missiles were coming from her left and right sides.

Acting swiftly, she deflected them, causing water to splash her in the face. Shaking it off and finding an opening, Harper transformed the shield in her left hand into a spear and hurled it toward the center of the water bubble. Winslow quickly raised his shield to block the spear, causing the watery protective barrier to rain down around him. Harper quickly closed the distance, bringing out her cutlass in her left hand.

The friends shared a smirk before their swords and shields clashed, standing face to face in their fighting stances.

"Okay, okay. Let's wrap this up. That is enough sparring for now," Wind said, weaving its way in between Wiki and Hap. "It's lunch time," the spirit suggested as it guided the kids to their lunch pails by the creek.

"Eat quickly children, we have more to cover before our time is done today," Water urged.

Putting away their weapons, Winslow and Harper scarfed down their food within a matter of minutes, their ravenous hunger driving them to devour each morsel with a fervor.

"Man, that hit the spot," Harper said, rubbing her belly.

"Agreed," Winslow stated, "I don't think I have ever been so hungry in my entire life."

"Well, that is good to hear. You are going to need plenty of energy for the next part," Earth said, as the spirit made its way to the clearing. "It is time you both learn to use your unique skills together," Earth paused and summoned ten animated training dummies.

"That is a lot of dummies!" Winslow exclaimed as his eyes widened. He stood up, wiping away the crumbs from his sandwich.

"That ain't nothing, Wiki," Harper rebutted with a wink as she jumped up from her spot at the creek. "This will be a piece of cake," she called out, bringing forth her cutlass and buckler.

Wiki, arming himself with Edge and Guard, stated, "Alright, let's do this!"

The group of puppets advanced forward, slowly surrounding them. With their weapons ready, Harper and Winslow stood back-to-back. One of the dummies on Wiki's left side swung its club, Wiki raised Guard and blocked the blow but didn't notice the dummy over his right shoulder taking a shot at him as well. Hap used her cutlass to parry the incoming attack on Winslow and quickly raised her buckler to block another swing coming from her right.

"Hey Wiki! Do you think you could make us some space?" Harper called over her shoulder while keeping her eyes on the incoming threats.

"I got you, Hap!" Winslow affirmed. He gripped his shield and began to imagine a burst of wind around them.

With their attention divided, neither had time to block the third dummy coming from Wiki's right. The club made contact with his right arm, dislodging Harmony's Edge from his grip causing it to dematerialize into the air. The disruption broke his concentration, turning his imagined burst into a wispy poof. Due to the lackluster performance, the remaining dummies closed in on the pair of friends, pinning them down.

"That's enough. Let's start over, you both were beat this time," Earth shouted.

With a stony snap, the clearing was reset, each of the puppets put back to their starting placement, encircling the friends.

"Can we have a moment to talk before we jump back in?" Harper asked, plotting her next moves.

"I don't see a problem with that. Just remember in a true fight, you won't have the time to plan," Fire stated.

Winslow and Harper huddled together to strategize. She suggested, "Alright, I really think we have got this. Do you think you can start us out by–"

"Making us some room?" Winslow finished her sentence, and the friends giggled.

"Yes, exactly!" Hap said, as they finalized their plan for the next fight.

"Okay! We're ready!" Wiki shouted excitedly as the friends resumed their fighting stances.

Winslow and Harper stood surrounded by the training dummies once more, this time with a plan of action. As the animated puppets began shuffling toward them, Wiki slammed Guard on the ground producing a circular gust of wind radiating out from around him, pushing the dummies back about fifteen feet.

"Perfect!" Hap exclaimed as she materialized Tidecaller.

Turning, she released two arrows that hit their mark, taking down two dummies on her far-right side before turning back. Using the Windwalkers, she darted toward an opening between the dummy directly in front of her and the one slightly to the right.

Ascending on invisible platforms, she fired while passing two more foes on the right, once at each. The velocity and rapid changes in elevation caused her to miss the first dummy, the arrow landing in the soil beside it. The second, while close to its mark, was deflected by the last training dummy on her right, who had enough time to adapt.

Jumping off an ephemeral platform at the edge of the circle of puppets, she landed while switching Tidecaller out for Firebrand, facing the dummy who was previously in front of her.

Winslow, noticing Harper left his backside, gripped Edge and imbued it with Fire before slashing toward his right. Flame waves burst forth, eradicating two of the dummies.

Harper spun the whip, its blazing tendrils slicing through the air and wrapping around the dummy's sword arm. With a flick of her wrist, she disarmed the dummy, taking the sword and its clay limb with it. The dummy responded by dashing forward and bashing her with its shield, causing her to stumble backward.

"This one has spunk!" Hap said, as she quickly regained her footing.

Wiki was feeling the pressure as the three remaining dummies in front of him began advancing quickly. Without much time to think of an attack, he slammed Guard down once more, creating a protective U-shaped wall of earth between him and the attackers, not fully encircling him.

"Hap! I need some help over here when you get a chance," Winslow called out in a bit of a panic.

Harper, finishing off the disarmed dummy with her cutlass, responded, "I will be right there." Turning her attention to the last two dummies she had fired at, who now stood side by side, she joked, "Ye be next, ye scallywags," before eliminating them in a fierce flurry of slashes.

Winslow hunkered in his barrier, now blind to the movements of the three remaining dummies slowly encroaching. He turned around to face the opening of the barrier, with his guard up and ready. Stressed, he called out, "Any moment now, Hap!" as a training dummy rounded the left wall of the protective barrier.

Hearing her friend's angst, Harper dashed over at an incredible speed. Using her momentum, she swung her right arm in a wide arc. Her buckler struck the dummy facing Winslow from behind with the force of a runaway freight train, shattering the clay dummy to pieces and causing her to wince in pain from the impact.

"That was cool!" Winslow said. Noticing her facial expression, he asked with concern, "Are you okay?"

"No time, I think there are only two left. Let's finish these guys!" Hap stated, breathing heavily before proceeding to deal with the puppet approaching from the right side of the barrier.

As Harper made quick work of that opponent, Winslow turned his attention toward the sound of a deep thud coming from behind him on the barrier's wall. He saw cracks where the dummy was attempting to break through. Lifting his right arm and bending his elbow, he transformed Edge into his war hammer. Striking forward with a precise blow, he sent jets of water that soared forward like crystalline spears, piercing through the barrier as well as the last puppet on the field. The figure's remnants hung loosely, resembling a tattered and porous relic as the streams of water dissipated into a fine mist.

"Bravo!" "Well done!" the spirits cheered for the children at their massive victory as the friends put away their weapons.

"Much better than the first round," Harper stated as her exhaustion and a slight pain in her shoulder took over. Rubbing the tender area, she said, "I may have hit that dummy a little too hard."

The water spirit glided over gracefully, saying, "You must be more careful not to injure yourself."

The spirit gently touched Harper's right shoulder, soothing the pain away.

"Thank you, that feels so much better," Harper said, showing gratitude.

Earth interjected, "You two have done well today but we know you have big plans for this evening, and we do not want to make you late."

Harper, lying on the ground still catching her breath, raised her left fist toward the sky, "Festival!..." with all the enthusiasm she had left.

Laughing, Wiki said, "It is going to be legendary."

"I can see that turkey leg now. Man, I'm starving," Harper grumbled as she was attempting to pick herself up off the ground.

"When are you not hungry, Hap?" Wiki jested before suggesting, "Let's head back to my house. We can grab a snack before we get ready for the festival."

"That sounds perfect! If... I can make it back to the house," she joked as they collected their belongings.

"Y'all have fun!" Wind called as the spirits began to leave.

Winslow and Harper turned their heads and yelled back in unison, "We will!" as they continued their walk.

Chapter 34

In the ritual room of The Fang's lair, final preparations were underway to hatch their nefarious plan. The acolytes raced back and forth, moving with a sense of urgency, as they responded to each demand.

"Quickly now, we don't have much time," Lillith shouted, commanding the members' attention as she picked up a piece of chalk and made her way to the prepped opening in the ritual room.

The floor was cold, rough stone, but it had been carefully swept clean. Every inch of the surface was free of debris, revealing its details. The meticulous care taken in cleaning the floor was evident, giving the space a sense of order and purpose despite its austere appearance.

Lillith began tracing the first of many intricate runes on the ground, her hand steady and practiced. This initial symbol was a central part of the necromantic web they were weaving, its curves and lines forming the heart of their dark spell, leaving a pentagram at her feet.

"Now get moving hastily. Seraphine will be down from her room shortly and the preparation must be complete," Lillith demanded as she pointed to the group of five members, awaiting her order.

They quickly followed suit, each of them taking to their section of the floor with chalk in hand. They worked in silence, the soft scratching of chalk on stone was the only sound heard. As the symbols took shape, Lillith moved among them, inspecting each one and murmuring corrections when needed. The ritual demanded absolute precision, even the smallest mistake could lead to catastrophic failure.

Once the symbols were complete, the acolytes returned to the crescent altar at the center of the lair.

"Now, take the possessions and split them evenly throughout the pentagrams," Lillith barked as she made her way to the wall of scrolls, looking for leverage in the upcoming confrontation.

Back in town, Mrs. Kinney raced around the house looking for a hairbrush.

"If only these kids learned to put stuff back where they got it, I could actually find things in this house," she stated as she scoured the living room, finally finding it. "Aha! ... How does it get this far down into the couch?" Ignoring her own question, she hollered, "Willow! Get down here. I need to brush your hair so I can start getting dressed."

"Yes ma'am!" Willow replied while hopping down the stairs like a bunny.

Sitting on the couch, Mrs. Kinney pointed to the floor in front of her, "Sit right here."

Willow, doing what her mother told her, plopped on the floor, crossed her legs, and sat upright.

Mrs. Kinney brushed through Willow's shoulder length hair, asking midway, "Would you like a ponytail or a braid?"

"Braid please," Willow responded, requesting her favorite style.

Finishing up Willow's hair, Mrs. Kinney called out, "Winslow! Harper! Can y'all come down here and help Willow with her socks and shoes while I get ready?"

Peeking his head out of the open doorframe, he yelled back to his mom, "Coming right down!"

Both friends then proceeded downstairs to help Willow and put on their own shoes.

As Mrs. Kinney started up the stairs, the phone in the kitchen rang. Stopping in her tracks, she turned around and made her way to the sound of the disruption, answering the call, "Hello?"

In the living room, Harper kneeled as she said, "Hand me your socks Willow," while reaching out her left hand.

Walking toward the closet near the front door, Winslow said, "I can grab our shoes."

"Hear you go, Hap!" Willow answered before handing over the socks.

"Hey! Stop wiggling your toes so much, this isn't easy," Harper said struggling to get the sock situated correctly.

Willow giggled, "It tickles. I can't help it!"

Wiki returned with the shoes, dropping them to the floor. Each of the kids grabbed their respective pair. Winslow sat down in front of Willow and helped get her shoes on and tied before putting his own on. All three kids were ready to go when Mrs. Kinney popped her head in.

"I just got the oddest call from Mr. Jenkins. He said his dog, among a few others in our neighborhood, have gone missing," she stated, looking concerned.

"Hey, some girls in soccer have pets missing too. Do you think a monster is eating them?" Willow spoke up while still sitting on the floor beside Winslow and Harper.

"You know monsters are not real," Wiki said, nudging his sister. "But that is really strange, Mom."

Attempting to change the conversation, Harper jumped up, saying, "Who's ready for turkey legs?" pumping her fist to the sky.

Everyone laughed before Mrs. Kinney responded, "Okay, well I still need to finish getting ready, give me ten minutes."

"Oh okay," Harper said, slumping with a clearly visible bummed-out expression.

Mrs. Kinney rolled her eyes as she walked upstairs, thinking to herself, "Will these kids ever stop being so dramatic?"

She shook her head from left to right, answering her own question and laughing as she entered her room to quickly change clothes.

Coming back downstairs a few minutes later, Mrs. Kinney grabbed her purse and slipped on her flip-flops, calling out with the subtle undertones of a chuckle, "Last train leaving the station. Be there or be square."

"Shotgun!" Harper declared as she raced to the door.

"Aw man, I never remember to call shotgun," Winslow retorted somberly as he followed behind.

"You can ride in the front on the way home," Hap said to cheer up her friend as they made their way to the driveway.

Everyone took turns loading into the car. Mrs. Kinney double-checked that everyone was situated before firing up the engine, throwing it into reverse, and backing out of the driveway. Putting the car into gear they began to make their way to the festival.

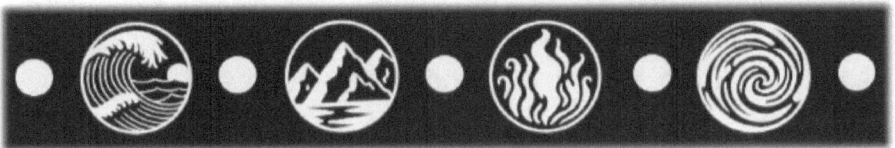

Bursting through the door of the ritual room, Seraphine, walking with a purposeful elegance, glided toward her five generals; Lilith, Alistair, Silas, Magnus, and Percival; standing just outside the salt barrier surrounding the prepared area.

"Have we procured enough essence for the Blood Crystal?" Seraphine asked while curling her lips fiendishly.

"We are close my priestess," Silas stated. "After tonight's festivities we should easily surpass the necessary amount to complete the summoning."

"Good, we haven't much time. We must be ready to summon upon the next blood moon to avoid giving the blessed more time to get stronger." Seraphine replied in an eerie, bone-chilling tone.

"The simple-minded townsfolk have no idea. We should easily be able to acquire the remainder tonight while they, and the blessed, are distracted," Silas stated with a maniacal laugh.

"Perfect," Seraphine said shortly while making her way to the center of the artistic display laid out by the acolytes.

A pentagram of pentagrams, each carefully inscribed within a larger, flawless circle of salt. The salt circle encasing the intricate design formed a barrier that both protected the casters and confined the potent magic within.

The central pentagram, etched in chalk and outlined with charcoal, radiated with dark energy. Surrounding it, five smaller pentagrams, without charcoal shading, were arranged meticulously. Completing the design, five lifelines of blood anchored each of the outer symbols to the center.

"It is time," Seraphine announced as she stood at the heart of the ritual site, prompting the generals to take their respective places inside the surrounding pentagrams. Each general made sure not to disrupt the possessions of the dead accompanying them.

The other members took their places around the outside edge of the salt circle, being careful not to disrupt the delicate artwork.

The high priestess spoke aloud, while raising her hands up from her side, "Defiled ones, hear our plea, grant us power, let chaos reign where balance should be." Immediately cuing the members surrounding her to begin chanting in unison, "Revertimini, Filii Sepulcri."

Each time they repeated the chant, their voices grew louder. The pentagrams on the floor started to come alive, pulsing with the rhythm of the incantations. Progressing, Seraphine's voice transformed into a deeply discordant, unsettling harmony. Speaking lowly, in a tongue unreproducible by humans, she continued until her voice reached a resounding pinnacle. The personal effects in the pentagrams began to glow faintly.

Seraphine declared loudly, three times, "Evigilate, milites mei!"

Thrusting her hands downward, channeling the amassed power into the ritual symbols beneath her. The glow from the personal items blazed brightly before dimming, confirming the energy had been transferred to the graves.

With a grim smile of satisfaction, Seraphine turned her head toward Lilith as she commanded, "Everything is in order. Escort them and make sure to do what needs to be done."

"Yes, High Priestess," Lilith answered with a bow before hastily departing to Ashenfall Cemetery.

Hundreds of miles away, Mrs. Kinney found a suitable spot and carefully parked her car. Wasting no time, Harper jumped out of the car, "I can smell the turkey legs from here!" Her overwhelming excitement prevented her from remaining stationary as she bounced up and down.

Winslow laughed, "Calm down, Hap!" The friends giggled as he joined Hap's side.

Interjecting, Mrs. Kinney stated, "Patience will get you much further in life children," while opening the back door for her youngest.

Willow reached out and grabbed her mother's outstretched hand, anchoring herself before she jumped out of the car, landing with a soft thud in the dirt. "I can't wait to become a beautiful butterfly," Willow said as she twirled beside her mother.

Mrs. Kinney, leading the way to the ticket booth with Willow's hand still nuzzled in hers, asked, "Y'all please stay close. You can never be too careful, people these days drive crazy."

"Yes, ma'am!" Winslow and Harper responded, excitedly following suit.

Arriving at the ticket booth, Mrs. Kinney pulled out her wallet from her purse before looking at Winslow, commanding, "Hold your sister's hand and stay right here while I get the tickets."

Winslow and Harper nodded, agreeing as Harper pulled five one-dollar bills from her pocket. "Here is the money my dad gave me," she stated, extending her hand toward Mrs. Kinney with the cash.

"All I need is two dollars for the ride tickets. I will cover the admission," Mrs. Kinney responded while only taking two of the one-dollar bills from Harper's hand. "That should leave you with plenty of snack money," Mrs. Kinney jested.

"Thank you! You're the best, Mrs. Kinney!" Hap replied, grinning from ear to ear.

The kids stood, waiting where they were told, their excitement barely contained as they fidgeted while glancing around at the bustling surroundings, eager for the adventure ahead.

Returning to the children, Mrs. Kinney stated, "Here you go," as she handed ten tickets each to Winslow and Harper, followed by giving Wiki a dollar for snacks.

"First stop, turkey leg station!" Harper exclaimed jokingly while pumping her fist in the air.

"Well, I want my face painted before I do anything else," Willow declared adamantly, as she stomped her foot.

"That settles it," Mrs. Kinney interjected. "Face painting is over near the food vendors. We'll walk with y'all over there." She began leading the children through the crowd, toward the food booths.

As they walked, they were enthralled by the sight of fire breathers, whose flames danced in mesmerizing patterns, as well as different characters on stilts, who towered above the crowd with their elaborate costumes and graceful movements. The vibrant performances and lively atmosphere captivated their attention, filling the air with excitement and wonder.

"This is amazing! Mommy, they look like dragons!" Willow stated, fully amused by the spectacle before her.

"It's really neat, huh?" Mrs. Kinney responded while keeping her focus on the kids, the booth in the distance, and working through the crowd.

With the food vendors in sight to their left, Mrs. Kinney called out, "Winslow and Harper, I'm going to take Willow to get her face painted. You two can go get your snacks and have some fun. I want y'all to meet me at the merry-go-round at nine," as she pointed toward the administrative building that stood as the centerpiece of Ashenfall Gardens, which bolstered a large clock clearly visible from the festival grounds.

"Yes, ma'am," the friends acknowledged as they parted ways. Harper snatched Winslow's hand and dragged him toward the food.

"Did you want a funnel cake or some cotton candy?" Hap asked Wiki as she let go of his hand.

"Not right now, I'm still kind of full from eating at the house earlier," Winslow responded as they took their place in the short line.

"What do you want to do first? Well, aside from food that is," Hap asked, buzzing with energy.

Winslow responded quickly, "I want to ride the Ferris wheel, I always love seeing everything from so high up."

"Great idea," Harper exclaimed as the friends stepped up to the booth's counter.

A young girl with blonde hair messily thrown in a ponytail, smacking on bubble gum, asked, "What can I get ya?"

Harper answered, "I want your biggest turkey leg, please!"

"Okay," the girl popped a bubble with her gum, stating, "That will be one dollar."

Hap eagerly handed over the money in exchange for the delicious treasure. Taking no precaution and diving in for a big bite, she immediately recoiled, "Oo! That's hot," as she blew on the steaming delicacy to cool it down.

The two friends made their way to the Ferris wheel and stood in line. As they waited, Harper continued to munch cautiously on her turkey leg while Winslow tried to look and see what games were available.

Not being able to see much through the crowd, Wiki asked, "Do you want to try out some games after this ride?"

"Yeah! That sounds like fun. We can try to win a prize for Willow," Hap suggested in between chewing.

"One ticket please," the ride attendant requested.

After giving the worker one ticket each, they stepped forward and were guided to their seats in the passenger car. Once their door was locked, the car jerked forward unsteadily before smoothly taking them up. As the huge wheel slowly turned, the world below them shrunk.

"Whoa! Look at how small the cars are!" Harper exclaimed pointing toward the parking lot.

"Yeah! And the people walking around look like ants," Winslow responded, laughing as the wheel reached its peak. "I'm trying to find Willow and my mom, but everything is so small!"

Giving up on the search, Wiki changed direction, suggesting, "Since we can't find them maybe we can at least figure out what else we want to go see while we're here."

Both kids looked around to identify different amusements.

"Perhaps we could do the shooting gallery, ring toss, fishing game, or strength test?" Harper proposed.

Winslow, honestly not caring what they did as long as they had fun, responded, "I can see ring toss right there," he pointed to the game booth near the right of the Ferris wheel. "Oh, and over there are some more games, it is just hard to tell which ones."

"Okay, so ring toss is next, but we should find the fishing game too," Harper said as the Ferris wheel stopped to load the car below, they dangled in the air as the bucket swayed back and forth.

"I'm pretty sure I saw that game not far from the entrance," Wiki replied as the ride began to move again. "We can definitely win something at one of those!"

The wheel creaked as it started bringing them back down, gradually returning their perspective to normalcy. Once it was their turn to disembark, they quickly left the passenger car.

"Come on Wiki! Let's go win a prize," Harper turned back and shouted as she skipped in the direction of the game.

"Maybe I should have gotten a turkey leg too, then I could keep up with you!" Winslow jested as he did his best to catch up.

Arriving at the ring toss game, Harper handed over her ticket and the attendant returned with a basket holding five red rings. With a focused expression, she grabbed a ring from her stack and narrowed her eyes at the array of glassy bottles on display before her.

Positioning her feet, Hap squared her shoulders, and with a smooth motion of her arm, released the ring. It arced gracefully through the air before descending, wobbling slightly, and landing with a faint "*Clink*." The ring teetered on the rim of the bottle before slipping off and falling between the rows.

Undeterred, she said, "I will win this prize," before lining up for her next throw.

Repeating the motion, she released it a moment sooner than her previous turn. It had the range it needed, but the edge of the ring hit the top of the bottle and bounced off.

"Aw man, I was feeling good about that one," she stated before rotating her shoulder to loosen up.

"Three more tries, Hap! You've got this," Winslow yelled out over the noise of the festival, encouraging her.

After missing two more times but still determined, she stood, focusing even more intently.

"It's the bottom of the ninth and the bases are loaded. Everything hinges on this last pitch," Harper said aloud, amping herself up. "All I need to do is strike this last batter out and we take home the prize."

She took a deep breath, feeling centered. With a swift, confident flick of her wrist, she sent the ring soaring. This time, it landed with a perfect "*Clink*" around the neck of the bottle, wobbling slightly before settling securely in place.

Winslow erupted into cheer as Harper's fists shot to the sky. "I did it!" she yelled as she jumped in joy.

The game attendant spoke up, "You get to pick from any of these small prizes," he gestured toward the petite stuffed animals.

"Which one do you think Willow would want?" Harper asked while turning her head to face Winslow.

"Um, I think she would love the pink teddy bear," Wiki answered while pointing to a tiny pink teddy bear with a white belly and a sunflower in its ear. The attendant handed over the prize before quickly turning his attention to the next customer.

"Let's go find her so that we can give it to her now," Hap suggested eagerly, anticipating Willow's excitement.

"Yeah, they were supposed to be by the face painter. Let's head that way," Wiki stated as the friends started walking toward Willow and Mrs. Kinney's last known location.

"Make sure to keep your eyes peeled, they probably aren't still at the face painter unless the line was super long," Harper said as she scanned the crowd. "Oh, look over there. Someone is juggling knives, that's so groovy!"

"That's rad, I wish I could do cool stuff like that," Wiki replied as he turned to appreciate the skillful entertainment.

Hap, turning her gaze back to Wiki, jested, "Well, I mean, technically you can do way cooler stuff than that now."

Wiki responded in a shakily, pseudo-confident tone, "Well, I suppose that's true–"

"Hey, isn't that your sister," Hap interrupted, catching a glimpse of Willow waving to Mrs. Kinney as she passed by, riding a noble steed, before disappearing once more as the merry-go-round continued to spin.

Winslow, turning to confirm, stated, "Yeppers, that's definitely them!" before pivoting to head in that direction.

As the friends made their way over to Mrs. Kinney, Winslow hollered, "Mom!"

This caused Mrs. Kinney to turn in the direction of the sound, and she began waving once she recognized Wiki and Hap.

As the friends neared Mrs. Kinney, Willow was getting off the ride. "Perfect timing," Harper stated, as she hid the prize behind her back.

As Willow rejoined the group, Hap directed, "Close your eyes! I got you a surprise."

Listening, Willow closed her eyes in anticipation and replied, bouncing up and down, "I'm so excited! What is it?"

"On the count of three, open your eyes," Harper guided as she pulled the teddy bear from behind her back and extended it toward Willow's face. "One, two, three!"

On her mark, Willow opened her eyes spotting the beautiful pink and white teddy bear, "I love it!" she said in awe with sparkles in her eyes, as she reached out and snatched it, bringing it in for a bear hug. Squeezing her new stuffy tighter, she looked up at Hap expressing gratitude, "Thank you so much!"

"I'm glad you like it!" Harper replied as a warm blush spread across her cheeks, painting them a rosy hue.

Mrs. Kinney spoke up, smiling as the gesture warmed her heart, "You kids can be so sweet sometimes."

Uncomfortable in these kinds of situations, Wiki interrupted the moment and said, "We're off to play some more games."

Mrs. Kinney reminded the friends, "Don't forget to meet back here at nine o'clock on the dot. Have fun!"

"We will!" Winslow and Harper said together as they waved and started walking in the direction of the fishing game booth.

"This next game should be a breeze for me since I go fishing all the time with my dad," Hap said as she flexed her bicep.

Wiki replied with a giggly undertone, "It's not real fishing so it might be more difficult than you think."

"We will just have to see about that," Harper retorted with a smirk, as they continued to weave through the crowd.

A fresh breeze surged past, whipping Hap's hair around as a familiar voice caught the attention of the friends. "Find someplace quiet where you can be unseen. We need to talk," Wind whispered urgently.

Both friends looked at each other to acknowledge what they had heard before looking around to find a suitable location.

Spotting the house of mirrors, Wiki nudged Hap with his elbow, gesturing with his head toward it, "What about there?"

"That's perfect," Harper thought aloud. "We've got plenty of tickets still. Let's head in."

After handing the attendant one ticket each, they made their way into the maze of illusion, curious to hear what the wind spirit had to say.

Chapter 35

As twilight settled over Ashenfall Cemetery, the humid air hung thick. The sky, painted in hues of deep orange and dusky purple, provided the last light of the day before it disappeared beyond the horizon. Ancient oaks, ever watchful sentinels, cast long shadows across the burial grounds. Stone markers, weathered by the time and elements, stood as somber monuments to the lives once lived, each one telling a silent story of those who lay beneath.

The oppressive air grew cooler, carrying with it the faint scent of flowery bouquets intermingled with decay. A sudden stillness descended, intensifying the moment with an unsettling calm.

Trembling ever so slightly, subtle vibrations traveled through the ground unnoticed by the living but reverberated through the very bones of the earth. The once-still cemetery became a place of restless activity as the tremors intensified.

From beneath the soil, faint, muffled sounds emerged, an uncanny symphony of scratching and scraping. The surface of the ground before each grave began to shift and bulge.

With a sudden, violent lurch, the first bony hand burst through the earth, fingers splayed in a macabre greeting as loose clumps of dirt crumbled and tumbled down. It was soon followed by another, and then another until the cemetery was a grotesque garden of skeletal limbs reaching skyward.

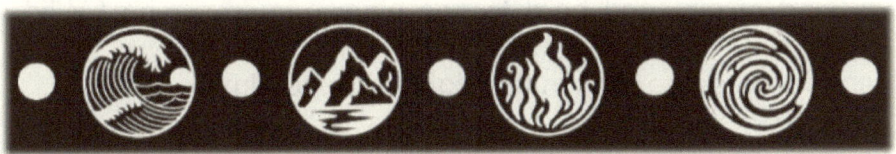

Meanwhile, back at the festival, Winslow and Harper delved into the dimly lit house of mirrors. It was quiet inside the illusionary maze as the floor creaked under the friends' shoes, and the smell of popcorn permeated through the air. As they stepped further in, they were surrounded by mirrors of all shapes and sizes.

Leaning over, Hap whispered, "Whoa, this one is kind of spooky, isn't it?"

"Totally! The last one we did was a lot brighter. This is kind of dim and hard to see where you're going," Wiki answered as he took in the sights around him.

"Yeah, that's what I thought too. Stay close so we don't get lost," Harper said as she made her way further into the silver-lined maze.

Following her, Winslow stated, "Agreed! I am right behind you."

Peeking to his left as they walked, he watched his image shrink and balloon, causing him to snort and chuckle which captured Hap's attention. She turned her head back just in time to catch a glimpse of a big-headed Wiki.

Pausing to delight in the distraction, she backed up to align her face with the same mirror, making her head appear comically large, like a bobblehead toy.

Unable to resist the urge, she began to make goofy faces at her reflection. She puffed out her cheeks, causing her eyes to magnify to an almost cartoonish degree. She stuck out her tongue, curling it in exaggerated loops, and wiggled her fingers next to her head like makeshift antlers.

The sight of her cartoonishly magnified eyes, along with the other gestures, caused both children to double over and burst into laughter. Hap began to lead the way again, but as she turned the corner, she smacked into a cool, hard surface.

"Oo, Ouchy!" she said as she rubbed her nose and reached out to prevent another mishap. "Well, it is definitely not that way," she nervously giggled before continuing.

"Look at this one," Harper said, standing in front of a mirror that made her legs look like they were made of jelly. "I'm a walking wobbly tower!"

Laughing, Winslow stood by her side as the two friends wiggled and jiggled their arms and legs, fully engrossed in their playful antics. Their laughter echoed through the room, carefree and lighthearted.

Without warning, a figure popped its head out from behind the mirror and shouted, "BOO!"

The unexpected appearance startled the children, causing them to jump back with wide eyes and gasps. As their initial shock wore off, they recognized the mischievous grin on Wind's face.

Laughing at the sight of Winslow and Harper's reaction, Wind chuckled, "I got y'all good! But seriously, we have a problem."

Ignoring the jesterly statement, Wiki replied with concern etched on his face, "What is it?"

"Looks like your nemesis is back at it again. The Fang has awoken the past to put you both and the town in danger," the wind spirit said, its usually playful tone now chilling and grave.

"Awoken the past? What does that mean?" Winslow asked, a tinge of dread bleeding through his expression.

"They have risen the dead of your lovely town in an effort to create chaos," Wind explained, a sense of urgency in its voice. "We must act quickly."

"The dead? You mean, like zombies?" Hap asked, her eyes wide open in dismay.

"Umm... Yes... and no," Wind replied, the tone shifting to one of careful explanation. "Zombies, also known as the living dead, act on basic instincts, driven by hunger and the need to spread. But the undead we're dealing with have been raised by magic and are commanded by their summoner to accomplish a specific task. They will not stop unless destroyed or their task has been fulfilled."

Wind paused, ensuring the children understood the gravity of the situation, before saying, "These undead are more dangerous in some ways because they're controlled, directed by a powerful force. We can't afford to underestimate them. That's why we need to move quickly and decisively."

"Whoa, that's cool… and also a bit terrifying," Wiki stated, his face a mix of excitement and angst as the weight of the situation began to settle in.

"What is their task?" Hap asked, her voice laced with concern.

"While we are not exactly sure what their task is, if I had to venture a guess, I would say it has something to do with causing harm to the blessed," the wind spirit replied, its words bringing a nerve-wracking realization to light.

Gesturing toward the mirror the kids had been staring at moments before, Wind stated bluntly, "Enough talk, we need to act now. Follow me."

As Wind made its way toward the familiar carnival staple, the mirror began to change before the friends' eyes. The once-clear reflection faded away, replaced by what appeared to be a glimpse of a distant scene viewed through a dirty lens. The image was hazy, with greyish hues dancing around its edges, creating an eerie, almost surreal effect.

"That's so beautiful," Hap murmured in awe as she watched Wind vanish into the ethereal scene. "We'd better not be late," she added with a playful wink at Wiki before stepping forward to follow the spirit through the portal.

Winslow, lingering a moment longer, stared at the swirling portal. "Aw man, I hope this doesn't trigger my motion sickness," he thought aloud, his voice mingled with a hint of reluctance.

With a deep breath and a resigned sigh, he hesitantly followed his friend into the unknown, bracing himself for whatever lay on the other side.

Instantly, Wiki landed in an environment surrounded by large trees and beautifully maintained grass. The abrupt transition left him temporarily baffled, and he looked around, trying to make sense of his new whereabouts.

"Where are we?" he asked.

Hap cleared her throat to get his attention before pointing toward a large clock perched atop the administration building in the distance. The familiar sight brought clarity, and Wiki nodded in understanding, realizing where they had been transported. As he continued analyzing his surroundings, he noticed the top of the Ferris wheel, a silent reminder of the nearby carnival.

"Based off their trajectory, they appear to be headed toward the festival," Wind informed the friends, before continuing, "We brought you here to be able to cut them off before they can rain chaos on the townspeople."

The gravity of the situation settled in as the friends exchanged quick, uneasy glances. They knew what was at stake and understood that they needed to act quickly to protect the festival and everyone in it. The peaceful surroundings now felt charged with tension, the calm before the storm.

"I'm not trying to be rude, but is there a reason that y'all can't take care of it?" Hap inquired as her brow furrowed in curiosity.

"That is kind of a good point. We have only seen a small bit of what you can do, and you are so powerful!" Wiki added, echoing Hap's concern.

"You raise a good question," Wind replied, its tone thoughtful yet firm. "To put it simply, this realm, along with infinite others, requires a careful balance. We cannot be in all places at once, so we choose and awaken the blessed within each realm to be our champions and assist us in maintaining that balance. Most importantly, we cannot directly interfere with corruption because it would upset the balance."

"But what about when we were attacked?" Harper quipped, her eyes narrowing as she recalled the recent event.

"Those boys were not corrupted," Wind explained patiently, "But rather, they were under the influence of blood magic. The caster used ancient magic to take control of anyone who dared wear the cursed object, granting them superhuman strength and speed in exchange. Because they were not truly corrupted, we were able to step in and protect you both, as well as those misguided boys."

"That makes sense," Winslow conceded, though worry still clouded his expression. "But if they weren't corrupted, then how powerful are the corrupted?" he asked.

Wind answered with urgency in her voice, "They are our counterparts. We embody righteousness and value the beauty of life while they are the bringers of chaos and destruction. The corrupted will never be gone, just as we will always be here. I understand this may bring more questions, but we must hold those for later as there are more pressing matters you both must attend to."

The seriousness in Wind's tone left no room for doubt. The friends knew they had to act, and quickly. The festival, and everyone there, depended on it. The short silence was broken by the unsettling sound of distant cracking bones, drawing their attention and sending chills down their spines.

"We will be watching, but we'll let you overcome this on your own," Wind stated before wisping away, leaving them alone to face the impending danger.

"Are we even ready for something this big?" Wiki asked nervously, his eyes darting around as the sounds grew louder.

"We have got this!" Hap exclaimed, her voice filled with excitement for the challenge ahead. "Just remember what we practiced in training, we keep space and take 'em out."

On high alert, they scanned the area, their eyes flicking back and forth as they prepared to come face-to-face with a real-life nightmare. The rustling of foliage caught their attention, the shaking leaves sending a new wave of shivers down their spines.

"Get ready!" Harper said aloud, equipping her battle-ready attire. Her beloved cutlass gleamed in her left hand and her trusty buckler was secured in her other, both originating from the Earthshapers. Accompanying them, her whimsical boots shimmered gloriously, eager for action.

"Ready as I'll ever be," Winslow muttered unenthusiastically as he called forth Edge and Guard. The familiar weight of his weapons brought some comfort, though the unease lingered in his eyes.

As the two friends unknowingly held their breath, the movement in the foliage intensified, right before three small creatures darted out from the underbrush. The burst of activity startled Wiki and Hap, causing them to instinctively step back.

"Whew," Winslow sighed with relief, wiping his brow. "It was just squirrels."

They shared a quick, nervous laugh, their tension momentarily eased, but it was immediately interrupted by another rustling sound.

From behind a twisted oak, a skeletal figure stepped forward, its empty eye sockets were dark voids that seemed to absorb the light of the moon. The creature's bones, yellowed with age, clattered softly with each movement. Moss and lichens clung to its ribcage, and the tattered remnants of burial shrouds fluttered like ghostly banners in the breeze.

Taking the initiative, Harper beckoned, "Follow my lead!" as she advanced toward the first sign of danger excitedly, breaking into full stride.

Understanding the limitations of her own body, she waited until she was approximately three feet from her target before launching herself into the air.

Drawing back her right arm, she thrust forward with her buckler just before coming into contact with the undead's skull. The sheer power of the strike rang out with an audible cracking sound. The impact was so ferocious that the skull was forced into an unnatural, grotesque misalignment.

The head twisted sharply to one side, the jaw now hanging askew, giving the once-human visage a nightmarish appearance. The neck bones, unable to withstand the force, crumbled and snapped, leaving the skull precariously perched at an impossible angle.

The undead staggered backward as Hap turned around to face Winslow, hoisting her cutlass in a victorious manner. "Got 'em!" she yelled.

Wiki's eyes widened as he noticed the undead regaining its footing. "Hap, look out behind you!" he warned urgently.

She turned back just in time to see the undead lurching forward, its skeletal form defying the damage it had sustained. Reacting quickly, she raised her left foot and kicked toward her opponent, releasing a gust of wind that pushed both her and the undead away from each other.

With a swift motion, she swapped her cutlass for Firebrand, the flaming whip igniting in her grasp. She cast the fiery lash forward, cracking it with precision. The whip sent out a spiraling pillar of flame that engulfed the skeleton and reduced it to ash in an instant.

"Well, that seems to do the trick," she smirked proudly before adding, "This is going to be a piece of cake!"

"Nice job!" Winslow called out. "All we have to do is completely destroy them, no big deal," he added sarcastically as he imbued Harmony's Edge with fire. "I just hope there aren't too many."

In that moment, Wiki looked up, realizing with a sinking feeling that he had tempted fate. More figures began to emerge from the shadows to Hap's left, a ghastly procession of the once-living, their decayed forms swathed in shrouds and ragged clothing that spoke of different eras.

Some were barely more than skeletons, their bones gleaming dully in the moonlight, while others had patches of withered flesh clinging to them, their faces frozen in eternal grimaces of pain and despair. The scent of rot and decay wafted toward the friends, mingling unpleasantly with the floral perfume of nearby magnolias creating a potent noxious odor.

"Way to jinx us there, Wiki!" Harper exclaimed as she darted toward the grouping of undead. Adjusting her grip on Firebrand, "I can take care of these. Keep an eye out for more," she yelled as she charged into the fray, her whip crackling with fiery energy.

"Ha, sorry about that. I had a feeling it wouldn't be that easy," Winslow muttered under his breath as he began to scan for signs of more enemies approaching.

Meanwhile, Harper, thinking she had devised the perfect plan—drawn from training—activated the Windwalkers, elevating herself step by step until she was directly over the three newly emergent undead. With the middle enemy in her sight, she cast Firebrand under her boot and cracked the whip before jumping backward. A spiraling column of flame shot toward the ground, engulfing the skeleton in the center and leaving the other two partially scorched and slightly damaged by the force of the impact, but still standing.

As Hap landed gracefully on the ground, the two remaining undead rapidly closed in on her. The first undead to her right, now missing an arm, raised a balled-up fist over its head. It unleashed a recklessly powerful downward swing. On the ready, Harper raised her buckler, blocking the attack with a solid clang and then added a forceful shove, sending the one-armed undead stumbling back approximately ten feet.

As the undead staggered back, a foul stench of burnt flesh filled the air, making Harper gag. "Oo, that is awful," she muttered, wrinkling her nose in disgust.

She tried her best not to choke on the putrid smell assaulting her nostrils but quickly turned her attention back to the encroaching sound of creaking bones. The second undead was closing in fast, and Harper readied her stance, gripping her buckler and Firebrand tightly, prepared for the next strike.

Winslow spotted more movement from beyond the trees as bushes and leaves were rustled. "I think we have more incoming!" Wiki called out nervously as he took a fighting stance, readjusting his grip on Edge and bolstering Guard.

An undead draped in overalls and a tattered plaid shirt, partially decomposed by years spent underground, shuffled through the brush. Winslow cautiously approached his target. The creature stumbled over a protruding root, causing it to lose its balance and fall. Seeing an opportunity, Wiki acted quickly as it tried to regain its footing, slamming Guard into the enemy with all his might, sending it crashing back to the ground.

Seizing the moment, Wiki reared his right arm back and thrust it forward, stabbing Edge into the hollow cavity that once housed vital organs. He focused his mind, imagining flames growing from the blade. The fiery tendrils that had been barely visible before now blazed brightly, growing exponentially in size and intensity. The flames quickly enveloped the undead, consuming it in a roaring inferno. The once-menacing figure was reduced to little more than an ashen pile.

Turning his head left to boast, Wiki hollered, "Hey Hap! I got one!" His voice filled with pride, the adrenaline of the fight still coursing through his veins.

"That's awesome, Wiki!" Harper called back as she ensnared the second undead with Firebrand, the flaming whip crackling as it wrapped around the creature. With a swift motion, she incinerated the undead, watching as it crumbled to the ground in a heap of ashes.

No sooner had the ashes settled than the last undead, which she had pushed back earlier, returned. In a grotesque display of macabre practicality, the creature—now clutching its scorched limb, darkened and charred at the edges–advanced quickly, wielding the arm like a makeshift club. With savage willpower, it raised its left arm into the air and swung wildly at Harper.

Anticipating the attack, Hap bolstered her buckler and met the blow head-on, the impact sending a shudder up her arm. With her right foot forward, she lifted it slightly before stomping it down hard, causing a violent burst of wind underfoot that flipped her backward through the air.

Landing firmly on her feet, without missing a beat, she quickly snapped Firebrand again. This time splashing a molten liquid that molded around the undead momentarily before dissolving the remains and hardening into something resembling a slightly askew burnt rock.

Amazed at the display he just witnessed, Wiki shouted, "Wow! That was super cool! When did you learn that?"

Harper smiled before she responded, "Just now! I've always heard I have a great imag– "

Her sentence was cut short as a small section of brush between Wiki and her began to rustle, followed quickly by more rustling sounds coming from behind her.

"Hey, Wiki, we should probably back up some," Hap suggested, cautiously scanning their surroundings as the sound of movement intensified.

Hearing the rustling growing louder and coming from many directions, Wiki replied, "I was thinking the same thing!" His voice was steady, but the urgency was unmistakable as he and Harper instinctively moved closer together, preparing for whatever might emerge from the veil of shrubbery.

As the two friends backed away in the direction of the administration building, they converged at the center of the gardens. They stood astounded by the sheer volume of undead seeping from around the trees and through the brush. The once peaceful garden was now a nightmarish scene, with the undead pouring in from several directions.

"What are we going to do now?" Wiki asked with panic taking hold as he struggled to comprehend the overwhelming numbers.

With a confident grin and a quick wink, Harper replied, "This ought to be fun! We can do this, just remember training. Make me a bit of space."

"I know exactly what to do," Winslow answered as he tightened his grip on guard. His expression turned serious as he focused on the task at hand.

As the creatures loomed closer, Winslow closed his eyes, blocking out the chaos around him, and began to imagine the perfect tactical solution. Once the image was clear in his mind, he slammed Guard to the ground with all his might. The earth responded immediately, a powerful tremor rippling through the ground. The soil erupted as towering stone pillars shot upward at diagonal angles. Each pillar was rugged and jagged, their surfaces marked with natural grooves and cracks.

The pillars crisscrossed in a precise pattern, forming an intricate web of stone that interlocked perfectly with the opposite rows. This created narrow channels that forced the undead to funnel through the paths it created, restricting their movement and leaving them with no choice but to navigate the tight, controlled corridors. The crisscrossed stone barriers guided the undead into strategic chokepoints where they could be more easily dealt with.

"Holy cow, this is so rad," Harper exclaimed, her eyes alight with excitement as Wiki's vision came to a finalization.

Realizing it was her turn to jump in, Hap took off with the Windwalkers and Firebrand, her movements swift and effortless as she soared over the battlefield. She wielded Firebrand with determined skill, though its wild nature made it a challenge to control.

Each snap of the whip sent searing waves and explosive bursts of fire across the gardens. Sometimes, the flames struck clusters of undead with devastating accuracy, reducing them to smoldering ashes; other times, the fiery tendrils veered off course, their unpredictable paths leaving charred scars on the ground.

Winslow, completely engrossed in his friend's fiery spectacle, was caught off-guard by an eerie groan coming from his right. Turning quickly, he found himself in the presence of a skeletal creature concealed beneath a once-immaculate suit.

The fabric, now frayed and worn, clung to the creature with a haunting elegance, as if it had been tailored for a man of stature in life. The suit, a deep charcoal gray, bore the marks of decay with small tears and dark stains that spoke of its journey from the grave. The shirt beneath, a ghostly white, tinged with the yellowed remnants of time, and the tie, a faded crimson, hung loosely from its neck, twisted in a way that suggests it was once carefully knotted.

Realizing it was still at least twenty feet away, Winslow took a deep breath, his momentary panic subsiding. He raised his shield to his chest, then exhaled slowly as he dropped to one knee, tilting his head forward and closing his eyes. Picturing immense winds barreling through narrow corridors, he opened his eyes and raised his head to see above Guard.

In a display of elemental beauty, strands of turbulent, spiraling winds flowed out of the shield, twisting and contorting through the passageways he had created. The force sent the tuxedo-clad gentleman tumbling backward, the sound of bone smashing against stone, echoing until it faded from earshot.

A satisfied smile spread across Wiki's face as he called out, "Hap! How did you like that one? If I keep this up, you can easily take them out!"

Without skipping a beat, Hap paused momentarily, turning to give him a nod of understanding and a thumbs up before getting back into her groove. Winslow, still holding his position, watched in awe as Harper danced effortlessly through the sky, conducting an orchestra of fire and flames with each controlled movement.

Hap spun in the air, the whip following her in graceful loops that traced intricate patterns, leaving trails of embers and smoke behind. Her performance was interrupted by a cry from a short distance away.

"Help!" the voice called out, laced with fear and desperation.

Harper immediately turned her head in the direction of the plea and spotted the grave keeper, Mr. Morrows, cowering in the crook of an old oak tree. She noticed three skeletons, also lured by the cry for help, advancing toward him with menacing intent. Realizing she had to act fast, Hap darted to his location, propelled by the wind. The urgency of the situation fueled her speed.

Arriving with minutes to spare, Harper landed gracefully near the oak tree. "Mr. Morrows are you okay?" she asked, concern evident in her voice as she approached the grave keeper.

"I'm okay for now, do you think you could get me out of here?" Mr. Morrows replied, extending his hand in a silent request for assistance getting to his feet.

Harper, always quick to help, sheathed Firebrand and the Earthshapers, reaching out her right hand to meet his. The grave keeper's demeanor suddenly shifted, his eyes glinting with an eerie light.

Before Harper could react, he muttered, "Magnes Vinculum."

Instantly, their hands were snapped together by an invisible force, the sudden motion causing an audible slapping sound as their palms collided. A sense of dread washed over Hap as she realized something was amiss. She tried to pull away, but it was too late.

"Dolor Captura," Mr. Morrows continued, unphased by Hap's struggles to retreat.

As the final syllable left his lips, waves of excruciating pain radiated outward from the point of contact, as though thousands of needles were piercing her flesh. Harper's eyes widened in shock as the pain surged through her, overwhelming her senses. Unwavering, she continued to struggle, but the agony quickly became too unbearable, preventing even the simplest of thoughts from entering her mind.

As she struggled in vain, words began to leave Mr. Morrows' mouth, but the voice that emerged was not his. It was cold, mocking, and unmistakably female—a sinister tone that sent chills down Harper's spine. The voice was filled with cruel delight, relishing Harper's suffering. The realization hit her like a blow: this was not Mr. Morrows at all.

The voice sneered, "You really thought you could save him, didn't you? So naive."

Harper had walked right into a trap; the real Mr. Morrows was nowhere to be found, and Hap was now caught in the enemy's grasp.

"That was easy. Kids are so gullible," Lilith teased as she released the binding spell.

Disoriented and dizzy, Hap struggled to maintain her balance, but the world around her spun uncontrollably, the spin intensifying with each passing wave of pain until her legs gave way and she collapsed to the ground.

Lilith burst into diabolical laughter, the eerie echo reverberating through the air, capturing Winslow's attention. He turned just in time to witness Harper's crisis as Mr.

Morrows' form began to twist and shift, the facade of the stout grave keeper melting away. Before his eyes, Mr. Morrows' features morphed back into those of Lilith, her true form revealed once more. The transformation was as horrifying as it was mesmerizing.

Being so engrossed in the transformation, Winslow unknowingly stopped channeling the persistent wind. Frozen in shock, all he could do was watch as Lilith opened a crimson portal and stepped through, her laughter lingering as the portal began to shrink, collapsing in on itself until it was no longer visible.

Snapping back from the paralyzing reality, he knew he had to jump into action to save his best friend. Wasting no time, Wiki sprinted directly toward where Hap lay incapacitated. Time seemed to slow as thoughts raced through his mind, his heart pounding as he noticed two skeletons blocking his path.

"*I don't have time to deal with this. My only shot to get to her in time is to barrel through these guys,*" Winslow thought to himself as he raised his shield and positioned the majority of his body behind it.

Running faster than he had ever run before, Wiki slammed into the first undead with so much force that it flew backward, knocking the one behind it down. Raising his head to gauge how much further he needed to go, he noticed three creatures creeping closer to Hap with each passing second. The sight caused his stomach to sink, but he pressed on, as he became more worried with every step.

As he got closer, a group of five undead filled the narrow corridor, forcing him to stop his advancement.

Seeing past them, he noticed that the undead were now standing over Hap's position.

Overwhelmed by the gut-wrenching horror that he might never see his friend again, Winslow unleashed a vicious roar, "Nooooo!"

In that instant, a transparent shockwave of immense heat exploded forth from Winslow's core, distorting his vision with its sheer intensity. The air around him seemed to warp, and the heat was so intense that the stone pillars around him glowed a bright, molten orange. The undead that had stood in his way, along with those looming near Hap, were instantly reduced to ashen statues of their former selves–frozen in their final moments, now little more than tributes to a forgotten past–no longer a threat.

With his path now clear, Wiki sprinted to his friend's side, his heart pounding in his chest. He dropped to his knees beside Hap and immediately wrapped his arms around her, pulling her close. Tears streamed down his face as he held her limp body, the fear and guilt overwhelming him. He could barely process the destruction he had just unleashed; all that mattered was that Hap was safe, even if she wasn't conscious and able to reassure him.

"I'm so sorry, you wouldn't have even been here if it wasn't for me," Winslow cried as he squeezed his friend tighter.

"Fear not, young one," the water spirit said reassuringly. "She is not dead."

Hearing the spirit's words, Wiki looked up as Water continued speaking. "She has been cursed."

"Cursed? What do you mean?" Winslow asked, wiping his face, trying to regain his composure after the emotional turmoil.

"The corrupt group, The Fang, used ancient magic to curse her, but don't be alarmed. We have seen this before," Wind spoke up, attempting to console him further.

"She isn't moving," Winslow said anxiously. "When is she going to wake up?"

"She is unconscious," Water assured as it moved closer to Winslow and Harper. "The curse placed upon her does not physically harm her but rather torments her psychologically. It is very unpleasant, but she is not in immediate danger, unless left uncured for some time."

"What do I need to do?" Wiki inquired, eager to do whatever was needed to help his friend.

Water answered quickly, "In the book we gave you, you must seek out the story of Sigurd. But first please rest her back down, we have other matters to address."

"Yeah, you made quite a mess here," Wind jested as it gestured to the landscape around them.

Following the spirit's gesture, Wiki's gaze swept over the battlefield. Towering stone pillars—some still radiating a glow from the heat they held, others plastered in soot—blocked his ability to get the full picture.

Earth, picking up on the look of confusion, stated, "Here, let me help," before lowering the pillars back into the ground.

As the stone returned to its rightful resting place, Winslow could finally see the extent of what he had done without even realizing it. Countless petrified undead, frozen in their final moments, littered the area. A large radial portion of the ground was scorched black, devoid of life.

"Wow, I did all of that?" Wiki asked, feeling a mix of shame and accomplishment.

"I knew you were gifted with fire, but this is unprecedented," Fire spoke up, trying to alleviate some of Wiki's guilt.

"I'm sure you have some better fire tricks up your sleeve," Winslow jested, trying to understand what the fire spirit was implying.

Fire chuckled before replying, "I have indeed seen many things done with fire but never something with this much raw passion and intensity. Even the most seasoned of the blessed would have struggled to flash-cook an undead horde."

The water spirit interjected, "Now it is time for one of the most important things you will need to know as an aid to the spirits. As important as it is to combat evil, it is equally, if not more so, to restore natural order."

Water made its way to the center of the charred ground, urging Winslow to follow. The spirit did not rush to mend what was broken; it first listened, feeling the echoes of the souls that had been disturbed.

As Wiki observed, the water spirit began its work, coaxing the scorched ground to soften, release its tension, and allow restoration to take place. Where the earth had been cracked and blackened, it now shimmered with a subtle glow, healing from within. Fresh grass emerged first, tender shoots that grew stronger with each passing moment, spreading a lush green carpet over the prior battlefield.

"You still have much to learn with controlling your power. Eventually, you will be able to avoid such accidental devastation," Water instructed, connecting with the land's sorrow. Continuing, Water stated, "For now, let's not harbor on what ifs and instead restore what was, and should be."

After uttering those words, the once charred and withered trees began to straighten, their bark regaining its rich texture, their leaves sprouting in a vibrant burst of green. The foliage regaining its thick luscious state, and the flowers nestled within, blooming with vivid colors adding a touch of decorative design.

Finally, Water turned its attention to the petrified ashen statues scattered about the field. Approaching the closest one, the water spirit gracefully twirled its hand-like appendage, generating a medium-sized cyclone from its essence. The spirit gestured once more, splitting the whirling vortex.

Strategically spaced out, the liquid torrents swirled with purpose, drawing in the ashes of the undead with a gentle but relentless pull. The micro-nadoes scoured the area, seeking out and gathering every trace of ash left on the field, both statues and piles alike.

Once all of the remains had been collected, the miniature cyclones returned to the spirit, converging and merging back into one larger, unified vortex. The swirling aquatic anomaly now held the essence of the fallen undead, a final act of cleansing.

"Lastly, we need to put these poor innocent souls back to rest. Let's walk over to the graveyard," Water instructed.

Together, they made their way to Ashenfall cemetery, with the elemental torrent in tow, leaving the gardens a serene landscape once more.

Wiki, with thoughts racing through his mind, nodded to signify he understood as he followed suit. After briefly cutting through the thick underbrush of the tree line, they emerged at the cemetery.

With another quick gesture, the water spirit sent the cyclone over the disturbed gravesites.

As the torrent passed over each grave, a light pulsed from within, coalescing and reforming the ashes with a deliberate grace. Like a master artisan sculpting from memory, the energy wove the fragments of bone back together, piece by piece. Once fully intact, it gently laid the reformed skeletal remains back to eternal slumber.

As the last bone was laid to rest, the torrent dissipated, raining its droplets to the ground. With another gesture from the spirit, the water flowed in gossamer streams that weaved through the dirt and grass, acting as sutures, stitching the ground closed and sealing them with a reverent touch. Wiki watched in awe at the elemental prowess on display, marveling at the power to heal and restore.

As he took in the scene, something caught his eye. "Hey, look over there," he pointed, drawing Water's attention to what he had found.

Winslow and Water moved over to the unconscious figure lying near one of the graves. To their surprise, it was Mr. Morrows, the grave keeper.

"This fragile man has seen things his mind will not be able to comprehend," Water stated, as it gently enveloped Mr. Morrows in a sphere of swirling water, slightly elevating him off the ground. The water spirit continued, "Let's replace those nightmares with something more pleasant."

As Water's calming influence took hold, Mr. Morrows' expression softened, and he was carefully lowered back to the ground, now resting peacefully. With their task complete, they returned to Harper's side.

Earth greeted Winslow with good news, "Look who is beginning to wake," it said, pointing to Hap as she began to stir.

Winslow's elation was evident as he rushed to her side. "Thank goodness! I was worried you were a goner," he said, relief flooding his voice. He gently helped her sit up before asking, "Is she still cursed?"

Interrupting, Hap said shakily, "The pain I'm feeling now is nowhere near what I was feeling before."

Jumping in to explain, Fire responded in a serious tone, "You may not be in as much pain now, but you are still very much cursed. This particular curse intensifies with time, the pain you felt initially was just a taste of how bad it could become if not dealt with promptly. You will have until the next full moon to find the cure before it becomes unbearable."

Earth spoke up, adding, "For now, I think it best you both return. Harper needs rest and Wiki you have a mountainous task ahead of you, so you will also need to be well rested."

At that statement, Wind took it upon itself to open a portal. Through the shimmering edges, Winslow could see the house of mirrors peeking through. With urgency, Wiki helped Hap to her feet, and together, they stepped through the portal, leaving the gardens behind.

Reappearing at the festival, surrounded by mirrors, the friends wasted no time finishing the maze, their playful mood from earlier, now replaced with determination. As they stepped back into the crowd, Winslow scanned the area for his mom and sister, his eyes finally landing on the merry-go-round.

After ten minutes of searching, he heard his name being called from behind.

"Winslow!"

He turned to the familiar voice and saw Willow standing in line with their mother, waiting for another turn on the ride.

"What's wrong with Hap?" Mrs. Kinney asked as the friends got closer, noticing that Harper wasn't her usual spunky self.

"I'm not sure. We were in the house of mirrors, and she just started to feel sick. Maybe it was the turkey leg?" Winslow shrugged, trying to downplay the situation.

"Well, I'm sorry, Willow, but we need to get Hap home now. Thankfully, you have already ridden this four times," Mrs. Kinney said, gently but firmly, as she began escorting the children back to the car.

The ride to Harper's house was mostly silent, with the radio playing quietly in the background. When they arrived, Mrs. Kinney helped Hap out of the back seat, up to the front door, and knocked.

Answering the door, Mr. Jones stated, "Y'all are early–" He paused as he captured a glimpse of his ill looking daughter, asking, "What's wrong, Champ?"

"I think the turkey leg is trying to take me out. I am really tired," Hap wearily responded as she made her way into the house.

"I have no idea what happened, Harper and Winslow said they were in the house of mirrors when she started feeling unwell. Then they came to find me, and I brought her home quickly," Mrs. Kinney explained, providing the details she had.

Mr. Jones replied, "I appreciate you taking good care of her," before turning his attention toward Harper, saying, "Let's get you to bed, Champ."

Mrs. Kinney, seeing that Mr. Jones had turned his attention to his daughter, bid them both farewell before heading back to the car. As they drove away, thoughts raced back and forth through Winslow's mind, the only constant was the name, Sigurd.

Chapter 36

Winslow laid in bed, but sleep did not come easily. He twisted beneath the blankets, as if even in sleep he could not escape the turmoil within. His brow furrowed and his lips parted in barely audible murmurs calling out Harper's name, his worry slipping through the fragile boundary of his dreams. Every few moments, he rolled to one side, then the other, sheets tangling around him like the snares of his anxious mind.

Suddenly, he bolted upright. His heart raced, his breath ragged as though he'd been running, driven by a sudden sense of urgency. A sharp clarity pierced through the fog of sleep, propelling him to full awareness in an instant. The room was still steeped in the soft dimness of early dawn, a pallid light barely touching the edges of the window. Squinting at the sliver of light creeping into the room, he realized he was awake earlier than usual.

With extra morning time and a singular mission on his mind, he leapt from his bed, pulled out his chair, and sat at his desk before 'The Spirit Blessed Chronicles.' Winslow's fingers traced the embossed title before he guided it toward the top right corner of the cover, paying extra attention to how it felt.

Gripping it with his pointer finger and thumb, he turned to the first page, its surface rough and brittle, the edges yellowed and uneven, as if touched by centuries of time. The faint scent of aged ink and dust lingered, and the texture felt almost like dried leaves, fragile under his fingertips.

In a font with elaborate flourishes and uneven strokes was large writing: "*Any attempt to exploit the spirits' powers for selfish gain or nefarious purposes would result in the withdrawal of their blessing.*"

Underneath the warning more words began to form before his eyes, "*Whom do you seek?*"

The question seemed to pulse with a quiet intensity, drawing Winslow in. He closed his eyes, letting his thoughts settle on Sigurd, the name given to him by the Wind spirit. He focused on that name, allowing it to fill his thoughts, uncertain of who Sigurd truly was or what he would discover.

As his mind centered on Sigurd, the words on the page shimmered. The ink twisted and reformed, spreading across the parchment like ripples in water until new words began to emerge, revealing Sigurd's story in vivid detail.

Winslow's eyes, delighted by the spectacle before him, waited for the words to settle before beginning to read aloud quietly. The story unfolding in the dim light of the room, its tone grave and laden with meaning.

It was the tale of Sigurd, Fafnir, and Regin, but not quite the version the world knew. This was the true story, hidden behind layers of myth and legend.

"Long ago, in the rugged lands where the cold wind sang of ancient secrets, there lived a mighty dragon named Fafnir. Once a dwarf of noble heart, Fafnir was corrupted by his father's cursed hoard of gold which he desired."

"The treasure, bewitched by the greed of those who had coveted it before, twisted Fafnir's soul, transforming him into a creature of greed and malice. His once-dwarven heart, beat with the rhythm of avarice, and his scales grew as hard as iron—his breath like molten fire."

"Fafnir's brother, Regin, watched with growing despair as the curse consumed him. Yet Regin, too, desired the gold, though he hid this longing deep within his heart. It was said that the gold could bring immense power, but only to those willing to bear its curse. Regin bided his time, searching for a way to reclaim what he believed was rightfully his."

"Into this tale entered Sigurd, a warrior of the Spirit Blessed. Sigurd was among the greatest of them, his mastery over fire, wind, water, and earth was renowned. He *was not driven by greed but by a sense of duty and the hope of freeing the land from the curse that darkened it."*

"Regin saw in Sigurd the means to his end. With a silver tongue, he convinced Sigurd to slay the dragon, weaving a tale of heroism and the glory that awaited him. He told Sigurd of Fafnir's tyranny, of how the dragon's mere presence poisoned the land and twisted the hearts of men. Sigurd, moved by the plight of the people, agreed to confront Fafnir."

"The hero set out to the barren, rocky mountains where Fafnir made his lair. With his ancestral sword and the power of the elements, Sigurd faced the dragon. The battle was furious, shaking the earth and scorching the sky. Fafnir's fire roared against the elemental fury that Sigurd unleashed. Wind and flame clashed, and the earth trembled

beneath their struggle. Sigurd fought with a strength and skill unmatched, but he did not fight with hate nor greed. His strikes were precise, his movements guided not by the desire to kill but to end the suffering."

"In the end, Sigurd struck a grievous blow. Fafnir, brought low by the wound, collapsed with a thunderous crash. As the dragon lay vulnerable, Regin appeared, his eyes gleaming with the greed he had long concealed. Drawing his blade, he moved to end Fafnir's life and claim the gold. But Sigurd, understanding the true nature of the curse, stood in his way."

"'Do not let greed guide your hand,' Sigurd said, his voice resonating with the authority of the elements. 'This gold is a curse, one that has already claimed your brother. To take it now would be to seal your fate as well.'"

"Regin, blinded by his desire, lashed out at Sigurd. The two clashed, the air around them crackling with energy. With a sweep of Sigurd's hand, he summoned a gale that knocked Regin back, leaving him breathless and dazed."

"Sigurd did not strike a final blow but instead reached out to Regin, not with force but with words. 'If you kill him,' Sigurd said, 'you will become the very thing you despise. Let us end this curse here and now, in a way that does not require more blood.'"

"Regin hesitated, his desire for the gold warring with the truth in Sigurd's words. In that moment, he saw the future laid bare—the endless cycle of greed and death that would follow if he took Fafnir's life. Slowly, he lowered his weapon. Sigurd, seeing this, began the final act of his quest. He called upon the deep magic of the earth, the ancient power of the Spirit Blessed, to banish Fafnir and the cursed hoard to a place beyond the reach of mortals. The ground opened, revealing a rift that led to a realm untouched by the desires of men."

"As Fafnir was pulled toward the rift, he wept, his tears shimmering in the cold light of the cavern. They fell to the ground, crystallizing into droplets of pure magic, capable of breaking any curse. It was his final act, a gift born from his own suffering–a way to ensure that others would not fall as he had."

"Sigurd turned to Regin once more. 'This is not the end, but a new beginning. The gold is gone, the curse with it. But you, Regin, you can live without its shadow.' Sigurd then used his power to summon forth riches from the earth, veins of gold and gems that would sustain Regin's wealth *and nobility. In exchange, Regin swore an oath to keep the secret of what had truly happened to Fafnir, letting the world believe the dragon had been slain."*

"And so, the tale of Sigurd and Fafnir was told in a different light. The world spoke of the hero who slew the dragon and claimed the cursed gold. However, those that know the truth whisper of a man who chose compassion over glory, who saw beyond the desire for power and saved not just the land but the soul of another."

After reading the story, Winslow felt a slight shift in the air, a gentle breeze that stirred the stillness of the room.

The curtains fluttered softly, and within moments, the familiar presence of the Wind spirit began to manifest.

"You seek answers, Wiki," Wind whispered, its voice a soft, melodic breeze. "Sigurd's story is but the beginning. There are many lessons within it–courage, compassion, and the danger of greed. It is an excellent example of how a Spirit Blessed should live their life and view the world around them. For now, however, we should stay focused on the task at hand. We don't have much time to talk, meet me in the woods so that we may discuss things in further detail."

Before Winslow could ask more, a sudden voice broke through the moment, grounding him abruptly back in reality.

"Winslow! Time to get up! Breakfast will be ready in five minutes!" his mother's voice called from downstairs.

Wiki turned his head and called back to his mother, "Yes, ma'am!"

As he turned to face Wind, the shimmering form of the spirit was already fading as quickly as it had come. He sighed, running a hand through his hair, feeling both the weight of what he had just heard and the pull of everyday life.

Despite the urgency of his friend's worsening curse, which gnawed at his thoughts, Winslow knew he had to wait until later to get more answers. With a fake smile, attempting to hide his intrusive thoughts, he gently closed 'The Spirit Blessed Chronicles' and stood up before changing clothes and making his way downstairs.

After breakfast, Wiki set out with the urgency of his mission pushing him forward. The morning sun had risen higher in the sky, casting a warm, golden light over the neighborhood as he walked briskly toward Harper's house. The branches overhead moved with a subtle creak, swaying uneasily as if echoing the restless, circling thoughts that swarmed in his mind.

He arrived at Hap's door, knocking softly but insistently, hoping she was alright. As the seconds stretched, Wiki's heart pounded with worry. Finally, the door opened, revealing Mr. Jones. He looked tired, with dark circles under his eyes, but he still managed a kind smile.

"Winslow," Mr. Jones greeted, his voice a mix of warmth and weariness. "Harper's still resting, she just needs time."

Winslow nodded, a weight still on his chest but slightly lighter knowing she was safe, at least for now.

"Thank you for the update Mr. Jones. I just wanted to hear that she was okay," he said.

"That's very thoughtful of you Winslow. I will be sure to let her know you stopped by to check on her," Mr. Jones replied caringly.

With a final nod to Harper's father, Winslow turned and headed down the path, his feet quickening as he made his way toward the woods where Wind awaited. When he finally arrived at the clearing, he felt the air stir around him, and within moments, the Wind spirit's form materialized.

Wiki took a deep breath, then spoke, "Wind, those crystallized tears from Fafnir's original banishment, can they still help Hap?"

Wind's form shimmered, the spirit appearing almost saddened. "Wiki, those tears are no more. Curses, you see, were once common, and many sought the tears' magic until nothing was left."

Winslow's heart sank, but he gathered his resolve, knowing there had to be another way. "Okay, but what do I do now? There's got to be something else I can try..."

Wind nodded, the breeze around them picking up slightly, swirling with an unseen intensity. "You must venture to Fafnir's prison, deep beneath the Earth's surface. It is there that new tears may be harvested, for Fafnir still weeps in his eternal confinement. But know this—Fafnir's prison is not easily reached. It lies far below, in a place of danger and darkness, branching off of the Terranexus."

The spirit continued, its voice becoming more somber, "Winslow, you must understand—Fafnir's prison is a place where no magic will function. This is because of the binding Sigurd placed upon Fafnir during his banishment. Sigurd gave up the ability to use his own magic within the prison to ensure that no magic of any kind could work there. You cannot rely on your elemental abilities once you enter."

Winslow's eyes widened, a chill running through him at the thought of being without magic in a place as dangerous as Fafnir's lair.

"Then... how am I supposed to do this?" he asked, his voice quivering slightly.

Wind answered, "That is why we must prepare you. There are artifacts and natural items that may assist you where magic cannot. First, you will need the petraflor; a rare flower whose scent is potent enough to overpower your own, masking your presence from Fafnir's keen sense of smell. Without it, he would sense you from far away, making your task impossible. Fortunately, I have brought one for you."

Wind extended its ethereal hand, and a delicate, vibrant blue flower appeared, its petals gleaming faintly in the morning light. "Take it, Wiki. This will help you on your journey. Simply keep it on your person and no creature will be able to catch your scent."

Winslow nodded, accepting the flower and carefully storing it away in the left pocket of his backpack, ensuring it was secure before looking back at Wind for more information.

"Now that we have a solution for Fafnir's sense of smell, we must address his eyesight," Wind said. "Dragons, being aerial predators, have exceptionally sharp vision. I have just the right tool for the job, a cloak woven with threads imbued by the ancient light of dawn, the Shroud of First Light. It reflects the surrounding light, rendering you nearly invisible. I crafted the cloak to aid the Spirit Blessed long ago, for times when magic alone would not suffice. It will help you avoid detection, but you must still tread carefully. The cloak does not hide sound, nor can it mask sudden movements."

Wind raised its arm, and a shimmer in the air began to solidify, forming into a cloak. Slowly, the Shroud of First Light appeared, its fabric seemingly woven from the rays of dawn itself. The cloak shimmered with a gentle luminescence, shifting colors from soft gold to pale blue, like the first moments of morning breaking over the horizon.

Wiki reached out, his fingers brushing the delicate yet sturdy fabric. It felt cool to the touch, and for a moment, the light seemed to blend with his skin, making his hand almost vanish before his eyes. A sense of awe washed over him, the enormity of the task ahead feeling just a bit more achievable with such a powerful artifact in his possession.

"Thank you," Winslow whispered, carefully folding the cloak, unzipping the backpack and placing it securely inside. "I really appreciate these gifts to help! One question though, how exactly do I get to Terranexus?"

"There is no way to reach the Terranexus through conventional means. Good thing you have me on your side," Wind said as it winked, asking "Are you ready?"

"It's go time!" Wiki said before nervously chuckling.

Wind raised its arms, and the air around them swirled, forming a shimmering portal of wind and mist.

"Remember, Wiki, the marking you bear will guide you. Trust in its power, and let it lead you through the darkness." The spirit paused, its eyes focused on Winslow, and its tone softened, "You have the strength to succeed, Winslow. Believe in yourself as I do."

Wiki nodded and swallowed hard before stepping toward the portal, ready to face whatever was on the other side.

As Winslow emerged, he found himself standing in the heart of the Terranexus–a vast underground cavern that was alive with movement. The cavern stretched out endlessly, its ceiling lost in shadow, while glowing fungi and iridescent crystals bathed the area in a soft, ethereal light. Among them, strange plants grew in clusters, their faintly glowing petals enhancing the otherworldly ambiance.

Winslow's eyes widened as he took in the diverse array of creatures around him. Tall, slender beings with sparkling scales and elongated limbs moved gracefully between the towering stalagmites, their eyes glancing his way with curiosity.

Small, furry creatures with luminescent eyes scurried across the ground, weaving between rocks and glowing vegetation, their noses twitching as they studied the newcomer.

Winged beings flitted about, their delicate wings catching the light as they flew between the towering formations above.

A large serpentine creature with scales that shined in hues of green and blue slithered closer, its eyes locking onto Wiki's. For a brief moment, he held his breath, but the creature simply regarded him before dipping its head in acknowledgment.

Winslow adjusted the straps of his backpack, reassured by the gifts he had received from Wind. He took a deep breath and raised his palm in front of his face, exposing the marking on his right hand. The wind element atop his mark began to pulse faintly, guiding him forward.

Wiki continued to navigate through the caverns with his mark. The air was damp, carrying with it a musty scent, mixed with the earthy aroma of moss and mineral deposits. His footsteps were muted by the thick layers of emerald carpeting that covered the ground, but the echoes of distant movement hinted at the presence of creatures hidden in the shadows.

After some time, Winslow found his path blocked by a massive creature that seemed to have emerged from the very walls themselves. Its skin was textured like stone, covered in patches of bioluminescent moss, and its broad form towered over him, casting a shadow that swallowed him completely.

The creature's eyes, deep-set and glimmering faintly like polished onyx, regarded Wiki with an inscrutable expression. It let out a deep, guttural sound, something between a growl and a word, a warning in a dialect that Winslow could not understand.

Wiki hesitated, feeling a momentary surge of fear. He could sense the weight of its gaze, the caution in its stance. Despite not understanding its words, Winslow instinctively knew that it was giving him a warning, testing his intentions.

He kept his posture relaxed, making no sudden movements, and after what felt like an eternity, the creature slowly shifted its massive form to the side, allowing Winslow to pass. Wiki gave a small nod of gratitude as he stepped forward, the path ahead now open.

Winslow pressed on, the air growing colder as he delved deeper into the Terranexus. The path grew increasingly treacherous, with jagged rocks jutting out at odd angles, slick with condensation. Despite the difficult terrain, Winslow moved with surprising ease. The rocks seemed to shift subtly, creating just enough space for him to pass. Narrow passages, though tight, allowed him to squeeze through without resistance.

As Wiki approached a narrow ledge, he noticed the sheer drop beside him disappeared into an endless darkness. The walls spanning the pit were rough and jagged, and he could feel the dampness clinging to his skin.

As Wiki stepped cautiously onto the ledge, he noticed the flickering glow of molten magma flowing from a crack in the cavern wall, spilling across his path before plunging into the chasm below. The magma hissed and bubbled, casting dancing orange and red shadows that made the walls flicker as though they were alive. The heat radiating from it was intense, a wave of warmth that should have been unbearable, but he was unfazed.

He took careful steps across the ledge, meticulously avoiding the liquid fire. The rock beneath his feet stayed firm, seemingly shifting ever so slightly to ensure he could pass without incident.

After traversing the ledge, he noticed the passage opened up in the distance. He moved forward until finally emerging into a large chamber. The ceiling arched high above him, the rocky surface glowing faintly from the crystals embedded within. At the far end of the chamber stood an imposing door, massive and wrought from a dark metal. Intricate runes and symbols etched into the surface, pulsated faintly, as if sensing Winslow's presence.

The marking on Wiki's hand began to fade as he approached the door. He glanced down, watching the pulse diminish until it disappeared entirely, swallowed by the powerful magical barrier surrounding the prison. The realization hit him that no magic would work beyond this point, amplifying his nervousness.

Wiki took a deep breath and stepped closer to the door. As he did, the runes flared to life, casting an eerie glow across the chamber. A deep, omniscient voice resonated from the door, reverberating through the air and into Winslow's very bones.

"You are worthy, but be warned, nothing within can be trusted," the voice echoed with a grim finality as the massive door creaked open, revealing the darkness beyond.

Wiki hesitated, the weight of the warning settling heavily on his shoulders. After a moment, he steeled his resolve and retrieved the Shroud of First Light. The cloak shimmered faintly in the dim light of the chamber, its threads reflecting the soft glow of the crystals around him. Winslow carefully draped it over his shoulders, fastening it securely before stepping forward.

Upon entering, Wiki was immediately struck by an overwhelming sense of unease. The air was thick and oppressive, carrying with it the unmistakable scent of damp earth and something metallic—perhaps the centuries-old tang of the gold hoarded within. The cavern was dimly lit, with only the occasional glint of gold catching the faint glow of luminescent fungi along the walls.

As Winslow took cautious steps forward, a whisper brushed against his ear, barely louder than the rustling of his cloak. The voice was soft, familiar, his mother's voice.

"Take it, Winslow. All of this could be yours. Think of what you could do for us," it said, a warmth that tugged at his heart.

The golden glint of treasure piled in the distance seemed to pulse with each word, a faint glistening that made the promise almost believable. Wiki shook his head, trying to push aside the confusion. He took another step, and another voice joined, this time Harper's.

"With this wealth, Wiki, you could protect me. You could save me," it urged, her voice laced with desperation.

Winslow clenched his fists, his knuckles whitening beneath the Shroud. The voices were familiar, comforting even, but he knew they were wrong, he knew they couldn't be real. The cavern itself seemed to press in on him, the shadows deepening, and the light from the crystals danced across the walls.

Then came his sister's voice, softer, almost pleading, "Wiki, think of all the power you could wield. Think of how you could change everything, how you could make it all better."

The words seemed to wrap around his thoughts, a tempting echo that refused to let go. His heart ached, the desire to protect, to do more, striking a chord deep within him.

He stopped, overwhelmed by the rising tide of voices, their insistent whispers pressing in on him from all sides. The gold seemed almost alive now, whispering, urging him to reach out and take it.

Winslow closed his eyes, trying to find something to anchor himself. Then, the image of Hap flashed in his mind— her face pale and her body weak, relying on him to save her. The stark vision cut through the noise, snapping him back to reality.

"No," he whispered, his voice trembling at first but growing stronger. "This is not real. You are not real."

He forced himself to keep moving forward, his eyes fixed ahead, refusing to let the piles of gold and the voices deter him. The whispers grew louder, more persistent, surrounding him from every direction, but Winslow drew strength from the image of Harper—hurt and in pain, relying on him. That image anchored him, filling him with resolve. His steps became steadier, each one a rejection of the lies, each one a promise to himself to keep pushing forward, no matter the temptation.

With every step he took, the voices began to fade, slowly merging into a low, almost growl-like snore that reverberated through the cavern. The distant drip of water echoed softly against the stone, blending with the rumbling sound. Wiki's curiosity piqued as the noise grew more distinct, and he continued forward.

As he rounded the corner of a massive wall, the dim glow of the cavern revealed the massive side profile of a dragon, Fafnir, his scaled head resting on a mound of treasure, his eyes closed, and his deep, rhythmic breaths filling the chamber.

A sudden, soft whimper escaped from Fafnir as the dragon shifted slightly in his sleep. The sound was almost pitiable, a fleeting glimpse into the creature's sorrow. Winslow watched, his eyes widening as a single tear rolled from the corner of Fafnir's closed eye. The tear glistened faintly as it fell, crystalizing, hardening into a small, glistening gem before striking the ground with a soft "*Clink.*"

Wiki held his breath, eyes darting between the sleeping dragon and the tear. He carefully moved closer, noticing the faint glimmer of dust-like particles scattered across the gold—remnants of tears that had fallen before, their essence forever mingled with the hoard. The gold around Fafnir seemed darker, touched by the sadness imbued within those tears.

Winslow knew what he had to do. He crouched down slowly, extending his hand toward the newly formed tear. His fingers closed around the solidified gem, its surface cool and smooth against his skin. Carefully, he placed the crystallized tear into his backpack, securing it in one of the inner pockets.

As he moved to hoist his bag back onto his shoulders, his foot brushed against a pile of gold, sending a few coins clattering across the cavern floor. The noise echoed sharply in the silence, and Winslow froze, his heart racing. He watched as the dragon's eye before him twitched, the heavy eyelid lifting abruptly to reveal a glowing slit-pupil, now fixed on the source of the disturbance.

Fafnir's head lifted slowly, nostrils flaring as he sniffed the air. His deep, rumbling voice echoed through the cavern, "That scent... it has been long since I smelled the petraflor. You're a clever one aren't you?"

The dragon's massive head turned slightly, his eyes narrowing as he scanned the darkness, searching for the unseen intruder. There was a moment of silence before Fafnir's tone shifted, curiosity lacing his words. "Who dares enter my lair? Come forth and perhaps I shall share my vast treasure with you. Riches beyond your wildest dreams lie here, and I am willing to share... if only you reveal yourself."

Wiki, not tempted by the dragon's false promises yet frozen in fear, scanned the cavern for a way out of his predicament.

Fafnir, growing impatient at the lack of response, let out a low growl, his irritation clear. The dragon's enormous tail swept across the cavern floor, the gust of wind from its movement scattering coins and sending sharp clattering sounds echoing through the chamber. The force of the movement was meant to spook Winslow into revealing himself, but he held his ground, refusing to move or make a sound.

After several more sweeps of his tail yielded no results, Fafnir's patience began to wear thin, his irritation transforming into rage. His slit-pupil eyes narrowed, and a guttural growl escaped his throat.

"You think you can hide from me, thief?" Fafnir snarled.

He inhaled deeply, his chest expanding as heat gathered in his core.

Winslow's eyes widened in terror as he realized what was coming. Without another moment's hesitation, Fafnir unleashed a torrent of fire, the intense heat blasting across the cavern in a sweeping arc.

Wiki dove to the side, narrowly avoiding the wave of flames as he scrambled across the uneven piles of treasure. The cloak shimmered, attempting to blend with its surroundings, but the movement made it difficult to stay completely hidden.

Fafnir caught faint glimpses of Winslow's form—a flicker of motion, a shadow where there should be none—and roared in fury. The dragon's fiery breath scorched the cavern once more, forcing Wiki to keep moving, each desperate step, a struggle to stay ahead of the raging beast.

Winslow, caught in a precarious situation, dashed between bursts of flame and piles of treasure, his heart pounding faster as Fafnir's fiery breath roared past him. The air was thick with the acrid scent of smoke, and each burst of heat made it harder to breathe.

Moving quickly, he ducked beneath fallen relics and weaved through a narrow pathway formed by the hoarded piles of gold before diving for cover behind a partially buried golden throne that lay on its side.

"Whoa! That was close!" Wiki thought to himself as the intense heat seared the air around him, grazing his arm and leaving a stinging reminder of the close call.

Taking a moment to analyze the situation, he realized that in the heat of the moment he had not headed back the way he came. Without the option to double back, he needed to devise another plan. Scanning the lair quickly, he noticed a rather small crevice at the junction of two massive walls in the center of the cavern.

"I think I can get through there," Wiki thought to himself. *"But I'll never make it without a distraction."*

Looking around for a way to create a diversion, he caught a glimpse of a red ruby peeking out from the gold pile next to him. Without hesitation, he snatched up a glorious goblet in his right hand. He reared back his arm and sent it soaring through the air toward the adjacent wall.

"Clink! Tink! Clink!" rang out as the goblet ricocheted off the wall's hard surface, struck the gold that acted as a metallic floor liner, and skittered to a stop.

The loud noise pulled the attention of Fafnir, as the dragon turned its head, Winslow made a run for the tight passageway, struggling to keep his footing as he raced across uneven piles of gold. The metal shifted beneath him, each step a precarious gamble as the coins threatened to slip out from under his feet.

Fafnir, catching a fleeting glimpse of movement despite the shimmering cloak, turned his massive head and bellowed, "There you are, mischievous one!"

The roar reverberated through the cavern, shaking the very foundation.

With a furious glint in his eyes, the dragon unleashed another fiery assault, a stream of fire surging toward Wiki's path. The flames lit up the darkened lair, reflecting off the mounds of gold and casting wild shadows across the walls. Winslow could feel the scorching heat on his heels as he made one final effort to dive toward the crevice and rolled through.

He could hear Fafnir's deep, enraged snorts and the scrape of his claws against the stone as the dragon pursued him, determined to flush out the intruder. After being nearly missed by the dragon's flame, he hastily got back to his feet and ran for the chamber door. The dragon's rage amplified and echoed behind Winslow as he made his way across the threshold, exiting the lair.

"*Phew! That was too close for comfort,*" he thought to himself as he peered down at his stinging arm.

"Hey Wiki! This way," a familiar voice called out from his right. Turning his head, Winslow noticed the portal was now at the chamber entrance.

"I thought you said I had to go through the Terranexus?" Winslow questioned.

"The trip through the Terranexus was for your benefit. You are the champion of the Terra Vitae realm. As such, your sole responsibility is to protect its inhabitants from the Corrupted's touch, ensuring balance. I thought it would be a good idea to introduce you to beings that you probably didn't even know existed," Wind said with a light-hearted, soft giggle.

Stepping through the portal, the dim lit atmosphere transformed in an instant. The familiar sounds of birds chirping surrounded him from all directions. With a quick glance, Wiki reassessed his surroundings; the lush green and soft brown hues immediately gave him comfort.

With a sigh of relief, Wiki asked, "So, what do I need to do now?"

"You've done quite enough!" Wind said with pride, admiring the young blessed one's bravery through such a trying quest. "For now, you should take care of your arm and leave the rest up to us," Wind reassured before continuing, "I just need the tear and to know a beverage that brings Harper joy."

Winslow nodded as he placed his bag on the ground at his feet, retrieved the tear, and handed it to Wind.

"She absolutely loves hot chocolate with marshmallows!" he declared, excitement lacing his voice as the thought of seeing his friend happy and healthy raced through his mind.

The spirit smiled, saying, "You really should be proud of your accomplishment today. Take solace in knowing that you've done everything you needed to do and give Harper a call in the morning."

With a wink, Wind faded into the breeze.

Wiki picked his bag up and took a seat on a tree stump nearby. He closed his eyes and took a deep breath of relief. Once his adrenaline wore off, the sting of his arm reminded him that his job was not done yet.

Opening his eyes, he removed his cloak, folded it, and placed it neatly in his backpack. After zipping it up and placing it on the ground, he repositioned himself on the stump to face the creek and proceeded to heal himself before heading home for a much-deserved dinnertime feast.

Chapter 37

As Lilith strode through the darkened chamber, her eyes flickered with fretfulness. The air was thick with the metallic scent of blood, mingling with the acrid smoke from the many torches that lined the stone walls. Shadows danced across her sharp features as she approached the large crescent altar in the middle of the room, where groups of members worked in stations, toiling with gruesome precision.

The first group worked over the altar meticulously, their faces impassive. Individually, in turn, tiny forms were brought forth, their lives ended swiftly with a precise motion. There was no ceremony, only the mechanical efficiency of their movements working to harvest the precious essence of the animals—once soft and innocent, now lifeless shells—into a foreboding hollow at its core, swallowing each offering in a quiet, endless thirst.

Nearby, another group handled the butchering, their crimson-stained hands working skillfully to separate what was needed from what could be discarded. The chamber echoed with the sickening squelch of blades slicing through tissue, each thud and crack resonating in the confined space. They worked in silence, their eyes reflecting the dim light, focused on the task of preparing each piece, ensuring the components were cut free without imperfection.

Further along, another group busied themselves by arranging the finished pieces, inspecting them carefully, as if they were precious relics. They lined them up with the utmost care, scrutinizing each for the perfect match and organizing them for efficiency. Each one was a small, macabre part of a larger vision, and the importance of perfection was evident in the stern gazes of those overseeing the work.

At the final station, one figure sat hunched over a raised platform, needle and sinew in hand. With deliberate, practiced movements, they continued stitching the individual pieces together. The needle pierced through, drawing thread and pulling the pieces closer, the sound barely audible over the haunting melody of the butchering station. Slowly, piece by piece, a creation began to take form, each stitch binding the power and purpose they needed. The acolyte's hands moved deftly, their expression blank as they worked, unaware or uncaring of the weight of the atrocities committed in the name of their dark purpose.

Lilith, while observing, made eye contact with Alistair, who was franticly navigating back and forth between the groups, ensuring they stayed focused and on task.

She inquired, "How much longer until we are ready?"

"The last groups have been dispatched to acquire the remaining innocents. We should be done within a few hours," he responded, not stopping as he continued to oversee the groups of members working diligently.

Lilith nodded curtly at Alistair's response, turned on her heel and began her journey to report to the high priestess, Seraphine. Lilith moved purposefully toward the stone spiral staircase, her footsteps echoing.

With each deliberate stride up the dimly lit stairwell, the flickering torches seemed to dance in rhythm with her movements, guiding her step by step until she reached the top floor of the underground lair.

Crossing through the archway onto the first floor, Lilith proceeded into a narrow corridor that led to the vast meeting hall, a chamber of dark grandeur. It featured theater-style standing spaces that encircled a platform at the center, giving an impression of a somber arena. Pressing on, Lilith's eyes remained forward, ignoring the empty standing areas.

As she approached the far end of the hall, her eyes fixated on Seraphine's door—an intricately carved masterpiece of dark wood, depicting scenes of conquest and sacrifice. The carvings seemed almost alive, the figures etched in the door twisting and writhing in the dim light, telling stories of victories and tributes offered to their master.

Lilith took a moment to steady herself, adjusting her cloak before raising her hand to knock, the sound reverberating through the empty hall. She waited, her eyes never leaving the door, her expression composed, ready to deliver her report.

Seraphine called out, "Who is at my door?"

Quickly responding, "It is I, High Priestess, with news of the ritual," Lilith answered, awaiting permission to enter.

"Come forth, my child," the high priestess invited.

Lilith opened the door and stepped into the chamber, her gaze meeting Seraphine's cold, calculating eyes.

She bowed her head slightly, a gesture of respect before she spoke, "High Priestess, the preparations for the summoning are nearly complete. We have secured all but five of the components, and our scouts are in the process of retrieving them."

Seraphine, seated on an intricately carved stone chair, her robes flowing around her like dark water, listened without expression. She nodded slowly, her fingers tapping rhythmically on the armrest.

"Good, Lilith," she said, her voice smooth and deliberate. "But there is something else I require of you."

Lilith's brow shifted slightly, allowing a glimpse of confusion to bleed through her stern expression though she quickly composed herself, waiting for Seraphine to continue.

The high priestess leaned forward and said, "There is a special task–one that requires your... particular skills," her eyes locking onto Lilith's with an intensity that seemed to freeze the very air.

Lilith straightened, her heart pounding beneath her composed exterior, "Of course, High Priestess."

Seraphine glided over to her wardrobe. She opened the dark carved doors and retrieved a silver ring. Returning to where Lilith stood, Seraphine extended her hand, her long-pointed nails glinting under the flickering torchlight. With a slow, deliberate motion, she offered the ring to Lilith.

Without hesitation, Lilith retrieved the band, her fingers brushing against Seraphine's in the exchange. The ring felt unexpectedly cool against her skin, sending a shiver running through her as she pulled it closer for inspection.

Her eyes widened slightly as she examined it in detail. It was polished to a mirror-like finish that reflected its surroundings with supernatural clarity. Faint etchings of spider-silk filigree wove around the outer surface, wrapping the silver in a subtle tracery of interlocking spirals and arcs.

"It's exquisite... so intricate," Lilith murmured, her voice filled with awe.

"Just wait, my dear, until you see what it can do," Seraphine replied as her lips curled into a faint sinister smile.

Chapter 38

Winslow woke early, feeling the jittery excitement bubbling in his chest. He couldn't wait to call Harper and check on how she was feeling. He tossed and turned in his bed, his eyes darting every few moments to the flip-clock on his nightstand, its numbers quietly cycling with a soft mechanical whir, as he tried to gauge when his mom might be downstairs. He knew he couldn't call Hap too early and risk waking the whole house, especially not without his mom's permission.

After what felt like forever, but was really only ten or fifteen minutes, Wiki decided he couldn't wait any longer. He pushed his blankets aside and swung his feet over the edge of the bed. The cool floor sent a shiver up his spine, but it also invigorated him.

He had just enough time to get dressed before his alarm went off. He pulled on his favorite shirt, a blue one with a faded logo, and tugged his jeans up, fastening them as he cast a quick glance at the clock. With a triumphant grin, Winslow reached over and squelched the alarm just as it was about to start buzzing.

He could hear his mom moving around downstairs, her voice calling up, "Kids, time to get up!"

Already awake and dressed, Wiki raced down the stairs, his heart thudding with excitement.

Entering the kitchen, Wiki found his mom pouring coffee into her favorite mug. The scent of breakfast lingered in the air, and he could see toast browning in the toaster and eggs sizzling in the pan.

"Mom, can I call Hap before breakfast?" Winslow asked, his voice filled with both urgency and hope.

He just needed to hear the reassuring sound of his friend's voice.

His mom turned, her expression softening as she looked into Wiki's hopeful eyes, "Sure, sweetheart. Just make it quick, breakfast will be ready soon."

Winslow nodded eagerly and grabbed the phone from its cradle on the wall, his fingers trembling slightly as he dialed Harper's number. Each ring seemed to last forever, but finally, he heard a click on the other end of the line and was met with the Jones' voicemail greeting, his heart sinking slightly.

He cleared his throat, preparing to leave a message, "Hey, Hap, it's Wiki. I just wanted to see how you're–"

Suddenly, he heard a click, followed by rustling in the background.

"Hey, Wiki!" Harper said, sounding a bit out of breath. "Sorry, I almost missed you."

Winslow replied, unable to keep the excitement from his voice, "How are you feeling today?"

There was a brief pause, then Harper's warm voice floated through the receiver, "I'm feeling much better today. It was kind of weird actually–I had a dream last night where the wind brought me some hot chocolate. It felt so real."

Wiki chuckled, a wave of relief washing over him. "That sounds like something the wind would do, doesn't it? I'm glad you're feeling better."

He paused for a moment before continuing, the idea that had been bouncing around in his mind coming to the forefront. "Listen, Willow has soccer practice today. She's been asking about you, and I think it'd be great to have you there. Besides, it's always more fun with you around. So... do ya want to come along?"

Harper let out a soft chuckle. "I'd love to, Wiki. I've missed you guys. And I could definitely use a little sunshine. Let me check with my dad, be right back!" she said before stepping away for a moment.

Wiki waited patiently, excited to hear her response as the smell of bacon continued to tease his appetite.

A few moments later, she picked the receiver back up, "He said yes! I need to get ready and then I will head over soon."

"Perfect! I can't wait," Winslow said, a warmth spreading through him. "See you soon, Hap."

They said goodbyes before hanging up the phone. Wiki turned to see his mom watching him with a knowing smile.

"Good news?" she asked, setting a plate of eggs, bacon, and toast in front of his place at the table.

Winslow grinned, nodding. "Yeah, Hap's coming to Willow's practice today. She's feeling better."

His mom's smile widened. "I'm glad to hear that. Now, eat up before your food gets cold."

"Glad to hear what?" Willow asked as she rounded the corner, entering the kitchen.

"Hap is feeling better, and she is gonna come to your practice!" Wiki interjected exuberantly.

"Yay! That is rad. I'm gonna try and scare her when she gets here," Willow chuckled as she sat down to eat.

Wiki and Willow quickly finished their breakfast when they heard a knock on the door. Winslow rushed to the front door and swung it open, the cool morning air rushing past him.

"Hey!" Harper said, her eyes lighting up when she saw him.

"Hey, Hap! Come on in," Wiki replied, stepping aside to let her in.

He led her into the kitchen where his mom greeted her warmly. Willow peeked out from behind her mom, her eyes widening in excitement as she spotted Harper.

"BOO!" Willow called out, running over to give her a hug, "Did I scare you?"

Harper knelt to Willow's level, hugging her back tightly. "You totally got me! Now, what are we doing while we wait for practice?"

"Harper, have you eaten yet? Would you like a plate?" Mrs. Kinney asked as she washed the eggs stuck to the pan.

"I did eat already, but I would never turn down bacon!" Hap said as she reached out, grabbing two slices, and scarfing them down.

The three kids—Wiki, Hap, and Willow—gathered in the living room and began brainstorming. It didn't take long before they decided to play some freeze tag in the backyard while Mrs. Kinney straightened up around the house. They stumbled out the back door, the morning sun warming the yard, casting long shadows of the trees over the grass.

"Alright, who's 'it' first?" Wiki asked, bouncing on the balls of his feet.

Willow raised her hand with a grin. "I'll be 'it'! But you all better run fast!" she challenged.

The game of freeze tag began, laughter and shouts filling the backyard. Harper's squeal rang out as she tried to dodge Willow, who was fast on her heels. Winslow darted around the swing set, barely managing to avoid getting tagged. The kids continued playing until they were all breathless, collapsing on the grass with wide smiles and flushed cheeks.

After a while, Mrs. Kinney called them in for lunch. They sat around the table, talking animatedly about their game and what they would play next. Once lunch was done, they decided to move to the driveway to play hopscotch.

Harper drew the hopscotch grid with a piece of chalk, and soon the kids were hopping along the numbers, cheering each other on as they tried to complete the course without losing their balance.

The sun had begun to climb higher in the sky, and the warmth of the day grew as they played. Mrs. Kinney eventually stepped outside, wiping her hands on a dishtowel.

She smiled at the sight of the kids playing, then called out, "Alright, everyone! Time to get ready for Willow's soccer practice!"

Willow froze mid-hop, her expression suddenly changing. Her smile faltered, replaced by a slight frown. She stepped off the hopscotch grid, her shoulders slumping.

"What's wrong, Willow?" Wiki asked, noticing a change in her demeanor.

Harper came over, crouching down beside Willow. "You were so excited earlier. What's going on?"

Willow looked down at her feet, her voice barely above a whisper. "It's just that we were having so much fun... and practice means... Kaylee and Sophia. They're the best players on the team, but they always make fun of me when I mess up." She sniffled, her eyes glistening as she continued, "They say I'm too slow, or that I shouldn't even try if I'm just going to fail. It makes me feel like no matter what I do, I'll never be good enough."

Harper's face softened as she exchanged a glance with Wiki, both of them understanding the weight of Willow's words.

"Willow, I know it's hard when people are mean, especially when you're trying your best. But remember, learning takes time, and one day you'll be way better than those girls will ever dream of," Hap said softly.

"Today is going to be your day. I can feel it! Don't stress sis, let's go get ready before we have Mom to fear," Winslow said with reassurance.

The siblings giggled and the three children ran inside to get ready.

Winslow and Harper were standing in the living room, shifting restlessly as they waited to leave. Winslow was tapping his foot, while Harper absently twirled a strand of her hair. Suddenly, Wiki's face lit up as if he'd just had an epiphany.

"I need to grab my jacket!" Wiki exclaimed, turning on his heel and dashing up the stairs two at a time, rushing to his room and shutting the door behind him.

Turning, he eyed his jacket hanging off the back of his chair, the faded fabric a comforting reminder of countless adventures. He walked over and grabbed it, slinging it on, the familiar feeling settling over his shoulders.

Moving to the window, he cracked it open slightly, just enough to let in the crisp morning breeze. He closed his eyes and took a deep breath as the cool air rushed in, bringing with it the scent of grass and distant pine.

Speaking up in a voice that was barely a whisper, but full of intent and a hint of urgency as he called out, "Wind, I need your help."

For a moment, the room was silent except for the faint sounds outside trickling in. Then, a gentle breeze swept in, swirling around the room, lifting the curtains and making the loose papers on his desk dance in the air. He quickly slapped his hand down, trapping the papers on the desk before setting his pencil holder on them, preventing their escape.

He turned around, and there, floating just inches from his face, was the wind spirit, its hands tucked under its chin as it stared at him with a playful grin. The spirit's eyes, like swirling clouds, seemed to twinkle with mischief as it hovered effortlessly.

"Wind!" he exclaimed, jumping back in surprise and immediately changing his voice to a whisper. "You have got to stop scaring me like that!"

The spirit laughed, "What is it that you need?" its voice was like a whisper carried on the wind, both distant and near.

"It's about my sister," Winslow continued speaking softly, hoping to avoid prying ears. "She needs help today, there's these girls on her team, Kaylee and Sophia. They keep bullying her, could you help with that?"

"Oh? Poor child. Hmmmm?" the spirit paused dramatically as it pondered. Its eyes widened for effect as it leaned even closer, booping Wiki lightly on the nose with a gust of wind. It winked playfully, a mischievous smile forming on its lips before it continued, "I think I have just the thing." Wind chuckled as it slowly faded away with the breeze, its form swirling gently out of sight.

Winslow turned and hurried back downstairs, rejoining Willow and Harper, his heart lighter than before.

Mrs. Kinney was in the kitchen, moving with efficiency only a mother could master. She filled the cooler with water bottles, arranging the oranges and other snacks, making sure everything was organized so that it was easy to grab during breaks.

With the cooler packed, she made her way into the living room and grabbed the various items she would need–Willow's shin guards, the first-aid kit, and extra towels. She hefted the cooler and supplies before going outside and methodically loaded everything into the trunk, her mind running through a mental checklist to ensure she had not forgotten anything.

Once everything was loaded into the car, Mrs. Kinney yelled out to the children, "Time to head out, let's go kids!"

"Yes, ma'am!" Winslow, Willow, and Harper called back in near perfect unison as they ran toward the door.

"Last one out needs to close the door!" Mrs. Kinney shouted as the children started coming out of the house.

Everyone piled into the car, the excitement palpable as Mrs. Kinney started the engine. Harper and Winslow sat in the back seat, chatting about the upcoming practice while Willow stared out the passenger side window, her fingers nervously drumming on her knees. When they pulled into the park, the car rolled to a stop near the soccer field.

Mrs. Kinney turned to her right, her eyes meeting Willow's as she encouraged, "You're going to do great, sweetheart. Just have fun out there."

Willow nodded but didn't say anything back.

As they all got out of the car, Winslow moved closer to his sister and bent down slightly so he could meet her eyes.

"Hey, you've got this, Willow," he said softly. "Remember, it's just a game. And we're all here cheering for you."

Willow took a deep breath, her eyes meeting Winslow's before she smiled. "Okay," she said, her voice steadier now.

Harper chimed in, her smile widening as she said, "Show them what you're made of Willow!"

Willow smiled back with a twinkle in her eye before grabbing her gear and running off to join her friends, who were already on the field warming up. Mrs. Kinney grabbed the cooler and supplies, before the three got settled in the bleachers.

The practice kicked off as the coach blew the whistle, setting the players in motion. Kaylee and Sophia's team swiftly took control of the ball, their speed and skill evident as they effortlessly passed and dodged Willow's team's attempts to steal it away.

As Sophia advanced toward the goal, Wind discreetly intervened, summoning a gust that sent the ball veering off course. Sophia stumbled and fell, providing an opening for Willow's team to gain control.

Spotting her chance, Willow sprinted toward the ball. With a powerful kick, she sent it soaring through the air toward the goal. Despite Sophia's efforts to recover, the ball eluded her grasp and found its mark, landing squarely in the net.

The parents watching from the sidelines erupted in cheers, and Willow bounced with joy, elated by her successful shot.

Mrs. Kinney jumped up from a seated position, pumping her fists in the air, overjoyed by her daughter's goal. "That's my baby girl! GO WILLOW!"

Kaylee and Sophia, red-faced and angry, engaged in a heated argument, their frustration palpable. The two girls, annoyed at losing, resorted to pushing, shoving, and playing dirty to get ahead. But every time they tried to gain an unfair advantage, Wind subtly intervened.

Kaylee shoved one of the opposing players, a sharp gust blew the ball just out of her reach, causing her to miss an incoming pass. When Sophia tried to trip Willow, the ground beneath her seemed to shift slightly, making her stumble instead.

Kaylee and Sophia, though still skilled, found themselves constantly struggling to keep control. Wind was relentless in its subtle corrections; ensuring that every push, every shove, every unfair advantage they tried to take was met with a gentle but firm resistance.

As the scrimmage drew to a close, Willow saw an opportunity. The ball was loose, rolling toward her. She sprinted forward, feeling the wind at her back, and with one swift motion, she kicked it straight into the goal.

The parents erupted in cheers once more, Mrs. Kinney's voice ringing out above the rest. Willow beamed, her face flushed with pride as her teammates surrounded her, cheering.

Hap's surmounting curiosity got the better of her. Leaning closer to Wiki, her voice low, she asked, "Wiki, did you have anything to do with this?"

Wiki glanced at her, hesitating for a moment before shaking his head. "Not exactly, but I did ask Wind for some help in dealing with the bullies teasing Willow. Other than that, it wasn't me." Winslow smirked.

Hap nodded thoughtfully, her eyes softening. "It was pretty amazing. Wind really knew how to put those two in their place without making it too obvious."

Wiki, Hap, and Willow approached each other, their faces illuminated with admiration.

"You were incredible out there," Wiki exclaimed, giving her a heartfelt hug.

Willow beamed with pride, appreciating her brother's support. "Thanks," she replied, her voice filled with gratitude and joy.

Hap chimed in, unable to contain her excitement. "You were absolutely amazing! We always knew you had it in you."

The trio stood together as Mrs. Kinney approached them, cooler in hand, asking, "Does pizza and games sound like a good plan?"

The kids erupted in cheers, and soon they were on their way to the local pizza parlor. The small restaurant was alive with the scent of cheese, warm dough, and the laughter of children playing in the arcade corner.

The moment they stepped inside, the bright neon lights of the arcade machines caught their eyes, and they were immediately drawn in. After ordering a large pepperoni pizza, they rushed over to the games, pockets jangling with tokens.

Winslow and Hap found themselves competing fiercely on the racing game, their laughter echoing as they bumped into each other's virtual cars, both trying to beat the high score. Willow, meanwhile, was captivated by the claw machine, her eyes wide with determination as she maneuvered the claw toward a stuffed bear that she had her heart set on. With some guidance from Hap, and a few near misses, Willow finally managed to grab the toy, her squeal of excitement filling the arcade.

The pizza arrived soon after, and the trio gathered around the table, their faces flushed from the excitement of the games. They devoured slice after slice, laughing over their victories and playfully teasing each other about their losses.

Hap leaned back in her seat, rubbing her stomach, joking, "I think I've officially eaten more pizza than anyone should in one sitting."

Winslow nodded in agreement, feigning a groan of discomfort.

After a couple of hours of arcade fun and a stomach full of pizza, they headed back to the car, their energy now pleasantly mellowed by the food and fun. As Mrs. Kinney drove, the car was filled with the soft chatter of the kids reminiscing about their favorite parts of the day and planning the next time they could do it again.

When they pulled up to Hap's house, the porch light was on, and Mr. Jones walked out of the house. As Mrs. Kinney and Harper stepped out of the car and approached him.

Mr. Jones asked, "How did Harper do today?"

"She seemed to be feeling just fine with us," Mrs. Kinney said as Hap made her way inside, "But I think she's probably worn out now."

Mr. Jones nodded, smiling warmly. "Thanks for taking her to have a fun day."

Mrs. Kinney returned the expression and said, "It was our pleasure. Have a good night," before returning to the car, and heading home.

The kids' excited chatter, now quieter, was replaced by the soft hum of the car engine. Willow leaned her head against the window, her new stuffed bear hugged tightly to her chest.

Winslow glanced at his sister, smiling softly at the sight. As they drove, they noticed the deep crimson glow of a blood moon hanging low in the sky, casting an eerie but beautiful light over the sleepy streets, accentuating their day.

Chapter 39

Beneath the haunting radiance of the blood moon, the Sonoran Desert seemed awash in an otherworldly red hue, with shadows twisting like spectral figures across the barren sands. The craggy silhouette of the mountains brooded over the land, their peaks faintly illuminated in the crimson glow.

Deep within the cool depths of the underground lair, Alistair moved with purpose, his footsteps barely a whisper against the stone floor. He paused for a moment before Seraphine's chamber, drawing in a deep breath to ease his nerves. The door loomed in front of him, heavy and foreboding. Alistair rapped his knuckles against it, the sound echoing through the dim, empty hallway, breaking the silence like a ripple across still water.

"Who is it?" Seraphine inquired with a sharp tone.

"Alistair, High Priestess. Everything is ready to begin," he responded.

"Very good. Have everyone take their positions. Lilith and I will be down shortly," Seraphine demanded.

"As you wish," Alistair said before turning to swiftly make his way back to the ritual room.

As he arrived at the bottom floor of the lair, Alistair wasted no time before barking orders to get the acolytes in place.

"You over there," Alistair yelled while gesturing to the right side of the room, "Line up on this side."

He then repeated the action to the members on the left.

As everyone began to take their places, Magnus approached Alistair, asking, "Are you mad? If the high priestess sees this atrocious pile of carcasses, she will devour our essence. Should we not clean it up first?"

"This was the high priestess's request, specifically," Alistair answered bluntly.

"Okay. But that is strange…" Magnus retorted under his breath as he proceeded to take his place.

Alistair continued directing the acolytes, his voice steady and authoritative as he ensured each one moved precisely to their assigned position. Slowly, the nervous chattering among them ceased, replaced by an anticipatory silence that seemed to thicken the very air.

When the last echo of whispers died, Alistair turned, catching sight of Seraphine and Lilith as they descended the final steps of the winding stairwell. Without hesitation, he moved swiftly to take his place among the generals, ready for the ceremony.

Seraphine entered the room with the Blood Crystal in tow, her robes flowing elegantly with each purposeful step as her gaze swept critically over the preparations. She paused, her sharp eyes taking in the gathered acolytes, the altar, and the horrendous heap of remains. A flicker of satisfaction crossed her features, barely perceptible, but enough to indicate her approval.

With a subtle nod, she resumed her path, gliding toward the rear of the ritual chamber, Lilith following closely. Lilith's steps were light and unobtrusive, her expression calm and deferential as she remained in Seraphine's wake, her attention focused solely on the high priestess.

Arriving at the rear of the chamber, Seraphine and Lilith positioned themselves before an elaborate tapestry that stretched from the altar at the room's center all the way to their feet, forming a ceremonial aisle.

The textile was a deep red, embroidered with elegant, abstract designs in gold thread that ran down the edges. On either side of this temporary aisle, her acolytes stood in a disciplined formation, their eyes fixated on the high priestess.

The four generals, two on each side, stood at the head of the assembly—markedly distinct with their imposing stances and richly adorned robes, setting them apart from the simpler attire of the acolytes. The generals' presence exuded authority, their watchful eyes scanning the room while the acolytes remained still, their expressions a mix of awe and apprehension.

"We stand on the precipice of greatness, ready to usher in a new era of chaos!" Seraphine said, causing the onlookers to cheer in response.

Raising her hand to command silence, she continued, "Your dedication, your tireless efforts, and the sacrifices you have offered are commendable. Together, we will complete this sacred rite, and our work will soon be immortalized in the annals of power."

"Let us begin!" she announced, her posture exuding confidence as she strutted proudly down the ceremonial aisle. Her steps were deliberate, her robes trailing behind her like rippling shadows, their movement giving her an almost ethereal quality. As she approached the crescent altar, its curved arms seemed to wrap around her in a welcoming embrace.

Standing before the heart idol, Seraphine gazed down at an abominable monument, forged from the amalgamation of a hundred innocent hearts. Each one contributed to the idol's grotesque form—some large and vibrant, others shriveled and blackened—entwined together in a tangled, horrifying display, stitched with sinews as tough as rope.

Appeased by the appalling sight, Seraphine continued with the ritual. She raised her arms, the Blood Crystal floating from her side to hover above the altar, its surface beginning to pulsate with a faint, unnatural glow.

"Absorbe essentiam de altare," Seraphine intoned, her voice reverberating through the chamber.

The Blood Crystal glowed more intensely, its dark depths swirling with crimson tendrils, responding to her command. The essence from the basin—a thick, viscous liquid—began to rise in thin, twisting streams, drawn toward the crystal. Crimson tendrils extended outward, interlacing with the rising essence and pulling it into the core of the crystal. As it absorbed the massive quantity of essence, its glow intensified into a more vibrant hue of garnet.

With the basin fully drained, Seraphine continued, "Gemma sanguinis, nutri idolum cordis."

Slowly, the floating orb drifted over to the heart idol, hovering above it, pulsating more vigorously than before. With a final, commanding gesture from Seraphine, the crystal released its absorbed essence in a brilliant surge of crimson liquid. The grotesque idol was enveloped by the sanguine fluid, which seeped into its twisted form until the crystal was emptied and returned to Seraphine's side.

The entire construct began to pulse, the twisted mass shivering before settling into a slow, rhythmic movement. Each beat grew stronger as the tangled flesh seemed to shift and tighten, veins swelling and contracting, with an eerie vitality spreading throughout the idol. With each pulsation, a deep, almost guttural thudding echoed, like the beginnings of a sinister new life.

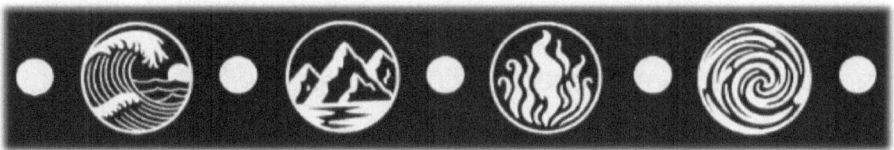

In the distant ethereal plane, the elemental spirits gathered, their forms alive with an ever-shifting radiance born of their respective elements. They conversed in urgent, resonant tones, their attention drawn to an unsettling disturbance—a connection forming between Terra Vitae and the Corrupted Realm.

Wind spoke first, its voice, once full of whimsy, now weighted with a somber edge, "Do you feel it? Something stirs–a darkness crossing the threshold."

The others nodded, each sensing the rift widening, an ominous tremor reverberating through the fabric of reality itself.

"We must act swiftly!" Fire declared, its voice ignited by the pressing danger.

"I agree, who will go fetch our champion and his companion?" Earth interjected.

"I shall go retrieve them. Meet us where the kids trained," the wind spirit said before wisping away.

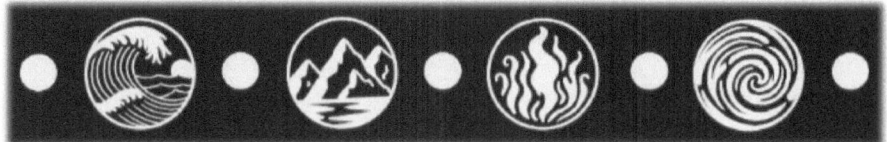

Back at the lair of The Fang, Seraphine finalized the ritual with one final command, "Per corda et sanguinem innocentiae, exsurge ad nos, Gluttulos!"

The idol throbbed with an uneven, unnatural rhythm, each beat sending subtle tremors through the ground beneath. A change began to ripple across the macabre structure.

The sinews binding the hearts stretch taut, pulling with a horrific creak as though they are resisting a great force. Suddenly, the hearts convulse, and with a sickening squelch, tendons and muscle fibers begin to emerge, snaking outward like the probing limbs of a distorted, sentient creature.

The fibers extended and wove themselves in a slow, deliberate pattern, branching and coiling as if alive. Raw and blood-slicked, they glistened dark crimson under the shifting light, a sinister hiss and crackle accompanying their relentless growth. The air, suffused with the sharp tang of copper, mingled with an acrid stench—burnt hair and sulfur—was an ominous prelude to an ancient, malevolent force slowly seeping into existence.

Seraphine glided effortlessly as she moved toward the end of the decorative tapestry, her powerful and resonant voice echoing through the chamber, "Behold the birth of the Stitch Reaper!" She gestured dramatically with one hand as she spoke, emphasizing her proclamation.

Upon reaching the end of the tapestry, Seraphine turned, her gaze locked onto the heart idol, her eyes ablaze with eager anticipation, a twisted grin tugging at her lips. As she watched, the muscle fibers surged outward, ripping an archway into the delicate veil of reality, as if clawing through the boundary between worlds, forming an entrance that tore itself open with a wet, rending sound.

The gap was framed by still-quivering tendons that tightened like coiled springs, pulsating and twitching. The newly formed portal's edges were slick with ominous black ichor, which dripped slowly down its fleshy, misshapen frame, staining the altar below.

A deep, sonorous hum emanated from the entrance, resonating with a bone-aching frequency. As the final heartbeats of the idol pulsed with desperation, the shadows surrounding the shrine coalesced, drawn toward the portal as if commanded. The edges of the gateway trembled, the tendons vibrating as though plucked by ghostly hands.

Then, with a sudden, sickening snap, the entrance solidified and widened, yawning open like the mouth of a nightmare. The space beyond was impossibly dark, except for subtle streaks of crimson.

Out of this chasm, the whisper of movement emerged, cold and sharp, heralding the Stitch Reaper's approach. The tendons framing the portal twisted and shuddered as if bowing before their master, stretching the gateway wider to welcome the entity that knows only pain and an insatiable hunger for flesh, blood, and souls.

Slowly, a massive crescent of blackened metal emerged from the darkness, its edge jagged and uneven, lined with cruel, serrated teeth that seemed to be forged to tear through flesh and bone. The surface faintly pulsated with runes, their energy exuding an unnatural menace. The spine, no less vicious, bristled with barbed spurs–sharp and twisted, like the coils of razor wire ready to shred anything daring to come near.

The blade scraped against the edge of the portal, the sound like nails dragging across a coffin lid, echoing through the chamber with an eerie finality. Digging into the archway, the weapon anchored itself firmly, its edge biting deep as though determined to pull its master through.

A monstrous hand followed, a deformed fusion of twisted flesh from countless creatures, its surface writhing as though each part fought for dominance. The fingers were thick, callused, and covered in patches of mismatched skin.

They twitched with terrible anticipation, groping along the ground with a primal hunger, as if already sensing the warmth of their prey.

The acolytes barely had time to react before the wandering hand latched onto four of them–tightening like a vice, the grip almost crushing. The unfortunate souls let out strangled screams as they were dragged into the dark void, their cries dissolving into the sickening sounds of crunching bones and tearing flesh. The wet, visceral noise of bodies breaking echoed through the chamber. Panic erupted, the air thick with frantic shouts and desperate cries.

The Stitch Reaper's meaty appendage reached out once more, grasping for sustenance, but found nothing within its reach. The acolytes scattered in a frenzy, scrambling in all directions, their fear keeping them out of reach of the monstrous hand. The fingers twitched, groping blindly, then with a sudden retraction, gripped the edge of the portal.

Slowly, eyes began to emerge—varying in size, shape, and color. Some were small and beady, others bulbous and bulging, each one unique, their placement seemingly random. It was almost spider-like, but with a lack of symmetry, giving the creature an even more grotesque and nightmarish appearance as the eyes scanned the room, hungry for more.

Amid the chaos, Alistair's eyes darted to Seraphine and Lilith, standing seemingly calm amidst the turmoil. He pushed his way through the confusion toward them.

"Seraphine! Lilith! We must get out of here!" Alistair shouted, his voice straining to rise above the cacophony.

There was no reaction, no flicker of recognition from either of them. They just stood there, unmoving, almost serene in their demeanor.

"Are you listening to me?!" he barked, his frustration building as he closed the distance between them.

Still, neither of them so much as turned their heads. A creeping suspicion began to gnaw at him, an unease that grew with every unacknowledged word.

Alistair's eyes narrowed. Something was wrong. He reached out cautiously, his hand moving slowly toward Seraphine's shoulder. The moment his fingers made contact, they passed right through her form, meeting nothing but empty air. The illusion shimmered for a brief instant before fading entirely, leaving only the empty space where they had once stood.

A chill spread through him as he realized the truth–they had left an afterimage behind. Feeling the sting of betrayal rise in his chest, Alistair's jaw clenched, his gaze hardening. He moved swiftly toward the twisting staircase, pushing through the panicking crowd, weaving past acolytes who rushed desperately to the living chambers on the second floor. Alistair continued forcing his way through the chaos, distant screams from the ritual room below reverberating up the stairwell.

Arriving at Seraphine's private chamber, Alistair noticed the door barely ajar. His pulse quickened as he approached, a growing sense of dread. He shoved the door open with force, the wooden frame creaking in protest as it swung wide. The room was dim, but Alistair's eyes immediately caught sight of the swirling energies of a portal beginning to close.

"Damn you both!" he growled, his voice filled with venom.

He lunged forward as if he could somehow halt the magic, but it was too late. The shimmering edges of the portal collapsed in on themselves, leaving only silence in its wake. He stood there, breath heavy, fists clenched, when suddenly, a deep, ominous rumble crawled through the walls—a low growl that grew steadily louder, vibrating the stone around him. It swelled into a rhythmic and relentless pounding.

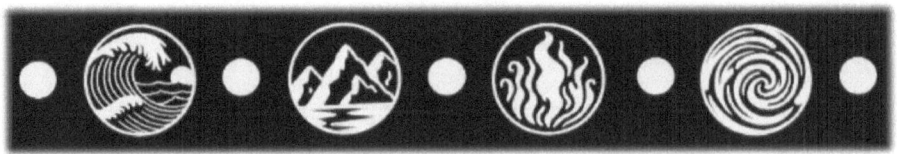

Back in town, at their secluded spot deep in the woods, the spirits and the children gathered beneath the trees. A sense of anticipation filled the air as the children waited for the spirits to begin.

"The thing we feared most has happened: The Fang has made a connection to Nocthara, meaning only one thing–they have summoned a creature from that abominable void. We must act quickly," Earth said, its voice a firm echo of authority and urgency.

"Aye aye, captain," Hap said, raising her hand to her forehead, saluting.

Wiki followed suit, mirroring Hap's words and gesture with playful precision, though there was an unmistakable hint of nervousness in his eyes.

"I commend your courage, young ones, for keeping your wits and humor intact," Wind spoke, its voice a whisper. "Yet heed my words, for what lies ahead is unlike anything you have ever imagined before." It paused, allowing the gravity of its statement to weigh upon them. "This creature hails from the depths of Nocthara, the Corrupted Realm—a place where light has been consumed, and hope is but a distant memory." Wind's expression grew somber as it continued, "The time for levity will return only once balance has been restored."

The Fire spirit stepped forward, its form flickering with vibrant, shifting hues of orange and red.

"Prepare your artifacts," Fire commanded, its tone crackling with urgency. With a sweeping gesture, it tore open a portal, the edges of which roared and licked with flame before turning to the children and saying, "There is no time to waste, children."

The children nodded in unison before they each summoned their artifacts–Winslow with Harmony's Edge and Harmony's Guard, the ethereal blade and shield appearing in a flash of light.

Harper summoned Earthshapers, the gauntlets enveloping her hands and forearms like a second skin, immediately forming a familiar buckler in her right hand. With her shield ready, she called forth Firebrand, the living flame whip. Finally, her Windwalkers wrapped around her feet, their magic rippling through the air like a heat wave, bending the light into a mirage-like shimmer that danced and wavered around her.

Wiki turned his head toward Hap, locking eyes with her. "Are you ready?" he asked nervously.

"Let's do this!" Hap said, her voice was steady and filled with resolve.

Together, the two stepped forward into the portal, their forms vanishing behind the fiery veil.

Arriving, they found themselves in a vast desert under a blood moon, the crimson glow casting eerie shadows across the sand. A deep rumbling echoed from beneath their feet, sending a shiver up their spines as they exchanged uneasy glances.

"What was that?" Winslow asked with concern lacing his voice.

"Great question, but where are we?" Harper replied, confusion in her tone.

"It looks like a desert, but I have no idea what…" Wiki began, but his words faltered as his attention was caught by the sight and sounds of robed figures emerging from the very earth itself, as if rising out of nowhere. Concealment magic shimmered briefly as they broke through.

"Looks like we have incoming!" Winslow called Harper's attention.

Harper turned her head before saying, "Ready yourself, Wiki."

Wiki and Hap readied their fighting stances, their muscles tensing, and eyes narrowing in focus. The acolytes, startled by their sudden presence, paused for a brief moment before sheer panic overtook them.

Without hesitation, they spun around, their robes flaring as they bolted in the opposite direction, their hurried footsteps kicking up the desert sand as they scrambled to escape.

"Well, that was easy," Hap smirked and the two exchanged confused looks.

Before Wiki could reply, the ground beneath them shuddered violently, a deep rumble echoing through the earth. A resonant boom followed, shaking the ground with such force that the children stumbled slightly, their eyes darting around, trying to locate the source. Another rumble, even more intense, shook the desert, accompanied by a thunderous boom that sent plumes of sand into the air.

Suddenly, a curved, gnarled piece of metal erupted from the ground, its twisted shape gleaming under the eerie light of the blood moon. Wiki and Hap's attention snapped to it, watching in astonishment as the metal slowly retracted, leaving deep fractures radiating from the jagged wound it had made in the earth.

With wide eyes, Winslow asked, "Whoa, did you see that? What was it?"

"I don't know, the sand made it difficult to see and it happened so quickly," Harper replied.

Suddenly, the hole where the fissures originated erupted, sending rocks, sand, and debris soaring into the air. As the heavier particles quickly settled, a massive arm came into view, covered in twisted sutures that crisscrossed in every direction. The arm retracted briefly before anchoring itself on the edge of the now expansive chasm.

Moments later, a large, curved blade shot out, securing itself on the opposite side. With a deafening roar, the creature propelled itself upwards, its enormous bulk causing the ground to quake violently as it landed on the desert floor. The force of the impact sent tremors rippling across the sand. The abomination stood with its back to the children, its monstrous form towering over them as Wiki and Hap remained frozen in fear and awe.

The fleeing acolytes caught the attention of the monstrosity. It turned its head slightly, releasing its grip on the massive, curved weapon, allowing it to dangle by a chain that disappeared into a swollen abscess in the middle of its forearm. The inflamed wound, covered in pustules, added to the creature's nightmarish appearance. With each organic *"Click,"* the ratcheting sound grew louder as the chain elongated incrementally, lowering the blade toward the ground.

When the spine struck the sand, a resonant *"Thud"* rippled through the air, the impact echoing across the desert. Acting on the auditory cue, the amalgamation fluidly swung its arm up and around in a counterclockwise motion, commanding the weapon to lash out in a wide, powerful arc.

The blade cleaved through its targets effortlessly, loose pieces catching on to the spur-like metal protrusions along its spine. The creature then extended its right arm outward, the familiar ratcheting sound echoing again–faster this time. With each organic *"Click!"* the chain retracted until the handle of the weapon returned firmly to its grasp in a matter of seconds.

The monster then turned its attention to the loose pieces of the acolytes still stuck to the blade. Though the children could not see, they heard the sickening sound of flesh shifting and staples being forced open with a wet, metallic snap. Its guttural groans and the wet, visceral sounds of consumption rippled through the air, each gulp resonating like a deep, hollow snarl.

After a moment, the creature turned toward the children, its mouth now visible—a large s-curved incision in the center of its protruding belly, slowly closing. Rows of vicious, jagged teeth could be seen, and its blackened, snake-like tongue slithered out, almost as if licking its lips.

The staples began to snap back into place, each one sinking into the flesh with a chilling *"Clack,"* the noise akin to bones cracking into alignment, until the incision was once again tightly sealed.

Wiki and Hap exchanged looks of complete terror as they both resisted the natural instinct to run.

"Well, that was horrifying. I wish I knew what this thing was, so we knew its weaknesses," Hap spoke up first.

"It is the Stitch Reaper. A creature from Nocthara that wields a large sickle-like weapon—a Soul Renderer," Wiki blurted out before he knew what he was saying.

"Where did that come from? How did you know?" Harper asked, looking over at her friend in astonishment.

"I have no idea. The words just popped into my head," Wiki replied, even more visually confused than his friend.

"Well, what else do you know? How do we take this thing out?" Harper inquired.

"It is able to summon an army at its command. It is driven by an insatiable hunger to consume flesh and souls. The more it consumes, the more powerful it will become," Winslow answered in a mechanical tone.

Harper replied, "So, since it just finished eating that means–"

Before she could finish her sentence, the Stitch Reaper unleashed a vicious roar, its voice echoing with primal fury. The creature's form began to swell, its bones breaking with a sickening crunch, then snapping back into place in a series of grotesque, sequential transformations. Each movement seemed almost ritualistic, as if its body were reshaping itself for greater destruction, until it towered above, visibly more muscular in appearance.

"Be ready to move," Hap warned Wiki as she decided to exchange her buckler and Firebrand for Tidecaller.

Winslow nodded, keeping his eyes fixated on the monstrous abomination.

"You children challenge me?" the Stitch Reaper growled, its dual-toned voice echoing with an underlying ancient language, audible beneath the spoken words like a dark and savage resonance.

The creature adjusted its grip on the handle of its weapon and hurled it straight above its head. The chain emitted a visceral, sinewy noise as it unraveled, propelled by the sickle's momentum. With a calculated motion, the Stitch Reaper clamped its hand closed, instantly arresting the upward surge. In the same fluid movement, it yanked its arm downward, forcing the sickle to whip violently through the air, the blade slicing forward with lethal intent.

In response to the attack, Hap dashed before letting out a battle cry, "RAHHH!"

Wiki raised his shield as the weapon rapidly approached. Imagining a giant turtle shell, Harmony's Guard reacted, transforming in a brilliant flash of light. The Soul Renderer struck the shield with a glancing blow, sending Wiki rolling backward as the blade crashed into the ground with a thundering impact. Quickly, he sprang back to his feet, resuming a defensive posture.

"What? It can't be. Such a puny thing is what passes for a champion of the blessed now? How utterly laughable," the Stitch Reaper sneered, its dual-toned voice dripping with contempt as it slowly retracted the chain, the metal links rattling with an eerie, deliberate rhythm.

"I'll show you just how powerful 'PUNY' can be!" Harper screamed, her voice echoing with fury.

She propelled herself into the air with a burst of wind, her body twisting gracefully as she released a barrage of razor-sharp ice arrows. Each shard trailed a faint mist, leaving a frosty arc in their wake as they hurtled toward their target.

One by one, the arrows found their mark, piercing the acrid flesh of the Stitch Reaper's right side. Each impact spread an icy chill, rapidly freezing the surrounding tissue.

In response, the skin convulsed, spitting out the frozen chunks with a moist, nauseating sound.

Almost immediately, the lost flesh began to restore itself in an eerie, fluid motion as fibers coiled and threaded together. Strands of muscle knitted seamlessly, glistening faintly as they stretched and fused with unnerving precision, while a subtle, rhythmic tearing accompanied the quiet hum of unnatural regeneration.

"What an annoying insect," the Stitch Reaper said in response to the lackluster attack.

"Insect, huh? I'll make you regret those words," Harper shot back, her eyes blazing with ferocity.

Shifting her approach, she summoned Firebrand. With a swift crack, the whip erupted into a serpentine blaze, unleashing an explosion of searing fire that struck the right shoulder of the Stitch Reaper, leaving behind a gaping cavity of moving muscle fibers.

"That tickles," the Stitch Reaper chuckled, its voice dripping with dark amusement as the torn flesh knitted itself together again, sinew and muscle writhing grotesquely until it was whole once more.

As the hilt of the sickle nestled into its palm, the creature's many eyes locked onto Hap, a malicious glint flickering in their depths. With a growl of irritation, it swung its free hand toward her with brutal, sweeping motions, its massive arm cutting through the air like a battering ram.

Wiki, watching Hap barely dodge the monstrous strikes, shouted with urgency, "Leave her alone!"

Channeling the power of wind, he unleashed a rapid barrage of slashes, each swing releasing an invisible blade that cut through the air with a sharp whistle. The attacks struck the Stitch Reaper's left leg in quick succession, carving deep gashes into its tough hide.

Tendinous strands writhed out of the gash, snaking through the monster's thick, scarred pelt with a repugnant fluidity. The fibers intertwined and pulled taut, stitching the wound shut. Its head turned with an unnerving slowness toward Winslow, its many eyes glinting with a dark, predatory focus.

"Wait your turn, I'll deal with you soon enough," the creature snarled, its voice a growl that reverberated like distant thunder. Its many eyes briefly flashed with malice before snapping back to Harper.

Aware of the Stitch Reaper's ravenous gaze fixed solely on her, Hap ascended further with graceful precision, circling left in mid-air. Her Windwalkers shimmered with latent power, each step bending light, creating rippling distortions in the bloodied moonlight. Firebrand cracked sharply in her grip, the whip's blazing tendril cast flickering light across the beast's towering frame.

With the Stitch Reaper's back once again fully visible to Winslow, he noticed newly formed massive, tumorous clumps protruding from its flesh, pulsating rhythmically as though alive. Alarmed by the unnatural sight, Winslow invoked the earthen element, summoning a viscous metallic liquid that oozed up from the ground. The liquid crept up the creature's legs with deliberate slowness, eventually encasing its entire lower half in a sheening, metallic shell.

With unwavering concentration, Wiki clasped his hands together, commanding the liquid alloy to solidify into a rigid, monstrous casing. Immobilized from the waist down, the abomination's attacks grew wilder and more desperate. It swung violently with its free hand, each motion more forceful than the last. Hap darted upward with agile precision, but the monster, displaying sudden and terrifying speed, brought its colossal weapon crashing down, sending Hap into a momentary panic.

In a split-second decision, Hap dodged to the right, narrowly avoiding the weapon's serrated teeth but suffering a painful nick from one of the large, barbed spurs jutting out from its spine. Letting out a sharp cry of pain, Harper plummeted from the sky, her weapons flickering out of existence as she fell.

Winslow, alerted by Hap's distress, reacted without hesitation. In a single fluid motion, he released his grip on Harmony's Edge, causing it to vanish in a flash. With practiced precision, he extended his right hand, summoning the desert sands to rise at his command.

The grains coalesced into a massive, elegant hand that surged upward to catch Harper mid-fall. The sandy construct cradled her gently, gliding swiftly back to Winslow's side with care.

"Are you okay, Hap?" Winslow asked, his voice tinged with concern as he ensured the wellbeing of his friend.

"I'm fine, it's just a scratch," she said, though her tone betrayed a hint of panic. "It doesn't really hurt, it itches more than anything. But... I can't seem to summon my weapons."

"I think I can help…just need to buy us some time," Wiki interjected, his gaze shifting warily to the looming Stitch Reaper. He gestured toward the jagged mountain range in the distance before adding, "We need to move. Let's put some ground between us and this thing."

Winslow sprinted forward with urgency, his eyes darting between their foe and the terrain ahead. Harper remained securely held in the sandy construct's grasp, her weight evenly distributed as the sand shifted seamlessly to keep her steady.

With a loud, guttural roar that reverberated through the desolate expanse, the Stitch Reaper hunched forward, its repulsive clumps convulsing violently. Thick, viscous fluid began to seep from the pulsating masses, transforming them into abhorrent pustules.

One by one, the clumps ruptured with nauseating *"Pop"* sounds, spurting with dark ichor. From the ruptures emerged shadowy aberrations, their twisted forms exuding malevolence as they scrambled down the creature's massive frame in relentless waves.

The Noctharian Terrors swarmed over the metallic encasement binding their master, their shifting forms coiling and unraveling. Dark appendages twisted and warped, blooming into claw-like protrusions that gouged deep into crevices with unnatural precision. Serrated edges materialized and dissolved in a blink, grinding relentlessly against the alloy's weakest points. Each strike unleashed a symphony of grating screeches, the friction sending sparks skittering into the gloom as shards of metal crumbled beneath their ferocious assault.

Amid the chaos, seven robed acolytes emerged from the shattered remnants of the underground lair, the movement stirring clouds of dust into the stifling air. The disturbance drew the attention of several spawnlings, who pivoted sharply, their shadowy forms rippling with malevolent intent. Without waiting for a command, they scampered down the metal encased leg after their prey.

As the terrors overtook the fleeing acolytes, they shrouded their victims in writhing tendrils of darkness, muffling their cries and movements entirely. The shadowy forms moved with chilling precision, dragging their captives effortlessly as they turned and made their way back to the Stitch Reaper.

Nearing the towering monstrosity, the mouth on its abdomen partially opened, *"Snap, snap, snap."* From within, its serpentine tongue slithered out, undulating as it extended to the ground, acting as a make-shift bridge. The terrors marched across, their captives still encased in shadow. As the final sustenance-bearing terror stepped onto the tongue, it coiled behind them with a slow, deliberate motion before retracting into the gaping maw, sealing shut with a series of wet, resounding clasps.

Arriving at the base of the mountain with no sense of an immediate threat, Wiki dismissed Harmony's Guard before guiding them to a safe plateau. Once they reached an ideal vantage point, he directed the sandy hand to gently lower Hap. Kneeling beside her, he inhaled deeply to center himself, then placed his hand over the wound on Harper's left arm. Focusing intently, he attempted to sense and share the pain his friend endured but failed to form the connection he needed.

In that quiet yet charged moment, the soothing, familiar whisper of the water spirit resonated in his mind, *"Nocthrallium, a metal from the heart of Nocthara that is formed from crystallized corruption. The slivers must be removed to restore her connection to the elements. Pay close attention to identify and single those shards out. Command her body to reject them."*

Focusing with unwavering intensity, he searched for the source of the obstruction hindering Harper's recovery. His senses locked onto several shards of jagged, foreign metal embedded deep within her arm, each radiating an ominous energy. The Nocthrallium slivers writhed subtly under his scrutiny, exhibiting a trait akin to urticating hairs, burrowing further into her flesh with each passing moment.

With meticulous care, he guided the first fragment to the surface, its sharp edges scraping against tissue as though clinging desperately to its host. One by one, he extracted each piece, the strain of their resistance palpable in his grip.

When the final shard surfaced, pulsing faintly and glinting darkly in his hand, he swept his senses over her arm to ensure no traces remained. Satisfied, he redirected his focus, summoning a soft, luminous energy that enveloped the wound, knitting torn flesh and restoring vitality with a gentle, radiant warmth.

"I think it's done. How do you feel now?" Wiki asked, his tone laced with uncertainty as he studied her expression for signs of pain.

"Only one way to find out," Hap replied. She stretched her arms behind her head, arched her back, and with a graceful burst of energy, flipped onto her feet in a single, fluid motion. "I feel like a million bucks! Great work!" she exclaimed, grinning as they exchanged a celebratory high five.

Suddenly, a thunderous roar erupted that seized Harper's attention sharply, the sound crashing against the jagged mountain walls like a tumultuous wave. She snapped her head toward the source, her ears ringing from the grating sound of metal rending under immense pressure.

"You gnats are mine!" The Stitch Reaper declared as troves of Noctharian Terrors leapt from their master's lower limbs with precision, their shadowy forms shifting and writhing unnaturally.

Each terror moved with a sinuous, almost hypnotic fluidity, their forms melding seamlessly into the surrounding darkness. Only the eerie crimson light of the blood moon revealed glimpses of their distorted silhouettes, casting fleeting shadows.

The fiends gathered near the Stitch Reaper's feet, their collective mass rippling like a living storm. Without pause, they surged forward, their inky tendrils elongating as they propelled themselves toward the children on the mountain, their movements swift and predatory, like a tide of encroaching darkness.

Another reverberating crack shattered the air as the creature wrenched its right leg free from the encasing metal, the gnarled remnants clattering to the ground. Moments later, its left leg broke loose with an equally jarring noise, shards of the alloy scattered like broken chains. The Stitch Reaper stood tall, its frame radiating an oppressive aura of raw, unrestrained power.

"Oh yay, it's free... and it brought friends," Harper muttered, her voice tinged with both sarcasm and unease as she summoned her Earthshapers, Tidecaller, and Windwalkers. "What... are those things..." she murmured, her brows knitting together as she squinted, trying to discern the distorted shapes.

"Whatever they are, it can't be good," Winslow replied as he looked over and saw the incoming horde.

Summoning Harmony's Edge and Guard, he hesitated, weighing his options before inspiration struck. A sudden spark of excitement lit up his face, eyes widening as he turned sharply to Harper and commanded, "Hit them with a tidal wave, Hap!"

Though uncertainty flickered across her face, Harper's faith in her friend outweighed her doubts. Envisioning a massive, surging wall of water crashing down, she unleashed an arrow with immense elemental force, propelling the water-laced projectile in a graceful arc toward the advancing horrors.

Briefly closing his eyes, Wiki relived vivid flashbacks of his harrowing encounter with Fafnir—the deafening roar of the beast, the searing heat of the flames that had come perilously close to incinerating him. The memory sharpened his focus, and his eyes snapped open, a faint orange hue glowing beneath their natural color, as if embers burned within.

With a powerful forward thrust of Edge, a torrent of flame erupted, surging like a living inferno toward the heart of the jagged mountain spurs and into the shadowy depths of the valley of nightmares.

As the fiery serpent barreled forward, an immense cascade of water erupted upward, forming a colossal, roaring wall of liquid might. The instant they collided, a deafening hiss resonated through the valley as blinding steam billowed out, engulfing the terrain. The scalding vapor swept across the valley floor, dissolving the shadowy fiends as over two-thirds of the formless legion disintegrated in a flash of sizzling intensity.

"Whoa, that worked better than I thought it would," Wiki said, his amazement lighting up his face as he locked eyes with Harper and raised his hand.

"Great job!" Hap said sharply, slapping his hand in acknowledgment before warning, "But we need to stay on our guard. Something feels off." She quickly began scanning the area with her eyes narrowed.

Winslow, leaning back with a grin, quipped, "Relax, we're in a safe spot. What's there to worry—"

At that moment, a faint ripple disturbed the misty veil. The disturbance grew quickly, taking on an overwhelming form that surged forward with staggering speed, its immense bulk becoming undeniable as it tore closer.

"Wiki, look out!" Harper's shout pierced the air as she threw herself into him with all her strength, driving them both into a roll across the rocky ground.

Their momentum carried them several feet away, dirt and debris scattering as a car-sized boulder slammed into the spot they had occupied moments earlier, sending a shower of splintered stone into the air.

Tumbling to a stop, they lay on their backs, dazed but breathing heavily as their senses slowly returned. Dust clung to their clothes, and the sharp tang of earth filled the air. Winslow turned his head and met Harper's gaze, her face a mix of relief and determination.

"Thanks–," he began, his voice filled with sincerity and the unspoken realization of how close he'd come to disaster.

"No time for thanks, we need to move!" Hap barked, her tone urgent and laced with a protective edge.

The boulder's thunderous impact against the mountainside sent tremors rippling through the ground. Jagged fractures snaked outward with alarming speed, triggering a rockslide that unleashed an avalanche of debris. Chunks of stone, ranging from pebbles to massive slabs, cascaded down with deafening force.

Scrambling to their feet, the children bolted toward the nearby mountain spur, their hearts pounding as they dodged the tumbling onslaught of rocks in a desperate bid to escape the chaos.

"So weak," the Stitch Reaper snarled, its voice dripping with disdain. "I guess it's true—if you want something done right, do it yourself. Return to me, you worthless parasites!"

The kids froze as the terrors abruptly halted their advance. With eerie synchronicity, the shapeless fiends turned and swarmed toward their master. One by one, the creatures ascended, climbing up to the Stitch Reaper's back before disappearing into the fresh gaping wounds.

The horrifying, yet mesmerizing sight rendered the friends speechless, their breaths caught as they tried to process the grotesque display.

Finally, Wiki broke the silence, a confident spark in his eyes accompanied by a crooked grin. "Get him to come closer to the mountain and keep him occupied. I've got an idea that might just work."

As the last of the terrors melted into its mass, the Stitch Reaper unleashed a thunderous war cry. The sound echoed across the valley, reverberating in their chests. Its sinister gaze locked onto Harper as she advanced swiftly, her grip tightening around her weapon, ready for the rematch.

"It's my turn!" Hap declared, her voice cutting through the chaos as she unleashed a sweeping arc with her cutlass.

The mid-air swing, a calculated maneuver, sent forth a cascade of sand tendrils. These strands twisted and coiled like living serpents, encircling the monstrosity before closing in from multiple directions. In a sudden burst, the clumps at the tendrils' ends exploded, pelting the creature's face with a blinding shower of gritty sand, forcing it to reel back in disorientation.

"Not so scary now, huh?" Hap said with a gleeful tone, a sly grin tugging at the corners of her lips as she taunted the monster.

"How dare you!" the Stitch Reaper growled as it clawed at its face to clear away the obstructive powder with jerky and frenzied movements.

Harper's subtle retreat did not go unnoticed. Catching a glimpse of her slipping further away ignited the abomination's fury. Its twisted form jiggled before it erupted into motion. *"Boom! Boom!"* The ground quaked under its massive strides as it devoured the distance in mere seconds.

With a wild swing, the Soul Renderer sliced through the air, narrowly missing Harper as she pivoted to the left, the force of its strike sending a shockwave through the space around it. Harper's sharp gaze stayed locked on the monster, her instincts alert to every feint and movement.

"That's all you got, big guy?" she called out, her voice steady and edged with a daring confidence, her every word meant to draw its focus.

Harper darted away, her movements swift and deliberate, creating as much distance as she could between herself and the Stitch Reaper to give Winslow the crucial time he needed.

Meanwhile, high on the mountainside, Wiki positioned himself with precision, selecting an overlook that provided a commanding view of the chaotic battle below. With a stern expression, he dismissed Harmony's Edge and Guard, shifting his focus to the rocky terrain around him. The uneven ground felt solid beneath him as he lowered himself to sit on the hardened earth, carefully scanning the scene.

Sitting cross-legged, Winslow let his hands fall limply to his knees, his posture deceptively relaxed despite the intensity of the moment. His eyes roved over the unfolding battle one final time before fluttering closed. In his mind, he envisioned the massive mountain spurs framing the valley, imagining their rugged edges bending and converging slowly.

Back in the valley, Harper heard the Stitch Reaper's heavy steps closing the distance once more. Swiftly, she swapped her cutlass for Firebrand and struck at the right-side mountain spur. The impact unleashed a violent eruption of shattered rock, billowing dust, and scorching heat, forcing the monster to pause its relentless advance.

As Hap glanced over her shoulder, her eyes caught the ends of the mountain's stony limbs in the distance, their jagged edges beginning to twist and bend unnaturally toward each other. Realization struck her like lightning– Wiki's plan was in motion. A mischievous grin spread across her face, and she wasted no time stirring the pot.

"Hey scrapheap! Is missing all you're good at?" Hap taunted, her voice brimming with bold confidence.

"Why are you so smug?" the Stitch Reaper snarled, its tone dripping with suspicion, sensing something amiss.

Noticing Harper's fleeting glance toward the mountain spurs, the creature whipped its head around. Its multi-colored eyes widened as it took in the impossible sight: the two massive rocky arms of the valley bending and melding together in an otherworldly dance, their rugged surfaces flowing like molten stone.

Composing its expression, the Stitch Reaper refocused its attention on Harper, sneering, "So, you think you got me." In a flash, its gaze darted to Wiki, continuing with a menacing growl, "Not if I get you first."

Harper instantly grasped the weight of the creature's threat. Seeing that Winslow was the target, she propelled herself forward with blinding speed. As she surged ahead, the Stitch Reaper hurled the Soul Renderer high into the air, the massive blade cutting through the sky with a flickering shadow trailing ominously behind.

Hap, recognizing the deadly attack from past encounters, reacted without hesitation. She accelerated toward Wiki, her mind racing with a clear purpose. In one fluid motion, she dematerialized her buckler and Firebrand. As she reached Wiki, she positioned herself between him and the impending strike. With a desperate resolve, she slammed her gauntlets together, silently pleading, *"Please protect us."*

The gauntlets pulsed to life, emanating radiant metallic strands that shimmered with a radiant glow. The filaments absorbed the ambient light, reflecting it back in shifting hues of deep violet, iridescent green, and spectral silver—colors that seemed to defy the natural spectrum. The strands coalesced into a smooth, curved barrier encasing the children. Its surface, though solid, rippled with a liquid-like fluidity, giving it the uncanny appearance of something both ethereal and unyielding.

The Soul Renderer slammed into the barrier with a deafening crash, its jagged barbs scraping against the protective surface in a cacophony of grating and metallic screeches. Sparks flew as the blade slid downward, each scratch amplifying the menacing din. The impact culminated in a thunderous thud as the sickle embedded deep into the mountain's rugged face, sending a cascade of loose rock tumbling down the slope.

As an uneasy silence enveloped them, Harper's ears strained to catch any hint of movement beyond the barrier. Slowly, faint, guttural growls reached her—low and simmering with frustration, yet growing weaker with each passing moment. The sound carried a note of fatigue, the anger dissipating into labored groans.

"How can a child possess this much power?" the Stitch Reaper moaned, its voice tinged with disbelief and weariness as its growls dwindled into exhausted murmurs.

Harper, sensing the imminent danger had passed, slowly lowered her arms. The barrier surrounding them shimmered briefly before obeying her intentions, retracting into her gauntlets as liquid strands of radiant metal. With her vision unobstructed, she gazed upon the awe-inspiring sight of the two mountain ridges completing their convergence. They enveloped the Stitch Reaper in an unyielding embrace, their jagged edges pressing in just below its eyes, muffling its wrathful exasperation.

Descending gracefully to the plateau, Harper landed beside Winslow. She glanced at him, her expression a mix of awe and concern, only to find him sitting still, lost in a trance-like state. Shifting her attention, she turned toward the Stitch Reaper's burial. The stone, once flowing like tar, began to solidify, regaining its jagged, unyielding structure.

The encasing rock seemed to pulse with finality, locking the monstrous being in place.

Wiki slowly opened his eyes, his vision adjusting to the surreal calm that had fallen over the battlefield. He spotted Harper and managed a weak grin.

"Hey Hap!" he called out, his voice tinged with exhaustion but warm as he noticed the awe sparkling in her eyes.

"That was epic! Totally rad, Wiki!" Harper exclaimed, her excitement bubbling over as she leapt into the air, unable to contain her elation.

Winslow blushed faintly. "Aww, it was nothing, Hap," he replied in a humble tone.

Harper's gaze shifted, her excitement dimming as she gestured toward the ominous presence of the dark deity. Its glimmering eyes seemed to watch them intently, sending an uneasy chill through the duo.

"What are we supposed to do now?" Harper asked, her voice tinged with uncertainty.

"We must deliver a mortal blow with the weapon forged from harmony," Wiki blurted, his tone distant, as if the words weren't his own.

"What?" Hap replied, her face twisting with confusion. "Where's that coming from?"

Wiki sighed, rubbing his temple. "I really wish the spirits would stop that," he muttered under his breath. "They mean Harmony's Edge," he added, his voice steadier now as he stood and summoned the gleaming blade into his grasp.

"Follow me," Winslow called over his shoulder, throwing Harper a teasing glance. "Think you can keep up?"

"You really think you can beat me in a race now?" she retorted with a playful smirk before springing forward with a burst of speed.

Winslow grinned, his hair whipped back in the rush of wind as he bent his knees and launched himself into pursuit. The gap between him and Harper narrowed swiftly, each stride gaining ground as his footsteps echoed against the uneven terrain. Adjusting his pace with practiced precision, he moved fluidly alongside her, their movements synchronized as they navigated the shifting landscape together. Sliding to a halt, Harper skidded across the loose gravel, throwing her arms up triumphantly.

"I won!" she proclaimed, her laughter ringing out as if the tension of the battle had momentarily lifted.

Wiki followed close behind, gliding in with effortless grace. "Cheated, is more like it!" he countered, his grin wide despite the mock indignation. "Next time, I won't fall for that trick."

The moment of levity faded as Winslow's focus shifted back to the entombed nightmare. With deliberate steps, he approached the creature's massive head, his shoulders squared and posture rigid with purpose. Standing before the monstrous visage, he locked eyes with its hollow, unyielding stare.

"This won't hold me forever!" the Stitch Reaper growled, its voice muffled but still seething with defiance.

"Not forever," Wiki replied, his tone firm, "But long enough."

Raising Harmony's Edge high above his head, its blade shining with a resplendent aura, he brought it down in a powerful, unyielding strike. As the sword pierced the abysmal creature, it unleashed an earth-shattering roar of anguish.

Blinding light erupted from the sinewy stitches all over its head. The radiant energy surged outward, crackling like untamed lightning, as it tore through the fibrous seams that bound the creature's form. The ground trembled violently, deep fissures began spidering out beneath its head like veins of destruction.

Realizing the imminent collapse of the mountainous form, Wiki and Hap leapt into the air, their movements precise as they soared to safety. From their hovering position, they watched as the once-mighty abomination caved in on itself, its form imploding with a deafening crash, leaving behind a colossal void.

"Well, you two have certainly made quite the mess," Wind remarked with a dry chuckle, its sudden presence startling them as it appeared there without warning, accompanied by the other spirits.

Harper spun around, before jabbing a finger in Winslow's direction. "He did it!" she blurted, her tone half-accusatory and half-teasing.

"Excuse me, we did this... together," Winslow countered, his voice carrying feigned annoyance as they both broke into nervous laughter.

"Yeah, but you're the one who punched a hole in the mountain," Harper quipped, nudging Wiki lightly with her elbow, a sly grin creeping across her face.

Winslow shrugged, his expression a mix of sheepishness and humor. "How was I supposed to know that would happen?" he replied, throwing his hands up in exaggerated exasperation.

"Well, you're not done yet, silly goose," the wind spirit teased, its playful tone cutting through the banter.

"Huh, there's more?" Wiki asked, his voice tinged with disbelief as his shoulders slumped and sadness wavered across his features.

"Devastation leaves plenty of fixing in its wake. Time to restore this land to its former beauty," Water said gently while gesturing toward the mangled mountainside.

"Oh, that's it? Thank goodness," Wiki said with a sigh of relief before lowering himself onto the ground once more and crossed his legs as he steadied his breathing.

Exhaling deeply, Winslow allowed the chaotic scene to fade away in his mind. Slowly, he conjured a vivid image of the mountains as they once stood—proud, untouched, and timeless. As the vision solidified, the broken earth around them began to shift, restoring the spurs to the position they once held. Rocks rolled back into place, jagged crevices sealed themselves, and the barren stretches flourished with greenery, all guided by the harmonious energy emanating from his focus.

Standing back up, Wiki brushed himself off, the dust falling in soft clouds around him. Turning toward Water, he asked with a calm but curious tone, "How is that? Is it close enough?"

Earth, visibly stunned, exclaimed, "It's perfectly restored! The precision, the balance—I knew you had great potential, but this... and everything you've done... I could never have imagined."

Fire, stepping forward with a flicker of intrigue, added, "It seems there is far more to you than we first suspected," its ember-like eyes glowing with a mischievous spark, the glinting light dancing across its fiery visage.

Earth, shifting its gaze to Harper with a look of both curiosity and admiration, asked, "How did you know what to use to protect you both?"

Harper tilted her head, "What do you mean? I just threw myself in the way and asked for protection," she replied, still uncertain about the events that had unfolded.

"The barrier you created wasn't just any ordinary shield," Earth explained, its voice carrying a tone of awe. "It was formed with Caelonyx–a rare and extraordinary metal that exists solely in the spiritual dimension. Your ability to summon it instinctively is remarkable. It seems Wiki is not the only one who has surpassed our expectations. Astounding!"

The spirits exchanged glances, their once-lighthearted demeanor shifting to one of solemnity. Their shimmering forms dimmed slightly as they moved in unison, forming a semi-circle around the children.

Fire gestured for them to come closer, its blazing figure now steady and serious, "Do not let this victory make you complacent," it warned, the embers of its voice crackling with intensity. "Forces far greater than this await in the shadows."

Earth nodded solemnly and then raised its hand, conjuring a portal rimmed with earthy textures, "Before you leave, look upon what lies ahead," it said gravely.

The gateway opened to reveal a distant realm, once a paradise of radiant beauty and abundant life, now shrouded in oppressive shadow and consumed by decay. Twisted, skeletal trees reached skyward, their barren branches etched against the horizon. The ground lay fractured and barren, riddled with withered veins. Creatures, warped beyond recognition, lumbered and slithered across the desolate land, their movements unnatural and unsettling.

"This is a world tainted by corruption," Earth continued, its voice heavy with sorrow. "If balance is not maintained, this fate could befall all realms. Remember what is at stake."

As the final word was spoken, the vision faded, the portal dissolved while Earth continued, "Now, return to your homes and find rest. Remain vigilant, and let your training continue to sharpen your skills. When the time is right, we will call upon you once more."

With a synchronized gesture, Wind swept its arms in graceful arcs, conjuring two distinct portals that swirled gently with translucent currents of air. Harper and Wiki exchanged glances, before stepping toward their respective portals, knowing they would soon return to their own homes.

Before crossing through, Hap and Wiki bid each other and the spirits a heartfelt "Goodnight."

The weight of the spirits' words, settling heavily on their hearts, a solemn reminder of challenges yet to come– and the certainty that this moment marked only the beginning.

www.ingramcontent.com/pod-product-compliance
Lightning Source LLC
Chambersburg PA
CBHW030738030726
47497CB00001B/26